DYNASTY

BY

DUTCH

www.dcbookdiva.com

ISBN-10: 0578029464
ISBN-13: 978-0578029467
Library of Congress Control Number: 2009936476

First Edition, December 2009
Printed in the United States of America

Publisher's Note

This is a work of fiction. Any names historical events, real people, living and dead, or the locales are intended only to give the fiction a setting in historic reality. Other names, characters, places, businesses and incidents are either the product of the author's imagination or are used factiously, and their resemblance, if any, to real life counterparts is entirely coincidental.

Edited by: A. Slye
Typeset: Linda Williams
Graphic Designer: MWS Designs

DC Bookdiva Publications
#245 4401-A Connecticut Ave
NW, Washington, DC 20008
dcbookdiva.com
myspace.com/dcbookdivapublications
facebook.com/dcbfanpage
twitter.com/dcbookdiva

PROLOGUE

Boy I need you bad as my
heartbeat… bad like the food I eat.
Bad as the air I breathe…baby I
want you bad.

The sound of Jazmine Sullivan's soulful voice filled the lavish banquet room of the Occidental Hotel in Aruba. It wasn't a public concert; it was a family reunion, an event the Bells always outdid themselves with. The Bells were a crime family out of New York that extended back to the Bumpy Johnson era. Tito Bell, the 33- year old head of the family, had arranged to fly his whole family, extended family and select friends to Aruba for the reunion. Jazmine Sullivan's performance had been a surprise for his twin sisters because they loved the young singer.

But for Tito, it was business as usual. His grip on the Tri-State cocaine market was slowly slipping away. He needed to expand, to move on to new markets and for that he needed his Uncle Guy and the Simmons family out of the

South. They had a stranglehold on the heroin market south of the Mason Dixon Line and therefore the clout and the pull to help Tito move his product in the south. Tito decided to arrange a meeting with Guy at the family reunion.

Tito glanced at his Presidential as he watched his sisters dancing with their dates. He turned back around and smiled when he saw his Aunt Gloria come in with her son Kev and Guy's other son, Tyquan. The door closed behind them and Tito's brow furled when he realized his Uncle Guy hadn't come. That was a bad sign, but at least he had sent his sons instead.

Gloria was greeted by faces she hadn't seen in years. She was a Harlemite at heart, but she hadn't been back home in several years; too many bad memories.

"Hey, big sis!" Tito's mother Theresa said and stood up to hug her. Theresa had been married to Gloria's brother, Eddie. "Girl, damn you look good! Where is Guy?"

Gloria shrugged. Everyone knew that she and Guy were divorced, yet they always seemed to ask about him. "You know Guy got remarried, so he's probably with his wife," Gloria told her simply, even though she still felt a way about it.

"Well, he's still family," Theresa replied, "so you tell him, next time if he don't come, the Bells gonna put a hit on him!" she joked.

Gloria thought to herself, *if you knew what I knew, you may put a hit on both of us for real.* But instead she said, "I'll tell him!"

"Kev! Boy, come give yo' aunt a hug wit' yo' fine self!" Theresa gushed, hugging Kev then turning to Ty. "And you too, Tyquan. I'm yo' aunt too!"

"Yes, Ma'am," Ty smiled then obeyed her.

"Hey, Gloria," her sister Pam said timidly.

Gloria sucked her teeth. "Bitch, you ain't dead yet?" Gloria spat coldly.

"Gloria?!" Theresa said in shock.

"No, it's okay. Only the Lord can heal our hearts. God bless you, Gloria," Pam said and walked away.

"God damn you, bitch!" Gloria said a little louder than she would've liked, causing a few heads to turn.

Theresa grabbed her arm. "Glo, you dead wrong for that," she whispered harshly. "That was a long time ago."

"Not long enough when your own sister was fuckin' yo' husband for years! Now the bitch wanna be saved?? Please." Gloria waved her off.

"People can change, Glo. Besides, Guy ain't exactly faultless," Theresa reminded her.

Gloria held up her left hand to show that her ring finger was empty, even though her middle finger was diamonded up. "Which is why I divorced his black ass!"

Kev cleared his throat. He already knew enough about his father's player ways to fill up a book. "Aunt T, um... where's Tito?"

"Oh, he should be—"

"Right here," Tito finished for her, hugging his aunt Gloria then his two cousins.

"Glad to see y'all could make it," Tito greeted.

"And miss a free trip to Aruba? Boy, bye," Gloria chuckled.

"What up, Kev? It's been a minute. Let's find somewhere to talk. We got a lot of catchin' up to do."

Kev and Ty excused themselves, then followed Tito out of the banquet hall and over to the hotel's spacious poolside area. The little Bell children were wilding out like little ghetto kids minus the Ritalin. The twins, Asia and Brooklyn, were out there with their dates until they laid eyes on Kev and Ty.

"Cuzzo!" they screamed in unison, making their way over to them.

Kev shook his head thinking *damn I wish they wasn't family.*

The twins were gorgeous. They looked just like the singer Rihanna; they even had the same color eyes. The only difference was they were thicker in the hips and both keep their hair long.

"Look at my country cousin!" Brooklyn chuckled. She was the oldest by only a few minutes.

Ty knew how to tell them apart, because usually with twins one twin's face is longer than the other's.

"Watch yo' mouth, Brooklyn... ain't nothin' country about me. I'm just southern," Ty quipped. The twins kissed them both then left the three of them to talk.

They sat around the poolside table and Tito opened up. "I hope everything is good wit' Guy. He isn't sick is he?" Tito implied.

Kev smiled because he knew that Tito was dying to know why Guy didn't come. "Pop sends his regards, but it couldn't be helped. But believe me... talking to me is like talking to him."

Ty hated the way his older brother assumed the lead role. He wouldn't speak on it at the meeting, but he planned on checking his ass later.

Tito peeped the look on Ty's face but kept it moving. "Cool," Tito replied, masking his disappointment, "that's what it is then. Let me get down to it. We've got the Tri-State area on smash. You've got the South on smash. Now being that our thing is coke and yours is dope, there's no way we could step on each other's toes if we decided to join forces,"

Tito proposed, then stopped to give Kev a chance to speak.

"I'm listening." Kev nodded. Guy had taught him when a man brings the deal you let him do all the talking.

Tito was hoping to get a gauge of where Kev's head was so he could tailor his idea to address Kev's concerns. When that didn't happen he continued, "Now with us, we've got our hands in a little of everything. From the hottest black owned record labels to construction... and of course more than a few politicians' backs. As I'm sure you have your hands in more than a few cookie jars and puppets yourself. My point is... we're both not getting the most for our money when it comes to the overall picture."

"How so?" Ty inquired.

Tito directed his attention to Ty. "Because, Fam... we got cops, district attorneys, politicians, and they all want a piece of the pie. Now with baking ourselves a *larger* pie, their piece stays the same while ours more than doubles," Tito broke it down.

"So what you're asking is... that we share markets and utilize each other's resources," Kev surmised.

"Exactly," Tito replied.

Kev smiled. "I feel your vision, Cuz, but we don't want to expand. New areas mean new problems. I can tell you now, Guy's gonna say, 'if it ain't broke don't fix it'."

"A fifty-fifty split of millions is far from broke," Tito quipped.

Kev chuckled. "I'm gonna have to decline your offer, Cuz, but I do have one of my own."

Tito was clearly upset but remained cordial.

"Like you said, we both have our hands in a lot of cookie jars. Where I think we can make the best match is in construction," Kev told him.

"Construction?" Tito echoed.

Kev nodded. "With the economy fucked up like it is and housing in the dumps, we can combine our companies' credit ratings and snatch up anything we want. Five years down the line we're talking about 4-5 times our initial investment."

Tito couldn't believe what Kev was saying. That fucking Guy was trying to belittle him and appease him at the same time! Tito was talking millions now, not five years! "Construction?" Tito chuckled. "Did Eddie give Guy a hammer when he came to him to get on?" Tito was referring to the fact that it had been his father Eddie that had initially put Guy in the game.

"So should I tell Pop you feel like he owes you, Cuz?" Kev asked calmly, but Tito could tell he was vexed.

Tito sighed. "No disrespect, Fam. Really. It's just... we family, and at the end of the day, it's all we got, you know? Do me a favor... talk to Uncle Guy; just ask him if I could talk to him face to face."

All three of them then stood up and Tito shook their hands.

"No doubt... I'll deliver the message, Cuz," Kev assured him.

The only good sign at the meeting was Tito could tell Ty was interested. He could see that look in his eyes. Kev may be content with the way things were but Ty was restless. He knew Ty saw the bigger picture. Tito thought to himself how it would be if Ty was calling the shots.

"Ay yo! What's all this, *you talkin' to Pops when you talkin' to me* bullshit?" Ty fumed, slamming the door to Kev's suite after they entered. "He sent us *both* down here!"

Ty felt like Kev had handled that all wrong. There were numerous times when he wanted to jump in and take control of the conversation, but held back as Guy had taught him to never air the family's dirty laundry to anyone.

"Look, that shit Tito is talkin' ain't in our best interest. Case closed," Kev shot back.

"Case closed?! Nigguh, how you know what Pop gonna say?!"

" 'Cause I already talked to him before we left. He knew Tito probably wanted to move shop down south and he ain't wit' it. How you think I was able to offer him the construction deal without Pop's approval?" Kev said with a glib smirk on his face.

Ty was heated but he was also hurt. Guy hadn't talked to him about the trip. Yeah Kev was the oldest, but he didn't have the foresight or sheer instinct Ty had. Guy had told him that himself, but little by little, it seemed like Guy was grooming Kev to take over the family business.

That made Tito's deal that much more important. He had to convince Guy. The Simmons didn't have to expand, but they could bring Tito in under their wing. Ty could personally oversee it and if everything went right, create his own niche between his family and the Bells. Because one thing was for sure, he refused to be under Kev should he become the head of the family, and was prepared to make sure that didn't happen...

CHAPTER 1

The ambulance's siren pierced the air like the wail of a woman in agony as it raced along the rain slicked streets. Pedestrians and drivers alike watched as it whizzed by with looks of apprehension etched on their faces. It was like they could feel the impending drama building in the air, because many of them already knew who was inside. The shooting occurred only a short time ago, but the streets were already abuzz with what had gone down.

Guy Simmons, the aging Don of the South, had been shot outside his favorite bar and grill on James Street. Both of his trusted bodyguards were murdered in the process. Everywhere gossip was rampant in the streets as to whom and why, they knew the Simmons family's response would be ruthless and brutal.

"Please, God, don't let him die! Please!" Gloria Simmons wailed as she sat beside Guy in the ambulance, gripping his hand. She held it so tightly it was as if she wanted to will her life force into him. "Guy, I know you can hear me," she said, bent near his ear. "Just hold on, baby, we almost there. Remember what you always said, 'they can't keep a good

8

man down.' "

His breathing was shallow and his eyes were closed, but he indeed heard her and it warmed him inside. Even though they had been divorced for a few years, they had been married for over twenty, had a child and an unbreakable bond forged through fire.

Seeing his eyes move under his eyelids, Gloria gasped and kissed his hand. "I'm here, baby. Always. I'm here," she assured him before asking, "Who... did it?"

Guy didn't know who had done it. But he knew that it had to be someone close to him because of how it went down. He definitely knew that. As he struggled to communicate his reply, he could feel his strength ebbing away and then was enveloped in darkness and silence.

Guy Simmons had been born and raised in Goldsboro, North Carolina. His father Willie was a brick layer by day and a gambler at night. He and his wife Mabel ran several successful liquor houses in and around Goldsboro. They lived in Webbtown, an area situated in the middle of Goldsboro, which served as the city's version of Black Las Vegas. The shotgun houses that teetered and leaned side by side offered every vice imaginable, and Willie Simmons had a hand in it all. From prostitution to gambling to bootleg liquor, the Simmons family lived high on the hog and city slick in a countrified way. Hustling was in their blood since all the way back to slavery.

Willie's great grandfather was lynched for horse theft after escaping the brutal whip of his slave master in Mississippi. Willie's daddy, born Geechie in South Carolina, ran moonshine across the south until he too was gunned down. Willie eventually relocated to Wilmington, then ultimately carried on the Simmons tradition.

As mentioned before, hustling was in their blood.

Guy was born with a ghetto silver spoon in his mouth — in other words, "nigguh rich". An expression that meant you was richer than most black folks but only slightly better than average to most whites. He was the child and was catered to accordingly. He excelled in everything he did, sports, women and school, everything that is except the family business.

"Boy, didn't I tell you to bring yo' ass heah afta' school directly!?" Willie huffed, chopping on his trademark cigar.

"I know, Daddy, but I had to go to the library to research my book report. Ms. Calvin says — ," Guy tried to explain but his father erupted again.

"The library?! The goddamn library?! Boy, here I is tryin' to teach you how to take care of yo'self and you tellin' me about a goddamn book!"

Willie turned his back, shaking his head and slammed the door of his illegal still behind him. He just couldn't figure his son out, but truth be told, Guy didn't want to follow the family tradition, he wanted to start his own. He was tired of living in the shadow of his family name. Instead he wanted to be the shoulders the next generation stood on. A sentiment his mother seconded and encouraged.

"Baby, don't worry about yo' daddy. I got him," Ms. Mabel told him one night after one of their arguments as she cleared the table.

"Why can't he understand?" Guy shook his head. As much as he wanted to be his own man, he also wanted his father's approval.

Ms. Mabel sat down and lovingly took her son's hand. "Guy, you know yo' daddy can't read and he don't trust what's in them books. His great- great- grand-daddy was a slave and he tried to read, which almost got him killed. That's why he turned to horse thievin'. The Simmons men, none of 'em could read, and they look at school as some-thing for uppity nigguhs," she explained.

"But I can read," Guy responded proudly, "and I am gonna be somebody. Not like dad – "

"Your father is somebody," Ms. Mabel reprimanded her son. "He provide you that roof up heah and that food in theah," she pointed at his belly then continued, "so don't think 'cause you can read you better'n yo' daddy, you hear me?"

"Yes, Ma'am," Guy answered with his head down. His mother lifted his chin.

"But you gonna be somebody too." She smiled that angelic smile that his father fell in love with. "A different kind of sombody... a new somebody. The time yo' daddy come from, we had to think that way to survive. But a new day is dawning, and the Lord is shining on black folk! You gonna be the first Simmons to go to college. And after that, anything's possible. Look at Booker T. Washington and all these great black folk. Times a changin' and before you know it; we'll have a black president. He might even be you!"

Guy laughed as he kissed his mother then rose from the table. "I don't know about all that. I ain't even get into college yet."

"You will."

And he did. He was accepted at Howard University in Washington, DC but never got a chance to attend, for a week later, he received a letter that would change his life forever.

"The Army?!" his mother exclaimed, clutching her chest. She had heard so much about the war in Vietnam, not just on the news but some of her friend's sons had been drafted only to return home in a box. "No, Guy! I don't want you going to nobody's war. What about school?!"

"I can still go once my tour is over, Mama," he explained. "Besides, I don't really have a choice. Once they draft you, you either report or go to jail."

11

He didn't mention that since he was the first born son he could be exempt from duty. Deep down he wanted to enlist. He had read so much about the Tuskegee Airmen that he too wanted a chance to add his name to history.

"Aww, Mabel, the boy'll be alright," his father said, "he's a Simmons and ain't no Simmons ever ran from a fight."

For once he agreed with his son. He'd rather see him in the Army than at some sissy school learning the ways of the uppily nigguhs.

"Then maybe you'll learn how to be a man and make me proud of you, my son," Willie added.

Guy turned and looked his father in the eye.

"All my life I've been Willie Simmons' son, but one day you'll be known as Guy Simmons' father!" Guy walked out, leaving his father with a slight smirk on his face.

...y'all brothers don't want it; I got the Godfather flow the Don Juan DeMarco; swear to God, don't get it twisted...

The sound of Jay-Z's "Can't Knock the Hustle" blared from the burgundy BMW 645 coupe sitting on 22-inch rims that the streets called shoes. Pappy, the owner of the car, leaned against the hood while kicking game to two beautiful red bones. Pappy was an average looking 21- year old brother, but it was his money that made him fine in the eyes of the gold diggers. A year ago the lanky boned, skinny young man would've never gotten a second word in with this caliber of chick, but since the come up of the Wolf pack, his crew, he was a bona fide hood star.

He wasn't the leader of the Pack, far from it. But just the

fact that he sported the diamond and ruby pendant of the NC State Mascot—and his crew's symbol—let the chicks know he could be their come up as well.

"So what up... y'all down or what? Fuck this club, the party is at my spot," he arrogantly spat, eyeing both chicks lustfully. They were outside a large club in Raleigh called the Factory. Candy coated whips filled the parking lot, and a lot of ballas were parking lot pimpin', but Pappy was easily out shining them all.

"It's whatever wit' me, baby," the shorter of the two flirted, eyes full of dollar signs.

"That's what it is then," he happily replied, leaning off the hood to make his exit.

"Yo, Pap," a gruff male voice called out to him.

He had been so engrossed in the heavenly bodies before him; he hadn't even seen the black MPV pull up on him. Pappy looked up upon hearing his name. He looked into a pair of Versace shades worn by the passenger.

"Kev said hi," the man announced while simultaneously pulling a .40 caliber pistol out and aiming the infrared for a dome shot.

On hearing the name Kev, his street instincts kicked in, but it was too late. The chicks dashed off in opposite directions as the laser light dotted his forehead dead center.

Whoosh! Whoosh!

The two silenced shots whistled through the air, entered his brain and blew the back of his head out. Pappy never even got a chance to lift the 9mm Luger he had tucked in his pants. His body was thrown back forcefully onto the hood of the car. Since the shots were fired through a silencer, the parking lot didn't break into a frenzy. Only a few alert ballas had seen what went down and quickly exited the parking lot. They were heading one way and the MPV another.

●●●●●●

"Damn, yo... I'm a daddy," Rico whispered to himself in awe. He held the tiny bundle of joy to his chest protectively as he stood by his girlfriend's hospital bed.

"What should we name him, Boo?" his girlfriend Pam asked, still a little woozy from her first birth.

Rico raised his child up, peered at his closed eyes and saw his little fists ball up. "Look at him! My lil' man a soldier!" he announced proudly, ignoring Pam's question.

She allowed him to have his moment then asked again with playful impatience. "Rico, you ain't heard a word I said!"

"Oh, oh yeah, a name... I got you. How about Tupac?" he suggested half jokingly. He loved Tupac Shakur like a dead brother.

"Picture that," Pam answered dismissively.

The nurse walked in to take the baby. He handed him to her carefully then watched as they walked out.

"Let me think about it a sec," he said, bending down to give Pam a passionate kiss. "You know I love you, right?"

Pam's heart fluttered. "I love you, Rico."

"I'm a daddy, yo," he repeated again proudly. "I-I gotta get some air real quick, baby. I'll be right back."

Rico walked out and headed for the elevator. Once he reached the lobby, he had a sudden impulse to buy cigars. He purchased a handful of "It's A Boy!" cigars from the hospital lobby and began passing them out as he headed out the front door.

He found an orderly standing outside smoking a cigarette. Rico handed him a cigar then began to split his open to smoke a blunt.

"I'm a daddy, yo!" he repeated again to the orderly.

"Congratulations, my man. Your first, huh?" the orderly surmised.

"That I know of," Rico replied with a chuckle. Living the life of a balla wasn't no telling how many baby mamas he potentially had. But this one would be real. It was his own family and he vowed to be the same kind of father his father was to him.

"You an NC State fan I see," the orderly questioned, eyeing his ruby and diamond pendent dangling from the barrel link chain around his neck. It matched his ruby beveled Rolex as well.

"Somethin' like that," Rico smiled inwardly. The wolf pack he ran with was on a different level of ballin', and the only shots he made were hollow tips. He was the second in charge of one of the most ruthless drug organizations Eastern Carolina had ever seen, and he repped it to the fullest.

The orderly thunked his cigarette into the parking lot and said, "Well, break's over. Congratulations again!"

"Too bad you won't enjoy it."

The voice caught them both off guard. The third man had crept up like an old memory, appearing out of the shadows.

"Huh?" was all Rico could say before the silenced hollow tips put his thoughts to rest.

The brain matter splattered the terrified orderly as Rico's body slumped to the pavement.

The gunman and the orderly's eyes met.

"Please don't...," was all the orderly could get out.

"Wrong place," the gunman replied chirping off two shots that crumpled the orderly right next to Rico. "Wrong time," he added then disappeared like a thief in the night.

CHAPTER 2

"Fuck Daytona Beach, dog. That shit don't excite me no more. I'm chilling," Vee spoke into the cell phone as he drove along Fayetteville Street in Durham.

He was behind the wheel of a blue Altima that was owned by the chick in the passenger seat. Her name was Cynthia and he had just met her earlier at Central University. Vee was hopping out of a cab to come check another one of his chicks when he eyed shortie coming out of the girl's dorm. He was dressed thug fashion in grey Dickies and a black hoodie, but one look at his Wolf Pack pendant and Cynthia knew he was ballin'. The rest was now.

"You gonna just talk on your phone all night?" she huffed with attitude; her arm's folded across her breasts.

"Nigguh, Luke bitches?! Luke wanna fuck *my* bitches!" Vee laughed arrogantly. "Miami hoes ain't nothin' special."

Cynthia sucked her teeth. "Vee?!"

"Yo, hold on," Vee spat then turned to her. "Ay yo, shut the fuck up, aight? Speak when spoken to or find something better to do wit' yo' mouth," he hissed with authority.

Any other nigguh would've talked to her like that and

16

Cynthia would've spazzed then put his ass out. But Vee wasn't just any other nigguh. He was the leader of the crew all the sack-chasin' hoes were creamin' their sheets to get next to, so she didn't want to blow her chance at hood celeb status. Besides the fact, Vee was the color of mocha chocolate with hazel eyes and enough waves to make you sea sick. He wasn't cut up or diesel, but word was he had dick for days. He was a woman's dream from which she wasn't ready to wake up.

Cynthia reached over and unbuttoned his Dickie pants, sliding her hand around the snake in his pants. She wet her lips seductively, eyeing him the whole time as she leaned forward. "You mean... like this?" she purred, taking his limp shaft into her mouth.

Vee smiled, "Yeah, exactly. Ay yo, Cuz, let me... DAMN... let me hit you back."

He dropped the phone on the seat and relaxed into the moment. As he drove the slurping sounds were the only ones in the car, because Vee never rode with the radio up. It was at that moment when Cynthia ducked her head that he saw the black MPV pull up beside him at the light. Had she not ducked at that precise moment, not only would her brains be in his lap instead of her face, he would've never seen the hit until it was too late.

"What the fuck?!" he blurted out as the driver and the back passenger opened fire with automatic weapons. On first glance he instantly hit the lever of the car seat, laying it all the way down, while simultaneously reaching under the bobbing neck of Cynthia putting the car in reverse. He knew he couldn't go forward because he was behind a car at the light. He drove top speed in reverse, not even looking back, as the gunfire had him pinned down.

"Oh my God! Oh my God!" Cynthia hyperventilated as the windshield shattered from the barrage of shots.

"Shut the fuck up!" Vee barked, trying to maneuver without sight.

The MPV gave chase and caught up quick, nose-to-nose with the Altima, blazing the hood and headrests. Vee remained calm. He knew sooner or later they'd have to reload. It had only taken seconds, so before Vee had gone a block in reverse a car came out of the intersection.

Screech! Boom!

The vehicle struck the rear flank of the Altima stopping it dead in its tracks. The shooter on the passenger side wasted no time in getting out.

"I don't wanna die!" Cynthia wailed.

Vee snatched her face to him. "Shut up! You ain't gonna die!"

"Yo, Vee!" the gunman yelled, cautiously approaching the car. "Game over, nigguh! Kev said tell God he said hi!" he yelled then lit the car up with another burst of gunfire.

The bullets whizzed so close over Vee's head he could feel the air piercing around him. He had yet to let off one shot of his Heckler & Koch .45 caliber. He was glad the gunman was so trigger happy, so he waited for his moment. It came when he heard the gun click on empty. Then he quickly made his move.

"Get out now!" he told Cynthia.

"No! He'll kill me!"

Vee put the gun to her head. "And I'm a kill you if you don't! Open the door... I got you!"

He flung the door open a nanosecond after the gunman ran out of bullets. He reached in his pants for his .40 caliber, the exact same .40 caliber he had just killed Pappy with. But by the time he pulled it from his waist, Vee had emerged from the car firing. The infrared can make anyone a marksman, so once the dot hit the gunmen's forehead, Vee dropped him with one shot.

The driver nutted up but managed to aim his Mac-11 out the window with one hand. The unsteady aim made his shots go wide, but once he trained in, each bullet hit Cynthia because Vee was using her as a human shield. Her body jerked and twitched but Vee kept his aim, centered his target and fired. The shot split the windshield and he saw the driver's head snap back and stay in that position. As the Mac-11 fell from his dead hand, Vee allowed Cynthia's mangled body to fall to the ground too.

"Good lookin', shortie," Vee chuckled, then began to jog off. He stopped in his tracks, went back to the car and retrieved his phone. While he had his head stuck in the car, he wiped down the steering wheel the best he could. As he jogged away, he pulled a small black pouch out of his pocket and kissed it. "You never let me down." Vee then dialed a number on his cell.

"We fucked up. He got away!" These were the words Kev Simmons heard when he answered the phone. Never mind the fake Scarface accent, Kev knew exactly who it was — Vee.

"Fuck you, you goddamn cocksucker! You're dead!" Kev based, trying to keep his voice low because he was in the hospital.

"Naw, won't be no next time 'cause now I'm comin' for you," Vee hissed on the other end.

"I ain't hard to find, nigguh. You started this war!" Kev replied.

Vee chuckled. "Naw, dog, I didn't. But I'ma damn sure finish it."

Click. The line went dead.

Kev was so heated that Vee would have the audacity to call while he was praying at the hospital that his father would pull through, he smashed his phone by hurling it into a nearby wall in the waiting room.

"Kevin! What's wrong with you?!" his mother Gloria asked.

The security guard quickly approached. "Sir, you're going to have to calm down or I'ma have to ask you to leave."

"I'm calm," Kev replied, eyeing the guard firmly.

"Baby, are you okay"?" his wife Karrin asked, taking his hand. He snatched it away.

"I'm good."

"Kevin, who was that on the phone?" Gloria asked.

Before he could answer he saw his half-brother Tyquan, Ty's mother Debra and three of Ty's henchmen approaching. Gloria followed his eyes and when she spotted Debra, sucked her teeth and rolled her eyes, like *here comes this bitch.*

Debra caught her expression and smirked to herself, thinking she had the upper hand. As they approached, Ty shook Kev's hand and pecked Gloria on the cheek. Ty's eyes met Karrin's, but he looked through her as if she didn't exist.

"How is he, Kev?" Ty inquired just as a doctor approached.

"Excuse me, doctor, but I'm Mrs. Simmons. Please tell me that my husband is okay?" Debra questioned with genuine concern.

"Mrs.? But I thought...," the doctor stammered looking at Gloria.

"No, no, doctor, *I'm* Mrs. Simmons... she's just the *ex-*wife," Debra announced proudly.

"*First* wife," Gloria shot back.

The doctor cleared his throat, trying to avoid a cat fight.

"Well uh-yes... Mr. Simmons' condition is extremely critical. He was shot multiple times. Right now it's touch and go."

Debra seized the doctor's arm. "Well, can I see him? Just for a moment. Please?" She eyed the doctor with those hazel eyes that made most men weak in the knees and the doctor was no exception.

Gloria chuckled inwardly thinking, *this fake bitch oughta get an Oscar.*

"I-I'm sorry Mrs. Simmons, but I have to say no. It's too early," he answered before walking away.

"Yo, Kev, let me speak to you a minute," Ty requested.

Kev looked at his mother, apprehensive to leave the two women together knowing they hated each other with a passion.

"Ma?" he asked as if to say, *don't cut up in here.*

"I'm a big girl, baby. I ain't got time for nobody's kids," Gloria answered the unspoken question.

With that, he, Ty and the three henchmen headed for the front door. Once they were outside, Ty's boys fanned out to secure the area. Ty and Kev walked side by side quietly. Although they were raised by the same man and acted so much alike, they had a strong distaste for each other. A feeling that was not only a gift from their mothers, but the brotherly rivalry enhanced by the life they led took on a dangerous edge.

"Yo, word is nigguhs pushed Rico and Pappy's wigs back tonight. You wouldn't know anything about that, would you?" Ty asked once they stopped walking.

Kev shrugged and lit up a Newport. "It was a G call."

"But you missed, Vee," Ty informed him. "What the hell was on your dome, dog??" Ty questioned.

"What the hell you mean, what's on my mind?!" Kev shot back, gesturing with his hands to the hospital. "*This* is

21

on my mind, nigguh! My fuckin' father is on my mind! So I holla'd back at the goddamn cocksuckers who put him here!"

Ty snickered in frustration. "And what if it wasn't them Wolf Pack nigguhs? Huh? Do you know what you did? You set off one war not knowing if the hidden enemy is one in the same?! Not to mention the fact that the police is waiting for us to show our hand and you just placed the whole deck face up!" Ty was seething and Kev's nonchalant attitude made him even hotter. Ty felt for sure his brother wasn't cut from the same cloth as him. In fact, if they didn't have the same father he would've killed him in a New York minute.

"Fuck you mean I don't know?! Of course it was Vee! Who the fuck else got the balls to hit Pop?!" Kev bellowed a little too loudly. Checking himself, he added, "and if it wasn't them, let them nigguhs be an example, you hit us, we bang first then ask questions LATER!"

Ty shook his head. "You ain't heard a word I said... look... you ain't in charge, and unfortunately, we in this together. You wanna be boss, cool, then be boss in your territory. Raleigh and Durham is *mine* so it wasn't your *G* call in the first place!" Ty based, thinking to himself, *as if you really is a G.*

Kev chuckled. "Then handle your business, nigguh. I wouldn't have had to move if you mowed your grass a little better. But I forgot, the Wolf Pack used to be your lil' squad, right? That is, till they decided to jump ship. Maybe you tryin' to protect em', yo."

"I'ma forget you said that, Kev. I'll holla," Ty responded then started to walk away.

"I mean tell me something, 'cause I'm startin' to question what side you really on," Kev accused.

Ty tensed up. His muscles flexed and twitched as he

22

walked back up to Kev. "What the fuck you say?"

Kev tossed his cigarette aside. "Nigguh, you ain't deaf," he hissed back.

"Motherfucka, don't ever question my loyalty to this family again," Ty growled.

Even though Ty's 5'10" height was 3 inches shorter than Kev, Ty was the better fighter.

"Kev," a female voice called out.

The two brothers eyed each other, ignoring the voice.

"Kevin!" Karrin repeated, walking up on the two.

"What?" Kev replied, not taking his eyes off Ty.

"Can we please go get something to eat?" she asked.

Although Ty tried to fight it, he had to look. He glanced at Karrin and cursed himself because she could still make his heart skip a beat. She was truly a beauty. 5'8 inches of cinnamon complexioned eye candy. Not video vixen thick but heavenly angel beautiful. But she looked darker than usual, like she had gotten a tan.

Kev caught the look of desire in Ty's eyes, but had he been looking at Karrin he would've seen the same thing. Kev smirked then put his hand on her ass. "Anything, baby. I'm finished here anyway." Kev and Karrin walked off leaving Ty to seethe in their wake.

Ty answered his ringing phone. "Yo."

"Peace, Fam, how you?" Tito inquired with concern. "I know that you messed up right now. My heart goes out to you and your family. My Aunt Gloria said she prayin', but I'm here prayin' you catch them nigguhs."

Ty nodded. "Good look, Fam. It is appreciated."

"I won't disrespect you and offer to send something thru there 'cause I know you can handle yours. But should the need arise, know you got an Army in BK," Tito promised.

"I got you." Ty replied.

"I know you ain't get at Guy yet on that. Just stay in touch, Fam. Peace."

◉◉◉◉◉◉

Vee hopped out of the cab in front of an apartment complex in north Raleigh. He intended on walking the last three blocks to his condo. Vee never took a cab all the way home, because he vowed never to be caught slipping. All it would take for a thirsty cat to do was see him jump in a cab then lay on that cab driver to find out where he took him. Vee was the type of predator that always covered his tracks.

When he got to the crib, he entered through the back door, as always. He placed his keys on the table then yelled, "Yo, Cat! I'm home!" He stuck his head in the fridge and pulled out a container of Sunny Delight, drinking straight from the jug. His girl Cat walked in and shushed him violently.

"Stop yellin' so loud wit' yo' ghetto ass! 'Cause if you wake Tata, *you* stayin' up wit' him."

One look at her and you knew why they called her Cat — even though her real name was Kionna. Her chestnut brown eyes slanted like a feline's. She had a slightly puffy dark brown skin face that gave her a Lisa Raye type quality.

Vee walked up and wrapped his arms around her waist and kissed her on her Kewpie Doll nose. "I missed you too, baby girl."

"Hm-mmm," she replied with her mouth twisted up even though she loved when he called her baby girl.

"Where my lil' man?" he asked.

"Asleep in his room."

Vee took the stairs two at a time until he got to his son's room. He was only six months old, but he already had all the toys he could think of. He even had a 48-inch plasma TV on his wall that stayed on the Baby Network. Vee looked down at his sleeping son and couldn't resist picking him up. As he did, Cat appeared in the door.

"Victor, please don't wake him up, 'cause I'm tired," she pleaded.

"I ain't gonna wake nobody up," he replied, looking at his son. "Taheem, what up boy? You gonna be a gangsta like yo' daddy."

"Shit, ain't no gangstas gettin' raised up in here," Cat toned firmly.

"I'm just playin'," Vee replied, putting Taheem back down.

Very few people saw this side of Victor Murphy—the side that could love. Cat and Taheem were his world, and that's why he kept them out of his life. He thought about his dead homies and the war that had been declared. He turned to Cat, all smiles gone and told her, "Y'all gotta leave town for awhile."

Cat looked at him confusedly. Leave town? Why? When? Where are we goin'?"

He walked her into their bedroom and began to explain. "Some major shit went down tonight, and I don't want you anywhere around when the shit hits the fan."

"Then why you ain't goin' too?" Cat wanted to know.

" 'Cause it's my beef and I'ma take care of it," he answered, turning to walk out like the subject was over.

"Oh hell, naw!" Cat protested, going around him to close the door then leaning against it with her arms folded. "You ain't goin' nowhere until you tell me mo' than pack yo' shit, Cat. Uproot your life, Cat. What about school?"

"Transfer your credits... I don't know, but you and Taheem outta here tomorrow," Vee announced firmly.

"Victor, why are you actin' like this? Don't I have a right

to know what's goin' on with you… with *us*? Why don't you trust me?" Cat asked, teary-eyed.

"It ain't got nothin' to do with trust."

"Then what happened?"

Vee took a deep sigh. "Pappy dead. Rico dead. The same day his son was born he got kilt! Right outside the hospital," Vee said, emotions raging but he willed himself to calm down. "But that's the game, but *this… us*, it ain't no game, so I'm making you go. Do you understand now?"

Cat wrapped her arms around his neck and sobbed in his chest. She cried for Pappy. She cried for Rico, Pam and their newborn son. But mostly she cried out of fear for Vee. She was terrified for him.

As Vee embraced her, he thought of the old root the lady Ms. Sadie had given him lying in his black pouch and worked the root that made him virtually untouchable. "I can give you everything you want but the price will be everything you love," she had told him.

He thought about how at the tender age of 17 he had nobody. No family…no one to love or be loved by him. He didn't even think he'd make it to 21. Now, here he is, three months into his 21st year and he had someone to love and be loved by him. The thought made him shudder. He didn't mind risking his life, but there was no way he'd risk his heart.

CHAPTER 3

It was the rainy days that always did it. Guy laid back on a small bed in a crammed, roach infested rooming house in Harlem. His hands were clasped behind his head and his eyes focused on the raindrops that streaked the window. The pitter patter of the rain and the boom of the thunder started a spiral into the past eighteen months.

It was almost as if he was still in Vietnam. Even wide awake he could hear the swish-swash of the bush as his Army fatigues brushed past it. The brutal boom of the thunder made him jump as if fired by the Viet Cong.

Then came the voices, the unintelligible gibberish of the Vietnamese, the hiss and squawk of the walkie talkies, the screaming, the wailing, the killing.... He had to sit up and cover his ears with his hands.

Guy grabbed for the fifth of cheap wine off the rickety night-stand and threw his head back until the alcohol burned in his throat and brought tears to his eyes. Then he lit up a Kool, inhaling in the rare moment of serenity. The twelve months he had spent in Vietnam were unlike anything he had ever experienced. He had gone in as a starry-eyed boy and come out a grown ass man. He was 6'1", 190 pounds of muscle, frustration and depression.

Vietnam had totally changed him and changed everyone he knew that went in. They never came out the same. Killing does something to a man's soul, and surviving Hell meant you had to come out burned, or at least singed.

Guy did his twelve-month tour and it seemed like ten years. He went in fighting for his country, but ended up simply fighting for his life, and killing was the only option. Before he had a chance to digest the first kill, they were followed by several more, until he was desensitized by it all. Men he ate with, laughed with and played cards with, one by one fell all around him. He anticipated being next; almost hoped for it so he could finally be at peace. But only by the grace of God did he make it to the end of his tour.

Upon returning to the States, he realized he wasn't ready to go home. Guy had changed and he needed a new environment to complement that change. One of his Army buddies, Blue, was from Harlem. He awed Guy night after night with eight million stories.

"If a man can make it in Harlem, he can make it any-where," Blue had told him.

He even turned him on to his cousin, Eddie Bell. Blue told Guy how a guy named Nicky Barnes had Harlem on lock and his cousin Eddie was a major player in this organization.

"When we get out this hellhole, Big Country, I'ma take you back home wit' me. Show you the prettiest women you ever seen and mo' money than you ever laid eyes on," Blue had bragged, but Blue never made it home.

Guy decided to give Harlem a try. Once he reached the famous city, he was awed by the bright lights and the hugeness of it all. It was Goldsboro times hundreds! But he quickly realized, making an honest living in Harlem meant breaking yo' back for nickels and dimes. It was the pimps, number runners and dope dealers that lived the sporting life in Harlem.

Slowly but surely he was drawn to that life. The life his father had wanted to give him, the life he refused. He could almost hear his father saying "I told you so," as he made his way to Bell's Bar and Grill. The place owned by Blue's cousin Eddie.

It was midday when he got there, so there weren't many people there; a guy at the bar and two Harlem females at a table. They were well dressed with their hair done up in that style he saw so many Harlem women wear. He could tell they were out of his league, just by the jewels and the minks draped over their shoulders — the kind that didn't pay a working man like him any mind. To Guy, they were all whores or some gangster's girl, so he didn't even acknowledge the brown skin vixen's inviting smile when he walked in.

"Who you here to see?" she asked, because he looked like a man on a mission. She gave him the once over and was instantly attracted to the stranger.

"I'm looking for Eddie," Guy replied without even looking in her direction.

The young woman wasn't used to being ignored. Once most men laid eyes on her, they'd be falling all over themselves to get with her. But he wasn't most men she could see and that angered her and intrigued her at the same time.

"Well we don't need no janitors," she quipped, looking him up and down and making her girlfriend giggle. "And all deliveries we take thru the back."

Guy wasn't fazed by her sarcasm... He sighed and said, "Look, is Eddie here? I got business to speak with him about."

"Business??" she echoed, "What kind of business could yo' broke ass have wit' Eddie? Humph, you need to get some business about yo'self and find some decent shoes. This is 1974 not 1954!"

Guy turned his stoney gaze on her stopping the giggle dead in *her throat.*

"Maybe my shoe'll look better when it's dead in yo' ass," he growled, tired of playing games.

At that moment, Eddie had stepped out of the back. He heard the stranger ask for him and he watched him closely, sizing him up. As soon as the woman saw Eddie she got bold and stood to her feet.

"Nigguh, who you think you talkin' to?! Eddie, you hear this muhfucka talkin' 'bout puttin' his foot in my ass?!" she huffed.

Eddie stifled a chuckle, thinking to himself, "Somebody need to". Instead he said, "Yeah, Gloria, I heard him, and I also heard you talkin' to a grown ass man like he a child."

Gloria sucked her teeth then sat down to sulk.

Eddie turned to Guy. "And dig, bruh, that's my sister you talkin' to, so I'd appreciate it if you'd do so wit' respect," Eddie stated firmly.

Guy nodded subtly, thinking to himself, so this is Eddie Bell. Right away he knew he was dealing with heavy paper because he looked like a million dollars.

Eddie was bone skinny and sported an afro. He was pressed in a purple silk suit with matching 'gator boots. Even his nails were manicured.

"Harlem nigguhs," Guy chuckled to himself.

"So," Eddie began, leaning on the bar, "what business you got wit' me?"

"I was in the Army with your cousin Blue, and he told me if I was ever in Harlem, you were the man to see," Guy explained.

Eddie's face lit up like 42ⁿᵈ Street. "My man Blue! Now that's a down stud. How he doin'? He out yet?"

Guy dropped his head then looked back up to meet Eddie's eyes. "Naw. Blue got killed…. He's gone."

The light went out of Eddie's eyes and he grabbed his temples. "Man, damn, not Blue…I told that nigguh not to go." He shook *his head then had the bartender fix him a drink, offering Guy one as well. "Goddamn, Blue," Eddie cursed, throwing the shot back. "I grew up wit' that nigguh. 122nd and Lenox. We wasn't really cousins, but we wasn't just friends, you know what I mean?"*

Guy nodded, taking back the shot. The bartender refilled both glasses.

"You two musta really cut into one another if he told you to look me up," Eddie commented, thinking Guy had to be a solid cat for Blue to hook him up with him.

Eddie looked Guy over, assessing the situation. It was obvious that the brother was doing bad. His bloodshot eyes showed Eddie he had already been drinking, and his baggy clothes said he had lost weight, which also showed in the sallow way his skin sagged. He could clearly see that Guy was down on his luck, but Eddie wasn't about taking in stragglers.

"So," Eddie said, lighting a Kool and pausing to light Guy's up, "what can I do you for?"

Guy took a long drag then thunked the ashes in the ashtray. "I need a job."

"Yeah? Harlem's a big place, why'd you come to me?"

"Blue said you were the man to see."

"He musta told you I run an employment agency, huh?" Eddie quipped.

Gloria and her girlfriend giggled. When Guy glanced over in their direction, Gloria gave him a look like "Well?"

Guy turned back to Eddie. "I can get any kind of job, but I ain't any kinda nigguh," he replied smoothly, looking Eddie in the eye.

"Yeah?" Eddie smirked, blowing out smoke towards the ceiling. "What kind of nigguh are you?"

"Loyal. I'm a jack of all trades, so I do everything well except kiss ass. I ain't never bent over for nothing, not even to pull my

31

pants up," Guy responded.

The comment made Gloria smile subtly. She could see the stranger was one of a kind.

"Yeah? So how you pull up your pants?" Eddie chuckled.

"I just leeean back," Guy answered smoothly in his southern drawl.

Eddie busted out laughing and so did Gloria's girlfriend. Gloria even had to chuckle.

"I like that, playa. Just leeean back, huh? Where you from...," Eddie asked, letting his question trail so Guy could fill in the blank.

"Guy. Guy Simmons. I'm from North Carolina."

"What part?"

"Goldsboro."

Eddie smiled. *"Yeah, I hear tell y'all have some mean skin games down there? You skin?"*

It was Guy's turn to smile. Willie had taught him every card game that ever earned a dollar. *"Somethin' like that."*

Eddie truly cut into Guy that day. It wasn't just his quick wit' or no-nonsense demeanor, it was his eyes. That look of hungry determination and the coldness of a man that had looked at death in the face and stared it down. Eddie would take it slow but he knew in Guy, he would have a true soldier.

After that day, Guy never looked back.

CHAPTER 4

Ty pulled his black Cadillac CTS up to the Rib Shack. The name had always amused him because they didn't sell ribs. Guy had once explained to him that it was a popular soul food restaurant back in the day, owned by an old hustler named Long Pockets. When Long Pockets died, another old gambler named Hawk Bill had bought it and turned it into a bar. Since everyone knew it as the Rib Shack, Hawk never changed the name.

Ty used to love to come here as a child because Hawk Bill always had all kinds of candy for him. But today wasn't about nostalgia, it was about the present. Ty wanted answers. The Rib Shack was the bar his father got shot outside of.

It was already well into the evening when Ty got there, so as usual there was a nice crowd inside. The place was a frequent for the older players that got together to reminisce about their days gone by. When Ty walked in, he was greeted warmly with hugs and condolences on the situation with his father. He knew many of the well wishers had larceny in their heart, because many of these men Guy had roughed up at one time or another or straight ran out of business. Guy was feared just as much as he was respected.

Ty took it all in stride heading for the bar. Hawk Bill was behind the bar watching champion boxer Bernard Hopkins fight Jermaine Taylor.

"Left, B Hop! Left! Teach that young nigguh a lesson!" Hawk Bill yelled at the screen.

Ty eyed Hawk Bill. He remembered when Hawk Bill was in his prime. He was always a little pudgy but everybody knew Hawk wasn't to be fucked with. He carried a curved rug cutter that was called a Hawk Bill, which is how he got his name.

"Ay, Hawk!" Ty called out over the blare of the T.V.

"Hold up!" Hawk answered impatiently, not bothering to look around to see who it was.

When the bell sounded the end of the round, Hawk turned around. When he saw it was Ty, his cold eyes warmed. "Get the fuck outta here!" Hawk Bill laughed, coming around the bar, "My man, Tyquan!"

Hawk Bill was only 5'6 but he bear-hugged Ty with all his 250 pounds, lifting him off the floor. Ty chuckled, allowing the man who was like an uncle have his moment.

As soon as Hawk put him down, he looked Ty in the eye. "How's your father?"

"Still in a coma, but it's only been three days," Ty replied.

Hawk nodded solemnly. He could tell Ty had something on his mind. "Come on in the back, young blood."

Ty followed Hawk into his office. It was a cramped little office/storage space, but it had a small desk in the corner. They both sat on crates while Hawk poured himself a shot of Henny. He offered Ty a drink but he declined.

"Yo, Hawk, I'm comin' to you… not because Pops got hit

right outside yo' spot. I'm comin' to you because I know he trust you like a brother," Ty explained, resting his elbows on his knees. "What happened?"

"Youngblood, I wasn't out front when the shots got fired. I was behind the bar. My old lady was here, you wanna ask —"

Ty held up his hand with a slight smirk. "Unk," he began purposely with the term of endearment short for uncle, "I know your love for my father and your loyalty to our family. I would never think to question that because the thought alone would break my heart!"

"Your father is like a brother to me," Hawk said, relieved to hear his name was in the clear. He may have known Ty since he was a baby, but he was a grown man now. He knew, even though Ty was only 23, that he had several bodies under his belt. So with the situation so serious, he knew to tread lightly.

"I feel you, Unk. Just tell me what you know?"

Hawk downed his drink then said, "Guy came in like he usually did, with a couple of his guys and a bad ass young girl."

"How young?"

"I don't know, maybe mid to late twenties."

Ty hadn't heard about any chick being shot. "Did she leave with him?" Ty probed.

"Of course."

Ty knotted his brow. "Describe her."

"I don't know, Youngblood, you know Guy likes 'em dark and built like a stallion."

Ty sighed.

"He kicked it wit' me and the fellas 'bout an hour, got his head right then he left."

"What guys?" Ty want to know.

Hawk shook his head. "I promise you, Ty, none of them would harm a hair on your father's head. Besides, they never left the bar when your pops left."

Ty nodded. "Then what?"

"Then we heard the shots. Had to be an automatic because the shit sounded like a machine gun."

Ty visibly tensed up just thinking about his father being gunned down. He couldn't wait to get his hands on the bastard. He took a deep breath to calm himself.

"So then we ran out and found Guy's bodyguard face down and your pop's head in Gloria's lap," Hawk added.

"Gloria?" Ty said surprised. "Where'd she come from?"

"I don't know, Youngblood."

Ty sat back letting it all sink in. Her presence would explain why she had been in the ambulance with Guy. *Could Gloria?* He dismissed the thought—for now. He needed to speak with her ASAP.

Ty stood up to leave and Hawk stood with him. They shook hands.

"Thank, Unk, I appreciate your time."

"We family, Youngblood. Anything I can do, 'cause you know my guns still bust," Hawk told him proudly.

Ty smiled. He had heard Hawk had put in major work back in his day. "I know."

Before Ty turned to leave, Hawk added, "This might be nothin' or it could be somethin', but Brah Hardy came home a few weeks ago."

"Who?"

"Brah Hardy. You probably don't remember the Hardy Boys, but they were some hell raisers back in the day. He been locked up 'bout twenty years," Hawk told him.

"What about him?" Ty asked, now giving Hawk his undivided attention.

"Well… he and yo' pops bumped heads before he went away for a body," Hawk explained.

"Bumped heads over what?"

Hawk smile sheepishly. "Your mother. She was wit' Brah first… before Guy took her. Brah felt a way and they got into it. Guy ended up shootin' Brah in the leg."

Ty was on fire. "Where Brah at?"

"Around. Let me make a few calls. Gimme a day or so," Hawk said.

"Unk, make it happen," Ty told him firmly, handing Hawk his number. He headed out the door and headed for Gloria's subdivision.

●●●●●●

Vee pulled up to the corner store in north Charlotte. He hopped out of the '98 Maxima feeling like a whole load had been lifted from his shoulders. Cat and Taheem had bounced to Baltimore, Maryland. Cat had chosen B-more because she could transfer her credits to Morgan State. He had seen them off with two hundred grand to tide them over until the war was over.

Vee glanced around him then entered the Arab store. Actually, the owners were from Afghanistan but everyone was Arab if they were from the Middle East in the hood.

The bell over the door tinkled as he entered. Inside, Vee heard what sounded like Egyptian music playing in the store. The pretty red-bone smiled into his eyes and licked her lips seductively.

"What's up, J-Rock?" she spoke, using his alias. It was the only name she knew him by.

"What up, beautiful… how you?" Vee responded.

The girl loved that sleepy bedroom look he had. It made

37

her pussy wet just looking into his eyes.

"Where Sami?" he asked.

"He in the back. Oh, you ain't come to see me?" she asked with a fake attitude and her hands on her hips.

"Next time, baby girl," Vee replied, not remembering her name.

"You say that every time."

"Then we both got something to look forward to, huh? Now, go 'head. Tell Sami I'm here."

The chick sauntered off with a vicious sway in her Buffy-like hips, making Vee lick his lips.

"Yeah, I'ma hafta bang that one of these days," he mumbled to himself. But today wouldn't be that day. His mind was on bigger things. Money, power, respect.

Sami came out the back with his trademark greeting. "J-Rock, my friend! How are you?" Sami said in his thick Afghan accent.

Vee smiled and stepped into his embrace. Sami kissed him on the cheek, something he hated but knew it was an Afghani thing.

"Come. We talk in the back."

He and Sami went into the storage room that Sami had sound-proofed. Sami often bragged that the room was so secure that he could hide Osama Bin Laden in the hood. They both sat on crates.

"You finished already?" Sami asked, surprised. "You movin' up in the world."

Vee chuckled. "Naw, I ain't ready to re-up yet. I need ammo and plenty of it. I need that shit that be flippin' buses, yo."

"What's going on?"

Vee felt comfortable talking to Sami. Not only was he his heroin and gun connection, he was thorough and street

savvy. Vee had met Sami in Raleigh at one of the many
corner stores he owned. He was known to move small-
caliber pistols in the hood, which is how Vee came to know
him. Tyquan had introduced them. Sami cut into Vee quick,
seeing his potential as a hustler. Sami didn't deal with hood
cats when it came to drugs because it seemed like if they
weren't trying to rob you, they wanted to dime you out to
the Feds. But Sami sensed something in Vee and took him in.

"What can you do with this?" Sami had asked Vee one
day, giving him an ounce of uncut heroin. Vee brought him
back fifteen grand in twenty minutes: that was the beginning
of the breaking off of the Wolf Pack from the Simmons
family.

Sami listened intently as Vee explained the situation.
"And for these you want some shit to flip a bus?" Sami
asked, after hearing the whole story.
"Hell yeah, yo! They want war, I'ma bring it to 'em
bangin'!" Vee vowed.
Sami shook his head. "J... what you describe is not war. I
have seen war. War is when the missiles shake the
foundation of your home. When the elders make you sleep
in your funeral garb just in case you don't wake up. *That* is
war, this is not. This is *business*. Dangerous business, illegal
business, yes... but business plain and simple."
"I hear you, Sami, but business sometimes calls for
drastic measures," Vee countered.
"Then start with your own crew," Sami suggested.
"Huh?"
Sami smiled. "J, think. You say you and two of your
people were targeted within fifteen minutes of one another.
How did they know how to find you so quickly?"

Vee sat back on the crate, nodding his head.

Sami continued. "I smell a rat, don't you? Find the weak link and trace it back to its source then you can strike quietly but effectively and bring your enemies to their knees."

"Nothin' beats a cross but a double cross," Vee mumbled to himself, cursing himself for not seeing it sooner. His blood was boiling thinking how one of his own had betrayed him. He stood up and Sami stood with him. "Maybe I won't need to flip a bus after all," Vee smirked.

Sami laughed. "No I don't think so. But if you do, come back. I got something that'll stop a tank!"

Vee wasted no time getting back to Durham and calling a meeting with the Wolf Pack. The crew was over fifty deep, but many of them were merely wannabes and block huggers just looking for something to rep. Their chains weren't even real. The main body of the Wolf Pack consisted of five Lieutenants and the six CEOs as they were known. Rico and Pappy, who were now deceased, Mike G, Banks, Rome and the HNIC, Vee.

They met at Rome's house because his crib was in a secluded area of Durham. Vee entered the basement to find the crew assembled and talking amongst themselves.

"Vee, what up, dawg?" Rome greeted him, followed by the others. "What's the plan, yo 'cause it's *been* payback time." The others murmured their agreement.

Vee stood in the center of the room. "Yeah, you right… it is payback time, but it ain't the Simmons I'm concerned wit'," Vee announced cryptically.

The nigguhs looked at each other, confused. By the time they set eyes back on Vee, he already had his gun out.

"Yo, Vee, what's really good?" Banks asked, eyeing the gun.

Vee walked up to Banks. He had known Banks the long-est. They had been in training school together. He looked Banks in the eye then said, "It's a rat in our crew, B... a fuckin' traitor amongst us, yo!"

"Word?!" Mike G's baritone boomed. He was 6'5" and cut like Ray Lewis. "Say the word, Vee? Who?" he added looking around.

"Why you say that, Vee?" Banks wanted to know.

Vee smiled but didn't answer. Instead he turned and addressed the whole room. "How the fuck did them nigguhs know where to find us at the drop of a dime?!" Vee barked.

"Word! Banks, didn't I say that shit earlier?" Rome growled.

Vee looked around the room at the five lieutenants. He walked up to a short light skin kid. "What you think, yo?" Vee asked.

"Man I—"

BOOM!

Vee blew his brains out all over the wall. Everyone jumped at the sound...

"Yo, Vee, I know that bitch-ass nigguh ain't set us up?!" Mike G asked.

Vee looked over his shoulder and smile demonically. "I don't know," he chuckled, "but somebody in this room know! I want answers! Pappy want answers! Rico want answers!" Vee walked up to a fat Lieutenant. "Well?" Vee questioned.

"Vee, I swear I don't—"

BOOM! BOOM!

Two more head shots rang out, leaving the fat cat dead and his leg still twitching. One kid threw up.

"Yo, dawg, you wildin'! This my house!" Rome scream-ed, but Vee ignored him.

"I don't want to hear 'I don't know'. I want the... fuckin'... answer!" Vee shouted, putting his gun in another cat's face.

"Please, Vee... man," he sobbed, "I-I—"

Vee cut him off, "Huh? What's that? You what?" he taunted the kid, putting his ear to his mouth. "Speak, nigguh!"

"It-it wasn't me, man, I swear," the kid sobbed.

BOOM!

"Bitch-ass nigguh, I never liked his pussy ass anyway," Vee spat, standing over the third body of the night. "Nobody knows shit, huh?! Huh?!"

"Yo, Vee... chill, dawg. What the fuck is goin' on?" Mike G tried to calm him down.

Vee got in Mike's face. "Why don't you tell me what's goin' on, Mike," Vee spat back.

Every muscle in Mike's body tensed and his fist balled up. "Yo, Vee... the fuck you tryin' to say?" Mike hissed.

Vee smiled at him and winked. He turned to walk out the door. "Whoever the bitch-ass nigguh is, I'ma find you. And if I find out somebody knew and didn't speak on it... I'ma kill his whole fuckin' family," Vee vowed.

"Yo, Vee? What about the bodies?" Rome wanted to know.

Vee looked at Rome and shrugged. "Clean 'em up!" Then he left without another word.

CHAPTER 5

"Oh yesss, Kev! Oh fuck yes!! Karrin panted, bent over the bed and clawing the sheets. Kev had a fistful of her hair and his thumb in her ass, pounding the pussy relentlessly.

"Who's the best, hmm? Who?! Say it!" Kev demanded, watching her pretty red ass jiggle like jelly with every stroke.

"Oh yes, baby, that's my spot!" she squealed.

"Say it!" Kev repeated, while long dicking her with the whole length of his 8-inch shaft.

"You are, baby, you are," she panted. Karrin knew why he was asking and to whom he was comparing himself, but his dick felt so good deep in her pussy, Karrin spoke for the moment but not from her heart.

Kev watched his dick slipping in and out of her creamy pussy, intensity building in his stomach. "Oh-h fuck, baby, I'm about to cum," he growled.

"Cum in this pussy, daddy," Karrin begged, throwing her pussy at him harder, "cum in this pussy!"

Kev's whole body shook and twitched until he got weak in the knees and let off deep inside her. Feeling his hot load coat her walls sent Karrin over the edge and made her cum back-to-back.

"Don't move," she commanded her whole body, too sensitive for any movement.

When they finally climbed into bed, Karrin laid with her head on Kev's chest while he gently caressed her back.

"You know I love you, right?" Kev whispered, kissing the top of her head.

"I know," she replied, snuggling closer to him.

"Whatever you want is yours."

"I already got what I want," she answered, then paused.

"You sure?" Kev probed.

Karrin lifted her head and looked at him. "What do you mean by that?"

Kev lowered his head. "Nothin'."

She lifted his head back up. "Kev, talk to me."

"Yo… I mean," he began, struggling to express his feelings, "I know you ain't seen him since the wedding, so I was just wonderin'… I don't know… how you felt seeing him again?" He finally got it out.

Karrin gently kissed his lips. "Baby, Ty is my past and you," she kissed him again, "are my present and future."

Kev looked her in the eyes. "Do I make you happy?"

"I wouldn't have married you if you didn't," she answered.

Kev nodded his head, but deep down, he couldn't shake the feeling he had when Ty and Karrin were in each other's presence. He felt… shut out, like he wasn't included in the energy. He felt like he was a third wheel. It wasn't that he felt guilty being with his brother's ex-girl. He always thought Karrin was too good for Ty; he just felt like the consolation prize.

Karrin was in her own world of thoughts as well. It was true she hadn't seen Ty since the wedding because he hadn't showed up. Since seeing him at the hospital, she couldn't stop thinking of him, couldn't stop hearing his voice in her ears. He had disregarded her like she didn't exist, but when he looked at her outside the hospital she could still see the love, the passion, the pain and the question... why? Karrin felt like she needed closure. If she could just talk to him, see him alone....

The 50 Cent "Many Men" ringtone of Kev's cell phone brought them both out of their thoughts.

"Yo," Kev answered. After a few seconds he sat up straight in the bed. "He did what?!" he asked, first with surprise then stifling a chuckle. "Yeah... yeah... okay look, calm down, aiight. If he knew it was you we wouldn't be talkin' right now, correct? Okay then... naw... yo, shit is good... don't fall back when we almost there... okay look, meet me at the spot. You know I don't do phones... yeah... fifteen minutes. One." Kev hung up with a smirk.

"Everything okay?" Karrin asked.

"Yeah, but I gotta make a run," he told her then kissed her on the nose. "Keep it wet."

As Kev got dressed, he thought about what his Wolf Pack mole had told him. How Vee had just flipped and murdered three of his own. The mole thought Vee had gone crazy, but Kev knew there was a method to his madness. His move had got the mole shook and wanting to fall back. Vee knew that would buy him some time and ensure no other hit was made any time soon.

Vee was smart; Kev had to give him that. But his mole was greedy. Kev kept him on a short leash promising to give him his own crew, connection and territory in exchange for them Wolf Pack nigguhs. Yeah, his mole was scared, but Kev knew his greed was stronger than his fear, because everybody wanted to be The Man.

⚫⚫⚫⚫⚫⚫

"Ty, if I wanted to kill your father, he would've been dead years ago," Gloria told Ty, sitting on her couch watching the Young and the Restless on TiVo.

"Mama Gee, I ain't tryin' to say —," Ty tried to explain, but Gloria cut him off.

"Ty, I *know* what you tryin' to say. You just like your father, always think you so damn slick! You wanna play junior detective and wonder why I was there," Gloria surmised correctly.

Ty had to smile to himself. He knew how Mama Gee was. She was an old school gangsta's wife. A no-nonsense type of black woman that you had to come correct with or don't come at all.

"Look at this bitch Jill," she said, mean mugging the screen, "somebody need to shoot her ass! Fuckin' bitch... I was on my way to Hawk's place 'cause I knew Guy would be there. I know that nigguh like the back of my hand, so when he stood me up I ain't appreciate that shit. I was on my way to tell his ass off and that's when I heard the gunshots... I-I seen your father lyin' there, and all that blood...," her voice cracked and the Harlem girl toughness cracked with it. What was left was a vulnerable woman trying hard to deal with the biggest threat she'd ever faced. Losing the man she loved.

Ty embraced her, allowing her to sob on his shoulder. Gloria got herself together after a few moments.

"I'm okay, Ty. Just... when I think about that night... your father done caused me a lot of heartache in my life, but I swear I didn't know what I would do without him," Gloria admitted, wiping the tears that started to fall again.

"You didn't see anyone leave? On foot? No cars pulling

off?"

Gloria shook her head.

"Mama Gee... who is Brah Hardy?"

Gloria looked into Ty's face.

"That depends... am I talkin' to a little boy or a grown ass man?" she quipped with the Harlem back in her voice.

"A grown ass man."

Gloria paused the TiVo and turned to face Ty on the couch. "Your mama's ex-pimp."

Ty had to blink to get his composure. "What?"

Gloria sighed. "Back in the day your mother Debra was into a lot of things. She wasn't but eighteen when Guy first laid eyes on her and she was already in them streets... used to live out in the jungle... Green Acres. Anyway, Brah Hardy was a hustler slash pimp and he turned Debra out. Brah and Guy couldn't stand each other. The Hardy's and the Simmons' was like the Hatfield's and the McCoy's, but that's another story," Gloria explained, stopping to catch her breath. "Your mother had a lot of dudes open, but you know Guy Simmons, he got to be the one on top. Well, he finally won out and got Debra."

Ty's head was reeling from what Gloria had told him. His mother, a whore? Guy needing to know if he was really his father? It seemed like the more he wanted to know about the future, the deeper the past became. "Mama Gee, I know you ain't lyin' to me, but...," his voice trailing off because he didn't know what to say.

Gloria took his hand to console him. "Listen, Tyquan, the reason I hate your mama ain't got nothin' to do with Guy marrying her. Hell, I divorced him! And it wasn't over her... or I should say it wasn't just her; it was *all* the other hers. A different her every time I turned around. That and the fact Guy killed my brother Eddie. The shit was too much,"

Gloria confided.

Ty knew about his father killing her brother, but he hadn't realized the toll Guy's womanizing ways had had on Gloria. Ty started to speak but he was interrupted by his cell. He didn't intend on answering but he checked the number out of habit. It was one he knew well—Karrin's.

CHAPTER 6

Guy's Stacey Adams clicked along the tile floor of the apartment lobby alongside Eddie's gators. The lobby was completely
quiet except the electric hum of the building and the sounds of Le
Chic in a nearby apartment. Guy pulled back the sleeve of his
camel hair trench and glanced at his expensive watch. Looking at
him, he definitely wasn't the same man that had walked into Bell's
Bar and Grill over a year ago. Good eating had bulked him back up
to his natural weight of 215, and his wardrobe, although not on
Eddie's level, was worth a working man's fortune.

He had been Eddie's driver/muscle, taking Eddie where he
needed to go, picking up and dropping off money and delivering
messages. He was a gangsta's gopher, but he was making the type
of money black executives in corporate America made weekly.

The elevator swooshed open, and he and Eddie got on, taking it
to the fifth floor. They were in the Bronx to collect a debt. Guy was
used to this, having done this over and over again. Everybody
wanted to get over and it was Guy's job to make sure they didn't.

"You heard about Nicky's party on Saturday?" Eddie asked,
looking up at the floor numbers.

"Yeah," Guy replied, thinking, who hasn't? Every major

49

hustler in town was looking forward to the event that was sure to be extravagant. It was the only way Nicky Barnes knew how to do things.

"Well dig, brah, I want you to roll wit' me," Eddie informed him, glancing at Guy for a reaction, but Guy kept the poker face.

Guy knew if he was being invited to the party, he was being introduced to the inner circle. "Cool," was all Guy replied.

The elevator opened up on the fifth floor. Eddie and Guy made their way toward 5C at the end of the hall.

"Who is it?" a raspy woman's voice called out after Eddie knocked several times.

"Eddie."

They heard the unlatching of four locks before the door opened and a short brown-skinned woman in a housecoat and rollers opened the door.

"Hey, Eddie! How you doing?" the woman asked, stepping aside to allow the two men to enter.

Guy could tell she was fairly attractive once she was dressed. Eddie ignored her question and instead asked one of his own.

"Where's Daryl?"

"He's in the back," she answered, seeing Eddie was in no mood for small talk.

As Eddie and Guy walked down the short hallway, the baby on the couch woke up crying. It was if the child felt the negative vibe the two men brought into the apartment. The bedroom door was locked so Eddie knocked.

"Daryl, unlock the door," Eddie grumbled.

"One sec, man, I-I'm comin'," was heard from behind the door. The shuffling of paper could be heard before the door opened up.

"Hey-Hey, Eddie man, what's up?" the scraggly brown-skinned dude named Daryl asked.

Eddie and Guy entered the room.

"What the fuck is up, nigguh?! Where's my fuckin' money?!"

Eddie barked.

"I-I got it, Eddie man. I know it took awhile but I got it," Daryl assured him.

Guy watched the dude closely, keeping his hand close to the .38 stuck in his waist. It was obvious the dude was a dope fiend. He was bone skinny and kept scratching his neck with his free hand while he dug in the dresser. He handed Eddie a wad of cash that Eddie quickly counted.

"$3,300??" Eddie barked, after counting the short stack. "This ain't even half my scratch, nigguh!" Eddie threw the money in Daryl's face hard and money went everywhere.

"Man... Eddie, please, I'm fucked up in the game! I'ma get my nuts out the sand, I just need – "

"Guy, teach this nigguh a lesson," Eddie said dismis-sively. He didn't want to hear the whining of a grown man. Daryl had been a good hustler until the monkey got on his back. Now he was just a shell of the man he used to be.

Guy wasted no time tearing into Daryl's tiny frame with massive body blows that cracked one of Daryl's ribs on impact.

"Arghh!" Daryl screamed in agony. You could actually hear the grotesque sound of his left arm breaking.

Guy beat him bloody and mercilessly until the woman in rollers ran in cradling the screaming baby.

"Please, Eddie! Please! I swear we'll get yo' money!" she begged.

"Too late, bitch," Eddie hissed, handing Guy his .38.

Guy took the gun and looked at Eddie.

"Kill this sorry muhfucka," Eddie ordered.

It had never gone this far before until then, Guy had only been asked to beat nigguhs up. He had put several in the hospital but never murdered anyone for Eddie.

Guy took the gun, his eyes locking with the woman's.

"Please don't kill him! He all we got!"

Guy leveled the gun at Daryl's bloody face.

"Oh God noooo," he moaned through swollen lips.

Guy didn't hesitate. He squeezed the trigger... then again and again... but nothing came out. Each metallic click made Daryl's whole body jump and he already had pissed and shit on himself.

The gun was empty. He turned to Eddie who was smirking. Eddie had to see if Guy was really cut like that. Eddie wasn't about to be around when a body dropped, but he wanted to see how Guy would handle it. From what he saw, he was more than satisfied. He took the gun from Guy, tucked it in his waist and said, "You see what I'm sayin'? You think I'm playin'? Consider yourself spared, nigguh. Now... get... my... money!"

Daryl nodded emphatically.

Guy and Eddie walked out and headed for the elevator. "Welcome to the Family," Eddie patted Guy on the back.

⦿⦿⦿⦿⦿⦿

The party was held in the Presidential Suite of the Time Life Building in Manhattan. It was definitely an Original Player's Ball. All the major players were in attendance and the cameras were snapping. Not the paparazzi, the Justice Department. That was the beginning of the Federal observa-tion game, and at the time, many of the player's didn't realize how serious it would get in the coming years.

Everyone came dressed to impress and nobody wanted to be outdone. The jewels blinged from every extremity as the game came out to celebrate the life.

Guy arrived with Eddie, sporting a dark blue pinstripe double breasted suit and his first pair of matching 'gators. The dark-skinned beauty on his arm completed his attire like a precious jewel.

Eddie, always the Harlemite, stepped out in a tailor- made

*purple double breasted suit and black ostrich boots. His black
Stetson was cocked ace-deuce and sported a purple feather. On his
left lapel was a corsage and on his right arm was his wife, Theresa.*

*Inside the plush suite, Guy found himself amongst the game's
elite. Eddie introduced Guy to everyone, including Nicky himself.*

*The females eyed the newcomer flirtatiously even while on the
arms of other nigguhs. Guy took it all in stride until his eyes fell
on Gloria. The vision he saw had him stuck. Her ebony thickness
was wrapped in a lavender sequined dress with matching head
wrap. Her heels exposed her lickable toes and Guy fantasized about
sucking each one, one by one. She was by far the most beautiful
woman in the room.*

*Since he and Eddie had been spending so much time together,
he saw Gloria frequently. But she always had something slick to
say or a bad attitude when Guy was around. Tonight would be no
different.*

*"Where the hell you get that monkey suit from?" Gloria
remarked snidely when she made it her business to walk over to the
refreshments table while Guy was over there.*

*He started to say something, but Eddie walked up and said,
"So how you enjoying yourself, brah? Nicky really know how to
lay it down!"*

*"Yeah, yeah, it's real mellow, Eddie," Guy answered, momen-
tarily distracted with grilling Gloria as she walked away rolling
her eyes. "Thanks for inviting me."*

*"Naw, brah, you invited yourself. I usually don't cut into cats
so quick, but I knew you was a solid stud from day one. I had to
give you the once over, but you proved to be a down blood. Now
dig," Eddie said, putting his arm around Guy's shoulder, even
though Guy was three inches taller. With his drink in his left hand
he gestured around the room. "Believe me, baby, this thing of ours
is a beautiful thing because it's organized. Just like the guineas,
except we a whole lot betta lookin'!" Eddie snickered, making Guy*

chuckle. "Look around this room. Every cat with a corsage on their lapels, like this," Eddie explained, pointing to his corsage, "is a part of the council."

"The council?" Guy echoed.

"Yeah, Nicky's roundtable. Me... and now you. Now, it ain't official yet, but once you get the nod, you'll get your own territory and a kilo of heroin to get on your feet. The way it works is, when it's time to cop, we cop big. Each member of the council puts up anywhere from a quarter mil to a half a mil. This way we get the best deal from the Guineas. You follow me?"

"Yeah, I follow," Guy answered, even though his head was reeling looking around the room at all the council members. He was just realizing the fact that he was in a room full of black millionaires!

"Did you hear me?" Eddie asked.

"Huh?" Guy remarked.

"I was saying, this is a brotherhood, brah," Eddie told him solemnly, "and we take that oath serious. That way we keep problems to a minimum. There's a few rules, but the three are, one, you never rat on your brother."

Guy nodded. He was too solid to even consider breaking that rule.

"Number two, no council member can trespass on another's territory without his permission," Eddie contin-ued.

"I got you."

Eddie stopped walking and turned to Guy. "And three, which is the easiest to break but least tolerated... never... never can a council member sleep with the wife or woman of another member. The penalty... is death." Eddie looked Guy in the eyes to make sure he fully understood.

"I can respect that," Guy assured.

"Make sure you do, because I saw how a few of these broads was checkin' you out. Remember, it ain't they life on the line... it's *yours. Enjoy yourself while I go find Nicky."* Eddie disappeared, leaving Guy to contemplate the life he was about to embark upon.

Guy danced with his date and conversed with different members. The night was going well, except for Gloria's funny looks and snide remarks. But the remark that was the one that broke the camel's back was when she brushed past him and said, "I don't give a damn who you think you is, you ain't nothin' but a backwoods country motherfucka."

Guy's blood was on sizzle, but he kept his composure, not even allowing Gloria to know he had heard her. But he had and waited for the perfect time to put her in check once and for all. That chance came fifteen minutes later when Gloria went to the bathroom.

Guy nonchalantly excused himself from his date then followed Gloria out of the room. Nobody peeped the move except Eddie because he always kept a close eye on his sister.

Gloria was a bit tipsy as she made her way to the bathroom. As soon as she entered, Guy was right behind her. She turned to see why the door didn't close and saw Guy lunging at her. Before she could scream his massive hand was around her throat, choking the shit out of her.

"Bitch, is you crazy?! You got a fuckin' problem?!" Guy snarled, biting down on his bottom lip.

Gloria tried to kick Guy, but only ended up losing a shoe. She hit at his arms and even tried to scratch his face, but he batted her arms away.

"Get... yo'... God...aargh!" she struggled to speak, trying to loosen the vice like grip he had on her neck.

"If you say some mo' slick shit... one mo' time... I promise you, bitch, I'll break yo' goddamn neck!" Guy hissed, with his body pressed up against hers.

Just as Gloria began to feel woozy, Guy let her go. Her knees buckled and she leaned against the sink, gasping for breath.

"Motherfucka you dead!" she gasped in a hoarse voice. "Just

wait 'til I tell Eddie!"

"I don't give a fuck what you tell Eddie!" Guy barked, ready to break Eddie's neck too, if he felt a way. "You talk like a woman but you ain't shit but a spoiled little bitch!"

"Nigguh, fuck you! You don't know me!" she screamed back.

Despite his anger, Guy couldn't get over how beautiful Gloria was. Especially now that she was angry. Her nostrils were flared, eyes ablaze and nipples poking hard through her dress. He bent to pick up her shoe then hurled it at her.

"Now go get yo' brother, and tell him he better bring an Army if he fuck wit' Guy Simmons!" he bellowed.

Gloria quickly retrieved her shoe then grabbed the door knob to exit. Guy grabbed her by the arm.

"Where you goin'?!" Guy barked.

Gloria quickly smacked the shit out of him but it hardly turned his head. He was already locked in on kissing her luscious lips. He pulled her to him.

"Get off —" was all she got out before Guy had her wrapped in his arms and his tongue half way down her throat. Gloria bit down hard on his tongue, but the pain only fueled his passion more. He pinched her nipple through her dress so hard, Gloria had to release his tongue to howl in pain and moan in pleasure. Guy's hand was already pulling up her dress and grasping at her stockings. Gloria's struggle against became groping for, groping at his back and neck trying to devour him with her body.

Gloria had never wanted someone so bad in all her nineteen years. She had wanted Guy since the first time she laid eyes on him, but he seemed to all but ignore her. She wasn't used to that, which frustrated and intrigued her more. Many nights she had dreamed of just what she was doing now, but she never dreamed they'd be fucking and fighting at the same time!

"This what you want?! You want it rough, huh?" Guy panted, snatching a hole in her stockings in the crotch.

"Hm-mmm!" she replied, biting and licking on his neck.

Gloria felt like she couldn't stop Guy if she wanted to, the way he was taking control and totally dominating the situation. She fumbled with his belt as he lifted her like she was weightless on to the sink. He already had her dress hiked up above her waist. Gloria was dripping like a faucet as she reached into Guy's pants. Her eyes popped open like silver dollars.

"Goddamn, nigguh, is you a mule?!" she gasped, push-ing Guy away from her.

"What?" he feigned ignorance, knowing exactly what she was talking about.

In the South they call it being 'ruint' or ruptured. In plain English, he had a dick that hung to his knees.

"Ain't no way, ain't no goddamn way!" Gloria cursed, pulling her dress down and scooping her shoe all in one motion. She shot out the door, hobbling on one foot trying to put her shoe on in midstride.

Guy chuckled to himself. He ran some water over his face and patted his mini afro back in place. He was used to that reaction from women, but he was determined to get Gloria.

He came back into the room to find Gloria talking to a few couples. She was trying not to be spotted, but once she saw Guy coming her way, her eyes got wide again and she froze like a deer.

"Get your coat," Guy whispered in her ear.

"Uh-uh," Gloria responded, suddenly sounding like a little girl.

Guy's smile never left his face as he gripped her elbow and repeated, "Get yo' goddamn coat... now."

His touch and voice sent shivers down her spine.

"Oh-oh okay," Gloria answered.

Guy escorted her to coat check then out the front door. As he left, him and Eddie's eyes met. Eddie smirked, nodded then raised his glass.

"Guy, please... don't hurt me," Gloria whispered as Guy braced himself to enter her. He knew she was talking about more than the intercourse; she was also talking about her heart.

Gloria felt like her pussy would split in two from the girth of Guy's dick. It was the most painful pleasure she had ever experienced. She laid spread eagle on her black satin sheets, gripping Guy's arms as he slowly slid deeper inside of her.

"Oh, Guy, no more... yes... yessss," she purred as her pussy got wetter the more he stroked her.

Guy looked down at her beautiful shapely body, twirling his tongue around each of her chocolate chip nipples that sat erect in her firm C cup breasts. Her pussy felt like pure cream, and it took every ounce of Guy's willpower not to cum. Gloria had already cum by the time he was eight inches deep.

"Tell me you can take it," he whispered in her ear.

Gloria arched her back and wrapped her legs around Guy's back. "Y-yes, daddy... awww fuck! I-I can take it!"

He pushed. Nine ... ten... eleven and Gloria's pussy farted as the air was pushed out of it. The way she was moaning, he knew the neighbors had to be listening.

Gloria pulled him tighter, panting over and over in his ears, "I love you... I love you... I love you."

Twelve... thirteen... then finally the entire fourteen inches slid in, and Guy began to grind his hips, causing Gloria's whole body to tremble. It felt like she could feel each stroke all the way to her brain as Guy built up momentum with his never ending long stroke.

"I'm squirtin', baby, Oh God... I'm squirtin'!" Gloria squealed as her pussy ejaculated like she was pissing.

Guy was ready to cum too as he placed Gloria's legs in front of his arms and lifted her half way off the bed.

Gloria gripped the sheets and her eyes rolled up in the back of her head as she moaned, "Guy, pl-pl-pl cum, I-I-I can't take any...

more."

Guy was in a zone. He had never seen a pussy so red on the inside. It looked like the inside of a watermelon. He loved watching his dick slid in and out, her pussy coming over and over until he pushed all the way inside her with a grunt and came deep inside her pussy.

He collapsed on top of Gloria, trying to catch his breath. Gloria cradled his head to her chest and kissed it gently.

"I love you, Guy Simmons."

CHAPTER 7

Ty looked down at his Blackberry as it vibrated in his hand. It had been so long since Karrin had called him. He hadn't erased her from the phone so he stared at the name — Karrin.

After all that Gloria had told him about his mother, now wasn't the time to relive painful memories or open old wounds. He let the call go unanswered. Instantly, she called back. Ty couldn't ignore her twice.

"What up?" he answered, looking up and down the block as he walked to the car.

Silence.

"Yo," he barked gruffly.

"Hello," Karrin said, her angelic voice sounding unsure, like footsteps on thin ice. "Are you busy?"

His pride willed him to say yes. Click! But his heart used his mouth to say, "No."

Karrin took a deep breath then said, "I need to see you, Ty."

"See me?" he echoed with a wounded chuckle, "See me for what?"

"Don't act like that, Ty, because I know you want to see me too," she spoke quickly so she wouldn't lose the nerve to go on. "I know our situation is… awkward, but if we could meet, not for long, but long enough so we can both speak our mind."

"First off, *we* ain't got a situation. That ended the moment you said I do. Secondly, the only thing on my mind to say is goodbye!"

He took the phone away from his ear, but he still heard her vaguely.

"…love me."

Ty put the phone back to his ear. "What?"

"I said… tell me you don't love me," Karrin urged him, scared of his reply.

"I don't love you," he answered, but without conviction or sincerity.

The words were like a dagger to her ears, but she knew it wasn't his heart talking.

"Please, Ty, just for a little while. Meet me at our old spot, okay? Please. After this I won't bother you again. I promise."

Ty sighed heavily. He knew this situation could lead to major problems, but he couldn't resist seeing her again, just one on one. Besides, he felt he owed her at least that. "Gimme an hour," he told her then hung up without hearing her reply.

Charlie Goodnights in Raleigh was a popular comedy club. It was the place that Ty had taken Karrin too many times. It was a regular cool out spot for them, Vee and Cat.

The place had a nice crowd when Ty walked in. The male comedian on stage already had the crowd in an uproar.

"….so I turn on the light and *then* she say I forgot to tell you!" said the comedian with the Chris Tucker type hi-pitched voice.

Ty spotted Karrin sitting up near the front. She was so beautiful to him. A cinnamony bronze that gave her skin the radiance of Egyptian gold. Her chestnut brown eyes gave off Sade's sultry seductiveness and had a way of hypnotizing Ty whenever he stared into them. He studied her as he walked up. She had her hair like he loved it. In an upsweep, one curly bang hanging down and slightly curling along her cheekbone.

She's your brother's wife now, he thought bitterly to himself, but he wondered if she was his brother's wife or had his brother married his girl. As he reached the table, Karrin started to get up as if to embrace him but he cut that short.

"Don't get up," he mumbled as he sat down.

"How are you, Ty? You look... good," Karrin said, but wanted to say fine.

She had grown up with him and watched him become a man. From the Timb boots, sagging pants and gaudy jewelry to GQ status, expensive understatements and tailor made suits. She smiled, to her thinking it was her that picked out the outfit he was wearing. From the Mauri gator sneakers to the Evizu jeans and Gucci button up.

The waitress came over and delivered their drinks.

"Henny and Coke, right?" Karrin smiled slyly.

"Yeah," he answered, not showing his appreciation for her remembering. He downed half his drink with one gulp.

Karrin leaned forward. "Thank you for coming."

Her comment dropped into an awkward silence. All that could be heard was the rousing applause as the comedian finished his set.

"What you got to say?" he asked directly.

"Why?" was her simple reply.

"Why what?" he retorted.

"Why didn't you return my phone calls? Why didn't you write me back when you were locked up? Why, all of a sudden did everything we shared have to end?" Karrin's voice broke, tears brimming in the wells of her eyes.

"The life I lead, I don't need any distractions, yo. I mean... I guess somewhere along the line I stopped feeling the same way," Ty tried his best to come up with a valid excuse, but he knew he was coming off sounding weak. He wanted to tell her the real reason, but he could never do that.

"I see," she said, lowering her eyes. She dabbed at them with a napkin.

"What about you?" he questioned. "Why'd you marry my brother?"

Karrin sipped her VSOP and replied, "It doesn't matter now."

"It matters to me."

She looked him in the eye and answered, "Because he asked."

Ty held her gaze with a confused look on his face. "Because he asked??? I don't get it. If what we had was so real how could you just up and marry my brother?!" His voice rose an octave, so he looked around to make sure no one heard him wearing his heart on his sleeve.

"I didn't marry for love, Ty. You're the only man that will ever have my heart. But I'm no fool either. If I'm gonna settle then I'll be damned if I'm a struggle too," she told him matter-of-factly.

"So you married for money."

"I married for security."

"You married for money," Ty replied, finishing his drink. "Better him than me, huh?"

Karrin sucked her teeth. "Don't play with me, Ty… you know what I mean! I would've eaten beans out the can with you, did a bid with you day for day if I had to, so don't even go there."

"Yeah well, we don't always get what we want, do we?" He stood, tossing a hundred on the table. "Congratulations on your marriage."

"Ty, wait," Karrin called after him, getting up.

Ty made his way through the club. Karrin caught up with him near the door. She grabbed his arm so he'd turn to her.

"I just…," Karrin began, but her words and emotions were all jumbled up inside. So instead, she expressed them with a kiss.

The kiss caught Ty by surprise, but when she wrapped her leg around his calf like she used to, he knew they had gone too far to turn back. Ty tongued her back, tasting the VSOP on her tongue and feeling the passion in the way she sucked his tongue. He finally found the strength to break the kiss, but he pulled away reluctantly.

"It's not over," Karrin whispered seductively as she walked past him.

Ty's mind was in a whirl as they stepped out the door, but reality struck quickly when a barrage of bullets was suddenly unleashed all around him!

●●●●●●

At the time, Vee was driving to Lagrange, a tiny town between Goldsboro and Kinston. It was also the place where he'd been raised. As he turned off highway 117 into the city limits, he spoke on the phone talking to Sami.

"Yeah, dawg, the cookout's Saturday, so come thru wit'

like thirty steaks!" Vee told him in code. The conversation never mattered; it was only the number that had meaning. It meant how many kilos of heroin Vee wanted.

"Well since it's your birthday, I'll pay for half," Sami replied, meaning half was consignment.

"If you feelin' that generous, you bring the drinks!" Vee joked.

"See you Saturday."

Click.

Vee was in a mellow mood because business was doing well. The Wolf Pack not only had a nice chunk of Durham on smash, they also had opened up shop in Greenville and Wilmington—two spots that were in Kev's territory. Vee's mentality was, if we gonna war let it be for something I did, not for something you think I did! Referring to the Guy Simmons shooting. He knew Kev would catch feelings but he felt like the Simmons' were over rated. Guy was an old timer and his sons never knew what it meant to be hungry. So how could they go to war with wolves?

But besides business, his soul wasn't at peace, which was why he was going home to Lagrange to see the old woman that raised him.

Vee drove straight through the city itself and drove along an old country highway bare of any street lights. The road was lined with trees. He felt like he knew these woods better than most animals because he spent his first seven years on this earth exploring them.

He turned a narrow dirt road. It was really a driveway about a tenth of a mile long. He came to a small white house with a tiny porch with enough room for one rocking chair. The front door was open as he always remembered. The screen door was the only thing separating the inside of the house with the outside elements.

He knocked once on the screen door then opened it. He smiled knowing that it would be unlocked. Anyone was welcomed and no one dared come with evil intent because Ms. Sadie may've been a kind woman but she was also a root worker.

Some days there'd be a line of people and cars waiting to see the famous Ms. Sadie. They came from miles around for various reasons. They never paid her because she didn't ask for money, but Ms. Sadie never wanted for anything. Vee didn't even know what money was until he was almost nine. But he never went to bed hungry.

"Mama?" Vee called out, entering the living room. Mahalia Jackson sang on an old am/fm transistor radio.

"In the kitchen, baby," he heard her tiny voice call out.

She almost sounded like a little girl, but she was clearly an old woman. No one knew exactly how old because even folks that looked her age had always remembered her looking the same when they were young. Vee knew old people had a tendency to exaggerate, but Ms. Sadie certainly looked the same when he was a child.

He bent over to hug her tiny frame then kissed her on her wrinkled cheek. Her hair was a grayish white but her eyes were still sharp as a hawk. She was snapping green beans into a pot when he arrived. Vee sat down at the small kitchen table catty-corner from her and slouched down.

"Victor, sit up. That's bad for your back," she quietly scolded him.

He leaned forward, resting his elbows across his knees. "What's poppin', Mama?" Vee asked with a smile.

"What's what? What's poppin'? Boy, I don't know what that foolishness mean. These beans is what's poppin', the bones in my back is what's poppin'," she chuckled.

"I know my favorite girl ain't gettin' old?" Vee joked.

"No, but I ain't gettin' no younger neither. How you? How's the baby and yo' girlfriend?"

"They good. They in B-More."

"Why?"

"A little heat, but nothin' I can't handle," Vee assured her.

"Hm-mmm. What I tell you about trouble? Take a minute to get into —"

"And a lifetime to get out of," Vee finished, having heard it a million times. "I ain't in trouble."

"If you say so," she replied, continuing to snap beans in silence then added, "You still got that pouch I give you?"

"Never leave home without it."

"You ever look inside it?"

"No."

"Don't," she replied firmly then met his eyes, "Ever."

Vee nodded solemnly.

"Now...," Ms. Sadie said, wiping her hands on a dishrag, "tell me about these dreams you been having."

A cold chill went up Vee's spine. No matter how many times she did it, it always managed to shake him. He hadn't told her about any dreams, but like everything else, she just knew. That's why he had never lied to her. It was useless. Vee rubbed his hand over his face then began.

"I'm walking in the pitch black. I can't even see my hand in front of my face... it's that black. But I can hear my footsteps... you know? The thunder flashes and I can see I'm in the woods. I get scared 'cause I don't know where I'm at, but I know I'm 'posed to be somewhere. All of a sudden I hear music and laughter... I look and I'm in front of a pool room but its back in the day. Somebody gettin' stabbed by some fat dude with a... I don' know, a fuckin' sickle like the grim reaper be carrying. I step over the dude and go in the

pool room. All the laughter stops and I see my mother...,"
Vee's voice trailed off, relishing the face. He had never seen
his mother but Ms. Sadie had described her so many times
he knew what she looked like. "My mother, she wit' a bunch
of gangstas... she walks up and hands me this... ring. But it
ain't gold or platinum or silver, it's like made of... ivory...
bone. I put it on and it becomes this fly ass gold ring with an
emerald in it. Soon as I put it on, the gangstas start shooting
each other, but the dude with the sickle kills 'em all," Vee
finished, shaking his head.

Vee looked over at Ms. Sadie. She had her eyes closed as
if she were seeing the dream with him.

"Then... I'm at a pool and Cat is there. She keeps calling
my name, but when I answer her she don't hear me. I tell
her, 'open your eyes,' because they closed. All of a sudden,
fish start jumping out of her into the pool. Next thing I see is
a beautiful fish jump out the pool with wings. As it flies off,
she tries to chase it. I'm steady callin' her name... but she
don't hear me."

Ms. Sadie took a deep breath and opened her eyes. "The
darkness is the unknown. The questions you have about
your past. The ring represents wealth and power. Once you
get it, the bloodshed will ensue, but death will assist you in
defeating your enemies. But the only way you can get it
Victor... you must find your mother."

Vee sucked his teeth. "Man, fuc... forget her," he spat.

"Honor thy father and mother that thy days on this earth
shall be long!" she bellowed.

"*You* my mother. I'm my own father," Vee replied.

Ms. Sadie smiled and took his hand. "Yes, Victor, you are
like a son to me. I raised you from a baby. But all the anger,
hurt and confusion that's so built up in you can only be
lifted with understanding. You're like a time bomb ready to

explode, but anger doesn't make you a man. A man would face head on, whatever stands in his way. Go… find your mother."

Vee sat contemplating Ms. Sadie's words then asked, "What about Cat and the fish? I remember you said fish mean somebody pregnant."

Ms. Sadie chuckled. "Most of the time," she said then her smile disappeared. "You need to check on your family. Spend time with them. All the money in the world can't replace that."

Inside, Ms. Sadie grimaced. She knew exactly what the dream meant, but there was no way she could prepare him for that and there was nothing she could do to stop it. He bent down and kissed her on the cheek. She watched him leave with a heavy heart. He had been through so much pain in his life and she knew it would only get worse.

CHAPTER 8

Ty sat in the hospital waiting room, seething. All he could see and taste was blood. Vee's! He couldn't believe Vee would make a move on him like that, especially with Karrin with him. He would've never made a move jeopardizing Cat, because Cat and Karrin were cousins. But that was before... before Vee showed him that it was truly war.

Ty knew the Wolf Pack hadn't put the hit on Guy, because they couldn't benefit from his death. Vee was ruthless, but he was a thinker as well. Ty was the only one that could've stopped an all out war, now Vee had made it personal and for that, he'd pay with his life. Ty was adamant about that.

The good thing was he hadn't been hit. But the bad thing was Karrin got shot. As they stepped out into the barrage of bullets, Ty's street instincts instantly kicked in, and he dove back in the club pulling Karrin with him. He had seen the two gunmen standing outside, but they were young, impatient and nervous. As soon as they saw Ty's face they let off at him; not wanting to give him a chance to put his hammer game down. They already knew Ty wasn't to be fucked with, so they didn't want to give him a chance to react.

The shooting of Karrin seemed devastating because there was blood everywhere. Ty was guilt stricken. He knew meeting with her would be trouble, but not like this! He had no choice but to call Kev, because if Karrin died….

Upon arriving at the hospital, Ty found out she only got hit in the shoulder. It was the shock and fear that made her lose more blood than the wound naturally warranted. For that fact, they wanted to keep her overnight for observation.

Kev entered with one of his men in tow. Ty could see the fire in his eyes. Ty knew the nigguh was heated, but he hadn't expected Kev to sucker punch him with a lunging straight right that sat Ty right back down in his seat. It happened so fast only a few people saw it.

"Stay the fuck away from my wife, nigguh!" Kev hissed.

The punch Kev landed had Ty's jaw throbbing and his eye twitching. His whole being wanted to jump up and mash Kev's ass out, but he knew he deserved it.

"You got that," Ty replied, rubbing his jaw. "But, don't ever do it again!"

"What you mean don't do it again?!" Kev barked and started at Ty again. This time Kev's man restrained him. Kev spun around and spazzed on his man. "The fuck is on your mind?! Take yo' muhfuckin' hands off me! This a family affair!" The dude quickly complied.

Kev turned back to Ty and bent down to eye level. "Don't you get it lil' *brother*?! Yo' bitch chose me," Kev smiled. "Don't tell me a chick got fly Ty fucked up in the head? I thought you respected the game, *playa*?"

"Yeah, I do. Just respect it when *you* see it… big *brother*," Ty smiled back. He wanted to tell Kev his wife wasn't

married to him; she was married to his wallet. But since they
say love is blind, he decided to leave Kev in the dark.

Kev stood back up looking strangely at Ty's lips. He
knew Ty's words had a hidden meaning, but he let it go for
now. "Still think them Wolf Pack nigguhs didn't set this shit
off?"

"Naw, but they got the right one now. And unlike you…
I won't miss," Ty assured him.

Kev smiled to himself as he walked away. The Wolf Pack
was history. He had met with his mole and he had calmed
his nerve. Well, the brick of heroin had calmed his nerves
and fed his greed. He had agreed to set them all up in one
spot for Kev. Vee had been elusive, but he promised Kev
he'd have him there. "Then you'll be the man in Durham,"
Kev had promised him while thinking to himself, *yeah the
man they find dead in Durham*. If he'd set up his own
homeboys for Kev, what would he do *to* Kev for a better
offer? It was a dirty game, but someone had to play it and
Kev planned on playing it to a tee.

Kev found out where Karrin's room was and he headed
for the elevator. When he entered the room, she turned to
see who it was. Their eyes met and locked, until her's
watered up and she dropped her gaze.

"I'm sorry, Kevin," she sobbed.

Kevin didn't reply. He silently shut the door and studied
her lovely face. The only thought on his mind was why she
couldn't see he truly loved her? Ty had all but left her for
dead. It was Kev that went through it with her. He gave her
anything she wanted and treated her like a queen. But it still
wasn't enough. He didn't see himself as a nice guy, the kind
women say they want but never appreciated. But more and
more he felt like one, standing in the room.

"Please, Kev, I know you're upset, but please say

something," Karrin begged him. The look of love in his eyes made her feel guilty that she didn't feel the same, but she didn't want to hurt him either.

"What you want me to say, Karrin? What *can* I say? That I'm sorry you got shot creepin' wit' my brother?" he retorted, his voice low but tense.

"We weren't creeping."

"Oh so, you expect me to believe if this wouldn't have happened, you were going to *tell* me you were with Ty?"

Karrin didn't respond.

"I didn't think so," Kev finished as he paced the room. "You want the nigguh that bad, Karrin? Huh? Just be woman enough to just say it to my face! You ain't gotta do it behind my back!"

"Kev, stop it! I love you, I do. I don't want Ty, I want you," Karrin lied, but since she willed herself into living an illusion, it flowed from her lips truthfully. "I... I just needed to know *why*, Kev? I just needed closure. Can you understand that?" she cried.

"So you called *him*?" he asked surprised.

Pause.

"Yes," Karrin admitted. Kev huffed loudly, so she quickly added, "I just had to get him out of my system."

Kev stopped and stared at her. "Did you fuck him, Karrin?"

"No!" she yelled, surprised but not shocked that he'd ask.

Kev approached the bed like a D.A. would a witness on the stand. "So you're telling me you went through all of this going behind my back, setting up a meeting spot and all, just to see him?!"

"I needed closure."

"You fucked 'im, Karrin," he said, his voice so low, it was

almost a whisper.

"No, Kev—"

"You fucked 'im?!" he barked, feeling sick to his stomach just thinking about it. Kev had her by the throat but he couldn't bring himself to apply pressure.

"No, no, baby, I swear I didn't!" she vowed.

Kev looked at her then slowly removed his hand. "But you wanted to," he mumbled.

Karrin sat up and grimaced as she did, "No, Kev, I didn't. I don't. It's over between Ty and me. There's... there's nothing left," she explained half truthfully because she was speaking from Ty's viewpoint.

Kev wanted to believe her with all his heart. He tipped her chin up and looked her in the face. "Did you kiss him?"

She looked him square in the eyes and replied, "No... I didn't."

It came out so smooth, so believable, he would've believed her had he not seen the smudges of lipstick on Ty's mouth. The same candy red Karrin loved to wear.

⊚⊚⊚⊚⊚⊚

"Yo, young blood, you got that Wolf Pack?"

"Let me get a bundle over here!"

"Let the Wolves out!"

The McDougal projects in Durham were abuzz with activity. The dope of choice was the one with the N.C. State Mascot on it—the one that belonged to the Wolf Pack. Fiends crept through the streets like zombies for that heroin that guaranteed to put your dick in the dirt.

The team of soldiers Vee had out there was truly solid. Ready for war and ready to eat. They just weren't ready for Ty. Like black rain, bullets began to seemingly fall from the sky, turning the black rain into deadly reign. The street team was totally caught off guard. They couldn't even locate where the bullets were coming from and a few ended up shooting each other. In a matter of minutes, the shooting stopped, and no member of the street team had survived.

When Ty hit, he didn't do drive-bys or even walk-bys— that was so West Coast. Ty brought in snipers, six of them, positioned strategically around the area. From where the snipers sat it was like shooting fish in a barrel.

The same thing occurred in Greenville and Wilmington. In less than five minutes, in three different areas, Ty had successfully reduced the Wolf Pack's army by half.

●●●●●●

"What's wrong wit' you?" Vee wanted to know. He and Cat had just finished fucking. She had rolled off him and laid down with her back to him. He knew something was wrong, because she loved to snuggle in the afterglow of sex.

"Nothin'," she replied without turning over.

Vee sat up on his elbow. "Nothin'? A minute ago it was 'Owww, daddy, daddy, daddy! I love you. I love you.' Now it's nothing?"

"I was horny. Thanks," Cat answered sarcastically.

Vee smiled at her back. He knew Cat had an attitude because he had taken so long to come see her and the baby.

Okay," he shrugged. "Thanks for the shot." He rolled over and turned his back to her, smiling. He knew she was boiling because he didn't urge to get it out of her.

Cat turned over quick. "Fuck you mean, thanks for the shot? I'm one of your hoes now?! Get the fuck out my bed!" she yelled, pushing her feet against his back.

"Chill, Cat." He laughed as he got up. "Damn, you just

thanked me! I'm sayin', you said it's nothin' then it's nothin'."

"You know damn well what it is, Vic, don't play wit' me! Oh, you think just 'cause you come sling a little dick I 'posed to be the happy little housewife?! Not happenin'!"

"Little dick?" he chuckled, gripping his flaccid six inches that stood erect at eight plus. "You wasn't sayin' that when this lil' dick had you shakin' and speakin' in tongues."

Cat sat Indian-style on the bed. "Don't flatter yourself, I've seen bigger."

"Yeah, but have you had better?" he quipped. He pounced on her unexpectedly and started tickling her.

Cat laughed until she cried, trying to kick and punch Vee. "Stop! Stop! You gonna wake Taheem!"

"No *you* gonna wake him laughing so loud," he shot back, tickling her unmercifully. "Now say it, say you the best Da-Da!"

"Hell no!"

He tickled her harder.

"Okay, okay!"

"Say it!"

"I can't catch my breath, I'm havin' an asthma attack!" she huffed.

"You ain't got asthma! Say it or the feet next!" Vee repeated.

Tickling her feet made Cat pee on herself, so she quickly relented, "You the best Da-Da!"

"And you know this!" Vee replied triumphantly, lying on top of Cat. He kissed her on the nose. "I know it took me a minute but shit is hectic back home."

"No, home is where me and Taheem is, so home is *here*," she retorted.

"True. Okay, it's hectic in N.C. but I'ma be *home* for a

minute, okay?"

"What's a minute?" Cat asked suspiciously, her cat eyes narrowed to slits.

Vee shrugged. "A minute minute," he answered evasively, not wanting to be tied to a specific time.

Cat sucked her teeth and began pushing him up. "You full of shit, Victor."

"Aw-iight, aw-iight. I'ma be here long enough so you know where my priority lies. So you know where my heart is… and you know all that street shit is for us," he told her then kissed her passionately.

The next day, Vee took Cat and Taheem for a much needed family day. He took Cat furniture shopping for the living room set. She already had most of the condo hooked up, so she knew exactly what set would compliment her taste. He took her out shopping for a whole new wardrobe before they had lunch at the famous Fleming's Steak House.

Vee was familiar with the city. He had gone there a few times to pick up dope before Sami became his connect, so he also knew a few players. His main man was a dark skin Puerto Rican dude name Tradero, but everyone called him Tre'. Tre' was a New York transplant that had come to B-more to get his hustle. He had been the main dude Vee was buying from back when Vee was just copping ounces. Vee decided to call Tre' and let him know he was in town. You never know when an opportunity to make money might arise.

Yo, who this?

Was the text Vee received back after his call to Tre' went unanswered.

Jay from N.C.

77

Vee texted back, using his street alias. His phone rang back instantly.

"Yo, what up, son?! Long time no hear? How you?" Tre' chimed with his gruff New York Spanglish accent.

"It's all love, dawg. Where you? I'm over here at the Fleming's," Vee answered.

"Oh word, you in town? Say no more. I'm on my way."

"Naw, naw, I'm wit' this cutie I just met," Vee lied, winking at Cat. "What you doin' tonight?"

"It's a spot called Eden's Lounge that be jumpin'. Gimme your hotel and I'll swing by and scoop you," Tre' told him.

"Cool. I'll text you. See you tonight."

"Say no more."

Later that evening, Cat dropped Taheem off with the babysitter she used when she had classes. Then they met Tre' in the parking lot of a local motel. Tre' was instantly impressed with Vee's come up. Vee only allowed his shine when he was out of town, so once Tre' saw Vee's money green Bentley Continental GT he knew he was doing big things.

"Damn, Bee, it's like that?" Tre' chuckled, leaning out the window of his BMW 745Li. This definitely wasn't the same kid from two years ago.

Vee followed Tre' to the Eden's Lounge where Vee saw Tre' was doing big things himself. The way the people greeted him as they walked in, the bottle of Louis XIV the house sent to their table and the three blood raw chicks he came with that catered to his every whim.

"Tre', this the chick I just met. Renee, this my man Tre'," Vee introduced Cat, using an alias for her too. He trusted no one.

"Pleased to meet you, ma," Tre' charmed, shaking her hand. "And this is so and so, such and such and what's her name… y'all introduce y'all self," Tre' said dismissively. The chicks introduced themselves.

"I'm Anita."

"I'm Shaneeqa."

"I'm Monica. Don't you go to Morgan?"

"Yeah," Cat replied with one word, letting the chick know she wasn't beat for conversation. She couldn't believe the disrespect some females were willing to put up with simply 'cause a man had a few dollars. As for Tre', she thoroughly disliked him as well.

Vee chuckled. "Damn, dawg, you definitely ain't doin' too bad for yourself."

"I can say the same thing for you! What's a recession?!" Tre' exclaimed, lifting the bottle of Louie in the air then filling everyone's flutes. Everyone laughed except Cat.

"Excuse me, I have to go to the bathroom," Cat said in a huff, sliding out of the booth.

Tre' motioned for his girls to go, too. The three chicks went with Cat. Tre' slid over closer to Vee.

"So, Jay, what brings you to Bodymore?" Tre' asked, sipping champagne.

"Just had a little spare time on my hands, so I figured I'd come see what's what."

Tre' nodded, exchanging acknowledgements with another balla who had just entered.

"Yo, shit is fucked up out here, B… the game that is. Muhfuckas playin' leapfrog when it comes to tellin' on each other. A nigguh'll tell on his moms for the Feds," Tre' shook his head.

"Shit, like Biggie said, 'Yo' mom'll set that ass up properly gassed up," Vee quipped.

"Real talk. My cuz just got twenty-five in the Feds. Guess who flipped?"

"Who?"

"His fuckin' pops, B! True story! Fuck that shit, I don't need the drama," Tre' said dismissively. "I even heard it's this C.I. down your way. Nigguh 'posed to be heavy in the game but he set cats up for the Feds. You know about that?" Tre' inquired, looking at Vee out the corner of his eye.

Vee turned to him, face screwed up. "Nigguh, what the fuck I'ma know about some hot nigguh in Carolina for?!"

"Naw, B. Be easy… I ain't tryin' to play you. Believe me, if I felt a way about you I wouldn't have returned your call *period*," Tre' told him looking him in the eye. "And if I did return it, I would've met you wit' a bullet… word."

Vee smiled, drinking his champagne. "You would've tried."

Tre' laughed. "But on the real, B, I'm out the game. I got a new hustle."

"Yeah? You a pimp now?" Vee joked as the ladies made their way back to the table.

"Naw… I'm into that porn shit," Tre' informed him.

"Booty flicks, dawg? Get the fuck outta here," Vee said unimpressed. For him porn seemed like some bootleg flea market shit.

"Don't sleep, yo, I been in the game eighteen months and I already seen over a meal ticket *after* taxes," Tre' bragged.

"A meal ticket?" Vee exclaimed. A meal ticket was a million dollars.

Tre' nodded proudly. "After taxes… and check it, I made like half of them online! I'm tellin' you, B, porn is a *billion* dollar industry, and nigguhs ain't up on it except as customers and actors! Few control the dollars."

Vee nodded. Now he was impressed. Tre' leaned his elbows on the table.

"But the *real* money is in legit films. Cats doin' these little DVDs on street legends, B.E.T. take the idea and run wit' it and make American Gangsters! B, I'm tellin' you shit is official, and I definitely could use a partner," Tre' alluded.

Vee looked at Tre' deep in thought. He had seen the DVD game on the street for years, now Hollywood wanted to jump on the bandwagon. He knew he couldn't play the street game forever and if porn was a billion dollar industry....

Cat sucked her teeth. She had heard enough. Porn? Hell no, not if she could help it! Having all those freak ass naked bitches around Vee on the daily. It wasn't that she didn't trust him, but a kid in a candy store? Sooner or later he's going to taste. "Umm, Jay, that's your name, right?" Cat quipped. "I really have to get up in the morning for school."

Vee looked at Cat and damn near read her mind. He turned to Tre' and shook his hand.

"Yo, keep my number locked in. I'ma be in touch for sho'!" Vee assured him.

"Say no more," Tre' replied.

"And, yo... on the hot nigguh... see if you can get a name," Vee asked.

"I'll see what I can do. Be safe my nigguh!"

CHAPTER 9

Guy was on top of the world. Nothing makes a man feel better than when his plan comes together. He had his first spot in Brooklyn and the money was coming in hand over fist. The dope the Council got from the Italians was top shelf and kept the fiends coming in. The Council kept everything completely organized, and Guy used that model for his territory.

He had a crib where the dope was packaged. In this house, six or seven naked women cut the heroin with quinine, lactose, dextrose and bonita then packaged it up in glassine envelopes. Since he wasn't a wholesaler yet, meaning he didn't sell large amounts of weight, Guy's money came from hand to hand deals that his runners took care of.

He had a studio apartment in Harlem's lower east. Eddie taught him the valuable lesson of never sleeping where you shit, meaning never live in the same area you do dirt in. Many hustlers had gone against that simple maxim and paid with their lives.

Guy lived a hustler's life with all the parties, Cadillacs and women a young man on the come up could handle. He also had something else every man wants. Gloria was pregnant with their first child. He and Gloria had quickly become a couple ever since

Nicky's party. Eddie approved of their relationship from the door.

"Nigguh, my sister been diggin' you since she first laid eyes on you. Yo' country ass was just too slow to recognize!" Eddie joked.

Guy truly loved Gloria, but a man's love is expressed differently than a woman's. Even though Guy had his share of women, Gloria was his only feminine priority.

Gloria also noticed that Guy was changing. She was a firm believer that money didn't change people, it just brings out what's already there. And at heart, Guy was a natural womanizer, as was his daddy and his daddy's daddy as well. Still, it didn't sit well with Gloria and they fought many nights about it until Guy finally told her, "Look, Glo, we can fight and fuss, break every goddamn dish and plate in the house, it ain't gonna stop me from doin' what I wanna do. If you can't handle that then there's the door. I love you wit' all my heart, but either you can hang or you can't."

"Guy, I hate yo' motherfuckin' selfish ass self! You ain't shit! You reel people in, that's what you do! Woo 'em wit' that country ass charm then you treat 'em like shit!" Gloria exclaimed with tears of anger running down her face. "I don't deserve to be treated like this and you know it, Guy!"

She couldn't hold back the tears because she was hopelessly in love with Guy and she knew, whether she could hang or not, she wasn't going anywhere. Guy knew it, too. He pulled her to him and allowed her to cry on his shoulder.

She allowed him to embrace her then pushed him, "Get off of me, nigguh! You know what? Fuck you!! I don't need you! Me and my baby'll be fine without yo' mannish ass!" Gloria got up and stormed out.

Guy didn't even make an attempt to stop her. He knew she'd be back and he was right... again and again through-out their stormy twenty plus year relationship. But at that time in Guy's life, everything was sweet... and was about to get sweeter than he ever imagined.

"Boy, when you comin' home again? Been damn near a year since yo' mama saw you last. We ain't gettin' no younger, you know?" Willie barked into the phone. Guy could tell his father was chomping on his trademark cigar.

"Yes, sir, I know. Matter of fact, I was plannin' on comin' down next week," Guy told him.

"Hmm-mmm. Then I'll see you next week."

Click!

The conversations with his father were always short and sweet. Truth be told he was missing his home. Even though he had gotten used to the hustle and bustle of the New York grind, as the old saying goes, there's no place like home.

Guy and Gloria had been broke up again, this time for three days before Guy went over to her mother's house in the Sugar Hill section of Harlem. Gloria's mother answered the door like a black woman of authority with an attitude.

"Hello, Mrs. Bell, is Gloria here?" he asked sheepishly.

"Hmm-mmm," her mother answered with her mouth twisted up with disdain.

"Can I see her?"

"Hmm-mmm," she grunted again, but didn't move out the door.

He wanted to say, today??! But he didn't want to disrespect her, so instead he added, "Please."

"Hmm-mmm," she repeated then reluctantly stepped aside so Guy could pass. She had never liked Guy because she had seen his kind before. "He too slick for his own good," she had told Gloria before. She wasn't fooled by the country charm. She knew underneath beat the heart of a killer, conniver and womanizer. He wouldn't do anything but break her daughter's heart.

Guy walked in then followed the sound of Gloria's voice into *the kitchen. He leaned against the doorway watching Gloria sitting at the table, talking to her sister Pam. Guy's heart wept every time he saw Gloria. She radiated a beauty few women could without trying. He wanted her to be his wife, he just knew deep down he could never be her husband.*

"What?" Gloria snapped, when she saw him standing in the door. She succeeded in sounding angry, but she really wanted to jump up and tongue him down. He looked so good in his silk suit; Stetson cocked ace deuce and that print that made women swoon and seemed to go on for days. She was like a moth drawn to the flame.

Guy smiled that cocky smirk. "How you doing, baby? I missed you."

Gloria loved when Guy looked at her like that. It made her feel like a little girl again.

"Hey, Guy," Pam spoke.

"Hey," he replied without emotion or even looking in her direction. He had fucked Pam several times, but his focus was on Gloria.

Gloria sucked her teeth. "What you want?"

"You."

"I told you its over," she said, like she had said many times before.

Guy came over and sat in the chair catty-corner from her. "I just stopped by to tell you I'm going home."

Gloria's heart dropped to her stomach and all she could think of was Gladys Knight's "Midnight Train to Georgia".

"I see."

Guy inwardly smiled. "Yeah, I just thought it was time I went to see the folks, they ain't gettin' no younger and it's been awhile. So I thought it was time for my mama to meet my wife."

Gloria looked up at Guy. "Wife??" she echoed, her heart-beat quickening.

Guy went in his inside pocket and came out with a small jewelry box. Gloria's breath shortened and all of Guy's past trespasses melted away the closer he got to one knee.

He grunted a little at the uncomfortable position of being on one knee and looked into her eyes. "Baby, I know I've made mistakes in the past, so I would understand if my plea fell on deaf ears. If so, then instead of being on one knee, I'll get down on both and beg you, Ms. Gloria Bell to be my wife," Guy proposed, extending the open jewelry box and exposing the five-carat diamond ring.

Gloria covered her mouth with both hands. She was speechless, but the sparkle in her clouded eyes spoke volumes. Trembling, she nodded yes.

"Is that yes? Tell me yes," Guy urged.

"Yes, Guy Simmons, I'll marry you! I love you," she exclaimed breathlessly.

Gloria stood up, pulling Guy up with her and hugged him as tight as her six-month pregnant belly would allow. Guy caught Pam's sour expression and winked at her. Gloria's mother saw the whole scene from the door and shook her head. She knew some women were foolish enough to think that a ring could change a man, and she hated to see that her daughter was one of those women.

"The hard-headed have to feel it to believe," she mum-bled to herself.

Gloria saw the disapproval in her mother's eyes as she turned and walked out and wished it weren't so, but Gloria was twenty-one years old and she had it all figured out, or so she thought. She knew what Guy was about. She just felt like his marrying her confirmed that he did truly love her. No other woman could claim his last name. Her mind was still on Gladys Knight...

I'd rather live in his world, than live without
him in mine…

Gloria had never been to the South before. She'd barely been
out of New York, except when she went to the Canadian side of
Niagara Falls. They made the trip in Guy's brand new 1980 pearl
white Cadillac Eldorado. Guy had bought it off the showroom floor
with cash. He vowed to drive nothing but Cadillacs, a promise he
never broke to himself even when he could afford better.

The experience was entirely new to a city girl like Gloria. All
the wide open spaces and rows and rows of tobacco, corn and
wheat made her think of the old days. "Is them slaves?" she half
joked, seeing several black men in the field picking tobacco.

Guy chuckled. "Naw, girl, them yo' cousins! Don't act like yo'
Geechie ass people ain't come barefoot from Charleston!"

Gloria laughed because her mother and father were from South
Carolina. "Ain't they scared they gonna run off or somebody
might steal 'em?" she questioned, seeing the cows and horses in
fields they passed.

"Naw."

"Why?"

"They just don't, is all."

"Why?"

"Gloria… turn up the radio." Guy smiled.

Gloria noticed Guy was more laid back. He wasn't as gangsta
as he was in New York. He even drove with his gators kicked off.
He sang the words of the songs on the radio, so she could see he
was happy to be home.

"Guy?"

"Yeah?"

"You don't live on no farm, do you?"

Guy just laughed.

They reached Goldsboro and things looked a little more familiar to Gloria. It was clearly a small town, but once they reached Webbtown, she knew she was in the ghetto. Poverty always gave off a certain stench. Guy drove to his parent's home. The home he grew up in.

"This is it," he announced, pulling into the driveway and parking behind Willie's blue Cadillac Brougham.

Gloria looked the house over. It was a nice brick ranch style home. There was only one floor, but the house was long and wide. There was a carport and a pretty green lawn that ran right up to the street, because not many streets had sidewalks besides the main thoroughfares.

Willie came out the front door to see who had pulled up. He stood there in his pants and his suspenders over his t-shirt. "Mabel! Yo' son heah!" he yelled back over his shoulder through the screen.

Guy helped Gloria out the car just as his mother came out the door.

"Guy!" she exclaimed, coming off the porch to meet him. Guy hugged her tightly then stepped back to look at her. She was a little more grey than she was a year ago, just like his daddy's hairline had receded and his belly exceeded what he had seen a year ago. The thought of his parents one day dying sent a chill through him and he vowed to come home more.

"Hey, Mama! How's my favorite girl?" Guy asked.

"Don't look like I'm your favorite girl anymore," Mabel chuckled, looking at Gloria's stomach. "Who is this pretty young thing?"

"Your future daughter-in-law," Guy replied.

Gloria smiled ear to ear. "Hello Mrs. Simmons, I'm Gloria. Gloria Bell."

"She sho' is pretty, Guy," Mabel complemented.

"Thank you," Gloria blushed.

"Come on in and take a load off," Mabel offered, taking Gloria's arm. They walked up on the porch.

"And this is my father, Willie Simmons."

"Hello, Mr. Simmons, it's good to meet you. Guy told me a lot about you," Gloria said.

"Then why would you marry this young-en, when his daddy is the real thing." Willie winked as he kissed Gloria's hand.

Gloria giggled like a schoolgirl. "I see where you get it from," she said to Guy. Gloria and Mabel went in the house.

"Eldorado, huh? Musta set you back a pretty penny," Willie signified.

"Thirteen five," Guy informed him.

"Must be doin' pretty well," Willie surmised.

"I'm doin' okay," Guy answered.

Willie looked at his son and smiled. He was shaping up to be a true Simmons. "Glad to have you home, son."

"Glad to be home."

"Go on in there and visit with yo' mama. Later on we gonna talk."

Guy and Gloria sat with his parents for awhile and had dinner. They talked about their future plans and told Gloria embarrassing stories about Guy as a child. Gloria enjoyed it thoroughly, but when the sun went down, Guy told her to get dressed. He was going to show her the real Goldsboro. He was anxious to see a few old friends because he wanted to bring a few of his thoroughest homeboys back to New York with him. He wanted men around him he knew he could trust.

They first made their way over to James Street. James Street back in the day was to Goldsboro what 42nd Street was to New York. Any and everything went down on "the block". Willie owned a pool room smack dab in the middle of the block with a club in the back. There were several pool rooms along the two block radius where most of the activity took place, but Willie's was the place to be.

Guy pulled up in that sparkling white Eldorado and double parked right outside the pool room. He blocked traffic in doing so, but he could do that, he was a Simmons.

"Baby," Gloria chimed as Guy helped her from the car, "you can't park here. You blockin' half the street."

Guy smiled. "Shit, I'm home. This my street."

The prodigal son had returned and returned with a vengeance. Guy stepped out wearing a tailor made gangsta black silk suit, red silk shirt and hankie with a black silk tie. His Ostrich boots were black with red topside. His black Stetson sported a red band and feather. His diamond ring and watch sparkled like the stars in the sky. He told Gloria to make him look good and she didn't disappoint. Even six months pregnant, she was killing the off the shoulder chiffon dress that V'd in the front and revealed her shapely legs. Over her shoulder was a mink shawl and her heels were gold heeled and open toed.

As they made their way into the pool room, the crowd parted like the Red Sea, whispering and pointing in their wake.

"Look who's here!"

"Guy's home!"

"My nigguh!"

Was all Guy heard entering the pool hall. Old friends and old girlfriends flirted, but Guy kept Gloria close and took the whole night in stride. Gloria was impressed with the night life in the small town. It wasn't New York by a long shot but it was obvious that the game was alive and well in the South. Guy's Caddy wasn't the only gangsta white walls spinning the block. True players slid up in Willie's to show that they too were on top of their game.

But the biggest impression made on Gloria was the way the other players respected and looked at Guy like he was the reigning

*prince. She saw that the scraggly dressed country boy that
wandered into her brother's bar didn't get his game from New
York; he had been raised with it.*

*"Ay, New York! Get yo' punk ass outta here fo' I drag you
out!" a voice growled from the front door.*

*Guy knew he was talking to him because of his New York
license plate. Gloria tensed but the smile that spread across Guy's
face relaxed her as Guy spun around.*

"You black ass nigguh!" Guy exclaimed, with gangsta glee.

*"You jive motherfucka!" the man bellowed back, before the two
closed the distance between each other and embraced like long lost
brothers.*

*"Hawk Bill Braswell! You still the uuugliest nigguh I know!"
Guy cracked at the shorter man. Hawk Bill was built like Joe
Frazier with a pug nose.*

*"And, nigguh you still the lamest! Lookin' like Petey
Wheatstraw the Devil's son in law!" Hawk Bill cracked back.*

*Guy noticed that Hawk Bill was dressed pretty well. He could
see he wasn't heavy, but he damn sure wasn't starving.*

*"This is Gloria, my fiancée. Gloria, you are now looking at the
only gorilla in the world that can speak. Hawk Bill."*

Gloria laughed. "Hello, umm, should I call you Hawk or Bill?"

*Hawk tipped his hat with a flourish. "Call me whatever you
like pretty lady, just don't forget to call me when you drop this
lame," Hawk chuckled.*

*Guy, Gloria and Hawk Bill kicked it at Willie's, danced at the
Carousel then gambled at Ms. Lillian's before they made it back to
Hawk Bill's liquor house located across town.*

*The house was packed, the liquor poured and the music played.
It was all good until three well dressed men came in, each with a
bad red bone apiece on their arm. The first man and Guy locked
eyes and the man smirked and winked. Guy didn't return his
acknowledgement.*

"What's up, Guy? Long time no see. That yo' Cadillac out there wit' the New York tags?"

"What about it? It goddamn sure ain't yours!" Guy spat back smoothly, but the venom was evident in his tone.

The man chuckled. "Same ol' Guy. Same slick ass mouth I see. Betta be careful, nigguh. See it don't get you in a fucked up situation." Guy smiled and downed his drink.

Gloria eased closer to him, feeling the tension building. "Guy, I'm ready to go." Guy looked at Gloria and she saw that same gangsta stare that he kept in New York.

"Be easy, baby. Brah is the neighborhood clown. He just came to dance for us," Guy quipped, making some of the patrons chuckle, even though most of them knew the history with the two men.

Brah Hardy was the oldest of the six Hardy boys. They made their money off weed. Ma Hardy raised the boys hard so not many wanted to fuck with the Hardy boys. Brah and Guy despised each other. What started out as a childhood rivalry had grown into a grown man's beef.

Hawk Bill felt under the counter for the sawed off.

Brah laughed. "Yeah, I love to dance, nigguh. Listen… you hear that? They playin' our song," Brah hissed.

Guy didn't hesitate. Before Gloria could pull him back, Guy was up and on his feet. Hawk Bill cocked the sawed off and followed the crowd outside. He went to make sure the other two Hardy's ain't jump in. By the time he got there, both men had their coats off and were going toe-to- toe.

Brah Hardy was a few inches taller than Guy and he had the reach, but Guy's hand speed was quicker. Guy managed to evade the telegraphed right cross, ducking it and catching Brah with a kidney punch. Brah bent double then Guy finished him with a swift uppercut that knocked Brah flat on his back.

Barely breathing hard, Guy straightened his tie and stood over the dazed Brah. "Next time," Guy paused to put on his jacket, "stay in yo' goddamn place." Guy kicked Brah in the ribs then calmly went back inside got Gloria and left while the Hardy boys stared daggers in his back.

"Guy... Guy... Guy!" Willie whispered harshly, shaking Guy awake. Gloria stirred slightly as Guy turned over to look at his father.

"Daddy?" he said, half sleep.

"Boy, get yo' ass up. How you gonna be a hustler? You sleep the day away," Willie scolded him quietly.

"What time is it?" Guy asked, sitting up. It felt like he'd only been sleep a few minutes.

"Five o'clock."

Guy's eyes popped open. "In the mornin'???" He had just gotten in after three. It was still dark outside.

"Naw, nigguh, in the goddamn evenin'. Of course in the mornin'. Now get dressed, I got somebody you need to meet."

As they drove along the highway, Guy tried to get some sleep before they reached their destination. Willie reached over and hit him in the chest.

"Boy, wake yo' ass up."

"Daddy," Guy replied impatiently, "I ain't get in 'til damn near four. It's five in the mornin'! Just wake me up when we get there."

"Then you shoulda had yo' ass home befo' twelve. Most nigguhs catch charges after twelve 'cause they out galavantin' and they get caught up," Willie schooled Guy, who was only half listening. "That's when the stick up artists catch you slippin'! Drinkin', chasin' a piece of pussy, shit like that. You got to wake the game up and put it to bed. A man don't need to be seen to be felt."

"Yeah, I hear you. Where we goin' anyway?"

"Winston-Salem."

They arrived a little after eight in the morning and drove to a small dilapidated house. Parked outside were a mid-sized pick-up truck and a van. Willie parked behind the van then he and Guy got out. Guy stretched his tired limbs then glanced at his watch. As they walked in the opened front door, two guys wearing tool belts walked out.

"Where's Charlie?" Willie asked.

"Back bedroom," one answered as they left.

Willie and Guy walked toward the back where they heard the sound of a hammer banging. When they entered, Guy saw the back of a wiry old man. The heaviest thing on him looked to be his tool belt, but he could tell he was in good shape by the way his muscles flexed as he swung the hammer.

"Be right wit' you," Charlie said, taking a nail out his mouth and sinking it flush in three bangs. He turned around, shook Willie's hand then shook Guy's as well. He had a firm grip and eyed Guy up and down. "So, I finally get to meet you, huh? I've heard a lot about you," Charlie commented.

Guy wasn't sure what to say. He had come three hours in the wee hours of the morning to meet a handyman? He shook his hand like, "Good to meet you, too."

Willie smiled to himself seeing the confusion on his son's face. "Guy, this is Charlie… Po' Charlie."

Willie had to admit, Guy definitely had a good poker face, but he saw the sleep instantly disappear from his eyes. Guy knew exactly who Po' Charlie was. He had heard his name several times. Po' Charlie was an old head that had a heroin connection straight from the Golden Triangle.

They called him Po' Charlie because even though he had crazy paper, you would never know it from looking at him. Guy had never seen Charlie and was beginning to think he was nothing but *a myth of the game. But standing in front of him now, he knew he was real. From that day forth, Guy got up at five in the morning, because that was the time of day he met the man that totally changed his life.*

Po' Charlie smiled. "I hear New York did you pretty well."

"Lotta opportunity in New York, man can't get it to-gether there, he ain't worth the shoes he stand in," Guy replied nonchalantly, even though his calculating mind was working a thousand miles a second trying to figure out how to play this opportunity. He knew if his father went through the trouble of bringing them together then big things were in the making. He just didn't know how big.

"Yeah, New York's okay, but it ain't nothin' but a second South to me," Charlie said.

"A second South?"

"Yeah, because everybody up there is really from down South!" Charlie chuckled, and so did Guy because he had a point. "But you ain't come all this way for a history lesson. Help me put up this drywall then we can go and talk." Willie had left the two men in the backyard of the house so they could talk one-on-one.

As they worked, Charlie and Guy got to know each other better. They had a common background in that they had both been in Vietnam. Charlie had retired a Sergeant Major three years prior. Charlie was sixty-eight, and looked good for his age. He told Guy how he bought houses to remodel and rent out. He had over seventy houses in Winston-Salem alone, but half of them he allowed his family to live in.

"That's the most important thing in life, Guy, your family. Everything else is second. They can take anything away but when it's all said and done, family's all we got," Charlie told him.

Guy nodded to show his understanding.

"That's why I got so much respect for yo' daddy. He knows

how to take care of family. Ain't a Simmons in Wayne County that's wanting for nothin'. Now that's a man," Charlie schooled him. "Why do you hustle, Guy?"

Guy paused for a minute to think about the question, the early birds chirping were the only sound until he answered. "Truthfully... I never wanted to be a hustler. My daddy used to try and shove it down my throat, but I didn't want it. I wanted to go to college. Be the first man in my family to do that... but that was a long time ago. I done seen enough, heard enough and done enough to know that the only thing I'm scared of is being black and broke in this white man's world."

Charlie nodded then cleared his throat and recited:

> *Man has been hustlin' for 50,000 years*
> *Every since the beginning of time,*
> *Since Satan tricked Eve and she believed,*
> *If she ate the apple, she'd be divine*
> *She traded pleasure for pain*
> *And there's no robbery in fair exchange*
> *But just the same I figure*
> *If Satan's a fact though he may not be black*
> *He's still one hustlin' ass nigguh.*

Then he turned to Guy and winked. "Po' Charlie, 1963".

Guy chuckled. "Yeah, the Devil is one helluva hustler."

"What you said, I can dig 'cause the best hustlers are usually the ones that ain't tryin' to be one. The ones that end up hustlin' 'cause they strugglin', not 'cause they seen Super Fly or just dig the feel of a pretty bitch's ass," Charlie told him.

"Yeah, 'cause when a sucka get lucky, a hustler don't stand a chance," Guy replied, making Charlie laugh.

"Nigguh, you ain't never lied!"

The two men enjoyed the laugh then Charlie spoke. "But it is a

Devil's game, Guy. Ain't no honor among thieves, and the only code is the unwritten one amongst real men. Motherfuckas'll cut yo' throat for chicken change, so you cut theirs first. This ain't a game for nice guys... you a nice guy, Guy?" Charlie smirked.

"Only when I'm meeting a bitch's mama," Guy told him truthfully and Charlie chuckled.

"I know you know what I do, and believe me, I know what you do too. I've been keepin' tabs on you every since you got your spot in Brooklyn."

Guy smiled knowing the old man was on top of his game.

"But I got a proposition for you, but you gonna hafta give up something to get it."

"Sorta like wit' the Devil, huh?" Guy smirked, knowing his soul was for sale for the right price.

"Nicky is through. Ever since he beat that first beef, the Justice Department's had a hard on for him. As of last week, Nicky had a warrant for his arrest, along with several members of the Council," Charlie informed him.

Guy allowed the information to sink in. "Was Eddie Bell one of the dudes?"

Charlie shook his head. "Not yet... probably not ever, unless one of 'em turns rat. Eddie deals with Nicky, but never directly. He was one of the smart ones... which is why I want him dead."

Guy quickly looked at Charlie. "What??" he barked, not believing his ears and suddenly feeling like at any moment they'd be coming at him, too.

Charlie was un-phased by Guy's outburst and continued to talk. "The Council is my biggest competitor. For years, Nicky and I have been engaged in a war to control the East Coast. He's backed by the Guineas so he's had a little advantage but I've done damn well because I'm my own boss. Ain't no Guinea — "

"What's that got to do wit' Eddie?" Guy wanted to know. Eddie was his main man and he felt a way about even talking to a

man that said he wanted him dead.

Charlie looked at Guy. "With Nicky out of the way that leaves a major void, because the Italians only dealt with Nicky. Now the majority of the Council are cats the Italians wouldn't even think about giving such power. But there are a few... four exactly, that even have a chance of becoming the next Nicky Barnes. With them out the way, the Council will totally crumble into non-descript little crews," he explained then added, "I'm offering you the chance to be the next Nicky Barnes... of the South. I'll put you in charge of distribution in North and South Carolina, if you — "

"Kill Eddie," Guy spat with more disgust than he really felt.

"Along with the other three as well," Charlie replied, then sat back to let Guy think.

Guy's thoughts were filled with Eddie's face. It was Eddie that had given him the opportunity to eat when he was living in a hovel sharing his one room flat with roaches the size of his thumb. It was Eddie that had showed him the ropes and guided his steps up the ladder. He hadn't kept him as a lackey; he had groomed him, took him to the Council and made him equal status.

"Let me ask you something. As heavy as you are, why me? Why not do it yourself? You can afford a top notch team of sho' nuff killers. So why me?" Guy wanted to know.

Charlie leaned back into the conversation. "True, I could. Then this move would have my fingerprint all over it. I don't want that. Then the Guineas and I would be in an all-out war, and in war no one makes money. Besides," Charlie smirked, "I'm not a gangsta... I'm a business man and this is a business."

"Yeah, but Eddie was the one who put me on in the game," Guy retorted.

Charlie knew Guy wanted to do it or he wouldn't even discuss it at such great length. "I'm aware of that, but now, let me ask you something? What do you think Eddie would do if he was in your shoes?"

What would Eddie do? Po' Charlie was offering him a multi million dollar deal. His own pie as opposed to a small slice of a slice of someone else's. It was a dirty game but didn't friendship count for anything? Not to Eddie. Guy had personally killed two men for Eddie that Eddie said he had grown up with. Men he had considered a friend at one time but because these men owed him money, Eddie had them killed.

Would Eddie do it? No question. But Guy wouldn't do it because he felt like Eddie would do it to him. Guy's decision had been made once Charlie offered him the Carolina's. Everything else was just justification.

"Who's the other three?" Guy inquired.

Charlie smiled inwardly. "Mo Jenkins, Chico Jones and J. Smitty. Now understand its all four or no deal. I'll pay you a kilo of heroin for each body in that case. But for the grand prize, it has to be all four," Charlie explained.

"Grand prize? What's this, some kind of test of loyalty?" Guy probed.

Charlie smiled. "Loyalty? I'm too old to be naïve. The dollar keeps a man loyal to opportunity, and that's what this is, no more no less. So... do we have a deal?"

Guy looked him in the eye and studied him for a moment then slowly extended his hand.

CHAPTER 10

Ty let the hot water run over his head, massaging the tenseness from his body. The whole bathroom was steamed up just the way he liked to shower. He lathered his body mechanically as his agile mind continued to work overtime.

It had been a week since the Wolf Pack had made an attempt on his life. His quick retaliation had gone unanswered and his people told him all three spots had slowed considerably. That was news to his ears because the next best thing to hitting Vee was hitting his pockets. His plan was to remove his army and force Vee into the open or to bounce. Deep down, he knew Vee would never choose the latter. Vee was too much of a thoroughbred to relocate. He would fight until he was the last man standing or the last man to go down.

The thought of going down made Ty think of his father. Guy was still in a coma. His condition hadn't gotten any better. Ty had sat with Guy all day the day before, and it sickened Ty to see his father so weak and helpless. Guy could be a motherfucka sometimes, but he was a stand up guy and he had raised Ty to be the same way. He had to know who had done this to his father.

When he had spoken to his mother, she was dumb-founded as well.

"Maybe they wanted to rob him," she had surmised, but Ty knew that wasn't the case. Cats of Guy's caliber don't just get robbed. And even if it could've happened, the fact that his bodyguards were gunned down instantly proved it was definitely a hit.

"Ma… who's Brah Hardy?" Ty had asked.

His mother had looked at him quizzically. "What about him?"

Ty didn't feel like it was his place to accuse his mother of being a whore, so he replied, "You know he came home about a month ago?"

"And?"

"And didn't Pop have beef wit' him back in the day before he went to prison? He even shot a kid, right?"

Debra waved him off like, "Boy, that's ancient history. Yo' daddy ain't thinkin' about Brah."

"That don't mean Brah ain't thinkin' about Pop… or you," Ty quipped.

Debra smirked. "I see Gloria been runnin' her mouth. What else she tell you?"

Ty shrugged. "Just that you used to be wit' Brah."

"Like I said… ancient history. I ain't thinkin' about no Brah Hardy."

But somebody was thinking about Guy.

Ty remembered the whole conversation. He had to find Brah Hardy and talk to him, but not even Hawk Bill could find him. That too sent up red flags. A man does twenty years, where else he got to go but home? Unless he met some pen pal and was shacked up with her or him thousands of miles away. Ty hoped that was the case. For Brah's sake.

Then another thought hit him like a ton of bricks. What about the Bells? Maybe Tito had found out that Guy had killed his father and tried to return the favor. It would fit their M.O. They had the type of killers on the payroll to pull off a hit like this. He hadn't even looked at that angle.

Ty quickly dried off and headed for the bedroom with nothing but a towel wrapped around his waist. He picked up his cell phone and speed dialed Tito.

"Ty, what up family? How you?" Tito greeted, with a lot of noise in the background.

"I'm good. Yo, you busy?"

"Never too busy for family, even though I am at the Garden. You know Tina Devoe?"

"Who??"

"Tina Devoe!" Tito yelled.

"Oh yeah, yeah. Sing that shit be on the radio all the time," Ty remembered.

"Yeah, she on my people's label."

"That's what's up. But, yo... remember the offer you made about the army?"

"Who?"

"The offer! You re—"

"'ey yo, Ty, let me hit you from the after party. It's crazy in here!"

Click.

"Yeah, you do that," Ty mumbled to himself.

Ty planned on taking Tito up on his earlier offer of sending a team down. Ty knew how gangstas thought, because he was one. If Tito had Guy hit then he more than likely would send his best shooters to carry it out. Now that Ty was asking, Tito would again send his best to avenge a hit they themselves had carried out. Gangstas loved irony. Ty planned on running their aliases by every hotel in the area, airport, bus and train stations. If he found out they had been in town during the time Guy was hit, Tito was a dead man. If not, at least he'd have another team to send against the Wolf Pack.

Ty's thoughts were broken when he heard his front door creak open. Without hesitation, he grabbed his nine millimeter infrared and kicked off the safety. The entire apartment was dark except the light in the bathroom. He got behind the bedroom door and held his breath, listening for footsteps. He could tell it was only one person, but he didn't know how many were still by the door. His heart was beating a mile a minute as he waited for the beef to kick off.

These nigguhs think it's that sweet?? He thought angrily to himself. *Well they better have an army, 'cause they fuckin' wit' a vet.*

The footsteps neared the bedroom and paused. They entered the bedroom cautiously. As they entered, Ty slid up slowly then quickly put the gun to the back of their head and began to pull...

"Ty!" Karrin gasped.

"What the fuck?! Karrin?!"

He slapped the wall switch and light flooded the room. Karrin stood there trembling.

"Yo, is you crazy?! Do you know what the fuck almost happened???" he yelled. His whole body shuddered thinking what he had almost done. He was within a hair of blowing her head off.

"I'm sorry, Ty. I'm sorry! Please don't be mad at me." She sniffed.

"How you get in?" Ty asked, the adrenaline beginning to subside.

"The-the key."

Seeing her old key in her hand, he remembered that he had never changed the locks. He sighed hard. "Give it here."

"Ty, I—"

"Karrin, give me my key," he demanded through clenched teeth.

She reluctantly removed it from her key ring and placed it in his palm. As he curled his fingers around it, she impulsively grabbed his hand.

"Ty, don't do this, don't cut me off," she begged.

"You have to go, Karrin," he replied, grabbing her forcefully by the arm and leading her back into the hallway.

"No, Ty, we still need to talk!" she said.

"Ain't nothin' left to say."

"No!" She jerked away, confronting him. "I love you, Ty, and… and I know you love me! You told me no one could ever come between us!"

No one except my father, Ty thought. "That was then, this is now."

Karrin pushed up on him. "Don't tell me that kiss didn't mean anything to you because I felt it, I felt *you*," Karrin surmised, pressing her body against his.

Ty pushed her away. "You're leavin', Karrin."

He grabbed her arm but she pushed Ty back with the weight of her body and kissed him like she did in the restaurant. Ty grabbed a fist full of her hair to get out of the lip lock she had him in. When she looked at him again, he could see the lust in her eyes.

"Fuck me, Ty," she whispered, biting her bottom lip then leaning into his kiss. Her hand had snatched the towel from his waist and was squeezing his dick, instantly bringing it to full attention. "I missed you, I missed you," she purred, covering his face with kisses.

"You gonna get us both killed," Ty mumbled, pulling up her Donna Karen mini skirt and finding out she didn't have on any panties.

"No one has to know, baby. I'll be his wife, but I'll be your whore," Karrin moaned as Ty lifted her off her feet and slid his nine-inch dick inside her dripping wet pussy, balls deep. Karrin hissed and clawed his back while she arched her pelvis meeting his thrust. Ty gripped her by her ass cheeks and spread her pussy lips with his fingers then began bouncing her on his dick harder and harder.

"Awww yesss, daddy, fuck me hard. Beat this pussy like I been a bad girl!" Karrin squealed in ecstasy and Ty complied.

He lowered himself to his knees then laid Karrin on the floor. He cocked her knees back to her titties and began sucking her toes while he banged the pussy mercilessly.

"I love you, Ty! I love... I love... I'm cummin' again!" Karrin moaned as her pussy creamed Ty's dick for the second time. Ty was the only man that could make her cum multiple times.

Karrin bucked wildly, tightening and loosening her muscles around Ty's dick. It felt like his dick was getting a pussy massage.

"Tell... tell me when you cummin', daddy!" she urged.

"I'm about to," he replied.

Karrin pushed him on to his back and wrapped her pouty lips around his shaft. She jerked it with one hand as she sucked and licked the head. When she felt his dick begin to twitch, she deep throated him, allowing Ty to cum deep in her throat. He grabbed her by the back of the head, making sure she swallowed every drop.

As he lay on his back with Karrin kissing up his chest, all he could think about was the consequences of what they just did if it ever got back to Kev.

"Damn," he whispered to himself.

Hello, you've reached Karrin Simmons.

Sorry, I —

Click.

Kev had called her four times and she hadn't answered. He decided to text her and was relieved to see she texted right back.

Sorry Baby, I was sleep. Hurry home.

He smiled and text.

No doubt. Keep it tight.

Always.

Kev flipped his phone closed and nodded his head to the music. He was in the Q club in Goldsboro meeting with his young team. Ever since the hospital incident, Kev's head had been in a whirl. Karrin had lied to his face. The look she gave him she had used many times, so the next logical thought was, how many other times had she lied?

Kev loved Karrin with all his heart, but he wasn't about to be anyone's fool. Why couldn't she get Ty out of her system and the bigger question, why couldn't he get his wife out of his system? He was young, rich and handsome, he could have damn near any woman he wanted... *except Karrin*. Kev thought to himself about the old saying, the ones we want never want us.

"Yo, Kev," young Hardy said, sitting next to Kev in the booth, "you good, big homie?"

Hardy brought Kev out of his own world. "Yeah, yo, I'm good," he replied, sipping his drink.

He looked around the hole in the wall club. It was definitely a hood spot, the kind of spot that ended with a shootout almost every night and closed in three months. It wasn't his type of spot at all. Yeah, when he was younger and had something to prove, but he was twenty-eight and on his grown man shit. He had only come through to check his little mans and them and give them status being seen with Kev Simmons.

"I'm tellin' you, Kev, we got the jungle on smash! Can't nobody move shit out there if it ain't us. This kid tried me, but I pistol whipped that nigguh so bad, I promise you he won't be back!" Hardy bragged. He looked up to Kev like a big brother because it was Kev that gave him a chance to eat. He was aware of the old Hardy-Simmons beef, but to Hardy it was just that. Old!

Kev was doing it big while most of the Hardy boys had become dope fiends and crack heads. All except Brah, but he had been locked up for twenty years or more, and he came home to nothing. At eighteen, Hardy was seeing more money than his uncles had ever seen. He was jeweled up and his crew was buying out the bar with the baddest bitches in the club drooling all over them. Hardy felt like he was on top of the world.

Kev saw the same thing, but he saw it differently. He saw a bunch of young boys making themselves hot fast.

"I feel you on that cat out in the jungle 'cause sometimes you gotta make examples, but that," Kev said, gesturing to the bar, "that ain't necessary."

"What you mean, dawg?"

"Look at your mans and them, tell me what you see?"

Hardy looked at his crew and smiled. "Them nigguhs ballin'!" he chuckled.

"Naw, lil' homie, they makin' enemies," Kev schooled him.

"Enemies??" Hardy barked, looking around and gripping the handle of the nine in his waist. "I wish a nigguh would bring that shit to me and mine!"

Kev shook his head. "Naw, they ain't gotta bring it like that. When these other muhfuckas see you wit' the money and all the pussy, that breeds envy. And you can't see that shit until the Feds is kickin' in your door 'cause a muhfucka made a call. This shit ain't for show, lil' homie, the game is only a steppin' stone to greater things. Stack yo' chips, stay under the radar and if a muhfucka try and test, handle the shit. But that ballin' shit is overrated. All it brings is heat."

Hardy nodded, taking in the jewel. "I hear you, big homie, and I got you. Don't worry… we gonna tighten up." He gave Kev dap.

Kev's phone rang. He saw the number and smiled. It was his Wolf Pack mole. "Yo."

"Kev?"

"Speak on it."

"Vee back in town."

Kev smiled. "Then let's make it happen."

"I'm on it. I'll hit you back soon."

"You do that," Kev said, thinking, *stupid ass nigguh*. Kev hung up and returned to his conversation with Hardy.

Vee was definitely back in town. As soon as Mike called him and told him in code about the Ty situation, he was headed for Durham, but not before Cat caught feelings.

"Victor, you've only been here a week!" Cat stressed, holding a crying Taheem.

Vee took Taheem in his arms and kissed him. He instantly stopped crying. "Cat, some shit went down unexpectedly," Vee explained.

"So why Mike and them can't handle it?"

"They need me."

"*We* need you, nigguh! You runnin' off to that bullshit and your family is all alone," Cat spat angrily.

Vee sighed. "Baby listen. I—"

"Don't baby listen me! Gimme my damn son! You ain't gonna be here to stop his tears so he might as well get used to it!" Cat huffed, taking Taheem from Vee. As soon as he was out of Vee's arms, he started crying again and reaching out to Vee. It was like he could sense whenever Vee was about to leave.

"Kionna... don't do this," Vee said softly.

"No Vic, *you* don't do this. Why can't you just leave that shit alone? It ain't like you ain't got money. You can do anything you want. Why you gotta keep playin' the game?" she questioned, tears running down her cheeks.

Vee came over and embraced her waist and played with Taheem's hand. "That's something I've been thinkin' about, but now ain't the time. I can't leave Mike and them out there like that when shit get hot," Vee said, trying to make her understand.

"Yeah I forgot, they need you," she remarked sourly. "Then go."

Vee tried to kiss her but she turned her head.

"Just go, Victor."

"I'll be back soon," he told her, and he meant every

109

word.

As he drove back to Durham, he thought about Ms. Sadie and wondered if this was what she meant about it costing him all that he loved. He and Cat were drifting apart so he knew he had to tighten up. He told himself as soon as shit calmed down he would take Kionna on a month- long vacation.

When he got back to Durham he told Mike to meet him at the mall. Ten minutes later, he changed it to the McDonald's on Pettigrew Street. Both times he watched Mike pull up. Vee wanted to make sure no one was following Mike. The Simmons had caught him slippin' once, but they wouldn't do it again.

Vee got out of the Bentley and got in the passenger side of Mike's Benz CL500.

"What up, dawg? Welcome back," Mike greeted him.

"So what went down?"

"It was some spur of the moment shit, man," Mike admitted, "but I figured, fuck it 'cause it was a golden opportunity."

"Mike, just tell me what happened," Vee replied a little impatient because Mike was beating around the bush.

"Yo, I was wit' this bitch in Raleigh. I'm ridin' wit' her on our way to the mo'. We come by Charlie Goodnite's and I see Ty's caddy. I wanted to hit 'em right then, just park and wait. But I had that bitch wit' me so I was like, 'yo, take me home.' She bitchin' or whateva but she do it. When I get there I call up them lil' nigguhs from Hoover. They follow me out to Raleigh and put in the work, but they missed the nigguh and ended up hittin' his girl." Mike broke the whole thing down.

Vee shook his head because it was a bad move. Ty would know he didn't hit his father, so he was the one factor Vee was counting on to bring some clarity to the situation. Of course Vee planned on getting Ty, but that would've come later. After he rocked Kev to sleep and made him think shit was sweet. Now he knew the hit had only succeeded in doing one thing, putting Ty in Kev's camp with both feet.

Vee sighed. "What about the spots?"

Mike shook his head. "We lost a lotta muhfuckas. Here, Greenville and the Port City. Ty holla'd back the same night," Mike replied, knowing he had messed up not hitting the nigguh right. Vee would've had a plan, and more than likely he wouldn't have missed.

Vee sat back and thought about his next move. Now he had both brothers against him. Of course Ty would support his brother, but if Vee had played his hand right, he could've got at Kev and then had only Ty to worry about. The Simmons may not have been his caliber but their money was entirely too long to go to war with.

The only good thing to come out of it was Mike had confirmed what Vee had assumed. He definitely wasn't the rat in the crew. So that left only Rome and Banks. Vee had thought about how to smoke out the rat while he was in B-more so he knew what he would do. Now that Mike had proved solid, he only had to set two traps instead of three.

Vee went to Rome's house and told him, "Look, we goin' hardbody at these nigguhs, you feel me my nigguh?"

"No question! What up?" Rome answered.

"We takin' it to Guy! We gonna send a team of nigguhs up in that hospital and finish that nigguh off," Vee told him.

Rome nodded. "I'm wit' you, dawg."

"But check it. Until the day we do it, I ain't tellin' *nobody* but you, you understand? One of us is takin' info back to the Simmons and I know it ain't me or you! Mike and Banks been actin' a little shaky... so, Rome under no circumstances do you tell *anybody*! You got me?" Vee asked.

"Yeah, yeah, dawg, I got you."

"Nobody, Rome. If it get out I know it can only be you," Vee explained.

"Come on, dawg, you know me. My lips is sealed," Rome assured him.

Let's hope so, Vee thought.

Next he went to Banks' crib and told him, "Look, B, we goin' hardbody on these nigguhs, you wit' me?"

"Nigguh, you know me! It's whatever!" Banks barked full of bravado.

"Aiight, this the plan. Kev man Dino gettin' married next Saturday. That's the 23rd, right?"

Banks looked at his diamond bezeled Jacob. "Yeah."

"Kev the best man so we know he gonna be there. Dawg, we goin' up in there and turn that shit from a wedding into a funeral! Feel me?" Vee chuckled.

"Hell yeah! It's the perfect time. The nigguh won't even see it comin'," Banks nodded with a smirk.

"*Exactly*, so that's what it is. But, B, I need you to keep this between me and you."

"Why, what up, dawg?"

"It's Mike and Rome. Them nigguhs been actin' shady to you?"

Banks shrugged. "Naw, Vee. I ain't see nothin'"

"Yeah? Maybe it's just me. Regardless, until I know for sure, keep this shit on the low, aw-iight?"

"Okay, Vee," Banks replied.

"Banks, I'm dead ass, yo! The only two gonna know until we roll on them nigguhs is me and you. So if Rome or Mike find out, I'll know who told 'em," Vee explained, looking Banks in the eyes.

"That's what it is then, dawg. I got you," Banks assured him.

Let's hope so, Vee thought to himself then bounced.

"You just can't let go, huh?"

Gloria looked up from the novel she was reading to see Debra standing in the door. Gloria humph'd then returned her attention to the book.

"Why is it every time I come to see *my* husband, you here?" Debra questioned as her six-inch Donna Karen heels clicked against the hospital floor.

"I guess 'cause I get here first," Gloria remarked, still reading her novel.

Debra stopped at the foot of Guy's bed, not three feet from where Gloria was sitting. "You got all the sense, don't you? Well I'd appreciate it if you used that sense to stay the fuck outta my family affairs!" Debra accused with her voice raised.

This time, Gloria looked up. "Excuse me?"

"You heard me…," Debra hissed through clenched teeth, "tryin' to belittle me in front of my son. Tellin' him all about Brah Hardy and my past."

Gloria smirked. "Why? You ashamed of it?"

"It wasn't yo' damn place!" Debra spat back.

Gloria nodded. "You're right. I'm woman enough to admit when I'm wrong. Ty asked me about him in connection with what happened to Guy, so I told him what I knew," she explained.

"What you oughta be tellin' is what the fuck you was doin' out there that night? How you miraculously appeared just seconds after Guy got shot," Debra replied. "I wouldn't put it past you if you had something to do with this."

Gloria closed her book, uncrossed her legs and stood up. "Look, *Debra*, believe me I would like nothin' better than an excuse to beat yo' ass after all these years, but now is not the time or the place. Right now, my only concern is Guy and with you bringin' all this negative energy it ain't helpin' the situation. So, if you'll excuse me." Gloria grabbed her purse and headed for the door while Debra glared at her.

"No, Guy is *my* concern, not yours! And as for beatin' my ass, bitch anytime you wanna try. But I'll tell you this, if I find out you had something to do with this I ain't gonna beat yo' ass... bitch, I'm a kill you," Debra vowed.

Gloria stopped and looked back at Debra. She wanted to go set it on Debra right then, but seeing Guy laying in the bed fighting for his life took all the fight out of her.

"Don't worry, Deb, you may get your chance sooner than you think," she replied calmly then walked out of the room.

"Bitch," Debra mumbled as she sat down in the chair and took Guy's hand in her own.

CHAPTER 11

Guy and Gloria drove back to New York in an eerie kind of silence most of the way. Gloria attributed his tenseness to the fact they were leaving. We gotta come down South more often, she thought. But it wasn't that. Guy had the plan in his mind.

For him, it had to go right. Too much was at stake. All four men Po' Charlie had told him. To make sure he was well equipped to handle the job, he had Hawk Bill and Scatter on a Greyhound on their way to New York at the same time. They were two of the most feared men in Goldsboro. Scatter was a high yellow dude with a pocked face. He got his name because he was known to pull that pistol on a nigguh, so when he came on the set, that's what hustlers did. Scattered!

Guy was back in Vietnam; the mentality of hunting the enemy down and killing him. Not once did he think about what it would do to Gloria or the children Eddie was leaving behind. He'd take care of Gloria, her lifestyle wouldn't miss a beat. As for Eddie's kid, well that wasn't his concern. He was on the verge of landing the deal of his life, and nothing would stand in his way. The deal would be signed in blood.

He dropped Gloria off at her mother's house. When he got his bags on the porch, Gloria turned to him and asked, "Baby, is there something wrong?"

Guy smiled. "Naw, sweetness, just… got a lot on my mind."

She moved closer to comfort him, caressing his face. "Wanna talk about it?"

He knew he couldn't be evasive with Gloria because she knew him so well. So he decided to tell her enough of the truth to appease her. "I was just thinkin', you know, with the baby on the way, I don't know, maybe we could move down south. Get away from the rat race and really settle down, you know?"

Gloria searched his eyes, hoping it was true. If a woman truly loves a man, there's nothing she would like more than to see him get out the game.

Just then Eddie pulled up playing Heatwave's "Ain't No Half Stepping." He came up on the porch, hugged Gloria and shook Guy's hand. "What up, playa? Welcome back. How was the trip?" Eddie beamed.

"Good, good," Guy replied quickly, avoiding eye contact with Eddie, "just tired. Glo, I'll talk to you later. I'ma get some rest." He gave Gloria a quick peck then left.

Eddie noticed how Guy avoided eye contact and was acting jittery, but he didn't think twice about it as he helped Gloria get in the house.

●●●●●●

Guy told Hawk and Scatter to catch a cab up to Harlem. He gave them the address to the same boarding house he stayed in when he first came to New York. As he climbed the rickety stairs, he thought about how far he had come since then.

He knocked on the door. Hawk answered it in his t-shirt, smoking a cigarette. He and Scatter were playing cards for money when he came in.

"So this New York, huh?" Scatter remarked in his syrupy thick country accent. "Where we at? In Brooklyn?"

"Naw. This Harlem," Guy corrected him.

"Guy, you shoulda seen this country ass nigguh." Hawk chuckled. "I thought he was gonna break his neck lookin' up at them tall ass buildings."

Guy laughed and Scatter even snickered.

"Man, fuck you fat nigguh, play cards," Scatter replied.

Guy was truly at home with his two childhood friends. If the deal with Po' Charlie would've involved killing either one of them, he would've told Charlie to kiss his ass. Hawk and Scatter were two of the best cats he knew. They'd give you the shirts off their backs. But if you were the enemy, you'd be lucky to get away with the shirt on your back.

"Y'all nigguhs ready?" Guy questioned.

"Nigguh, fo' fifteen grand a body, I was about to ask you the same thing," Scatter quipped.

"We gonna need a car. Hawk, you got us covered?" Guy checked.

"If it got fo' wheels, nigguh, I can steal it," Hawk boast-ed.

Guy knew everything was in place. He just wanted to double check and if need be, triple check. He took off his coat and pulled a chair up to the table. There was nothing left to do but wait until nightfall.

"Deal me in," Guy told them.

Chico Jones stepped out the bar on Flatbush Avenue and lit a cigarette. He was tipsy but not drunk and ready to fuck the shit outta the young thang on his arm.

"Psst, my man," Scatter whispered, leaning against the wall.

Chico turned around.

"You wanna buy a brand new watch?"

Scatter held out Guy's diamond Rolex. The bar light reflecting against the blue diamonds made Chico take notice. He could tell it was an expensive watch, so he came over.

"Nigguh, who you steal this shit from?" Chico asked.

"Dig, bossman, you askin' a little bit too much. The important thing is, I got it," Scatter replied.

Chico picked up on his country accent and smiled inwardly, thinking he could fast talk the country nigguh and get the watch for a song.

"Nigguh, you know who I am? Huh? I'm Chico Jones and this is my muhfuckin' block!" he boasted, stunting for the chick. "Now yo' best bet is to look out for the house, so that the house may look out for you."

Scatter smiled. "I can dig it, bossman."

"Now how much you want for the watch?"

"Yo' life!" Hawk hissed, grabbing Chico from behind and shoving him in the alley beside the bar.

Before the chick could scream, Scatter had already gutted her with his six-inch blade. Jerking in an upwards motion, he silenced her forever and snatched her into the alley.

Hawk Bill wasted no time slitting Chico's throat ear to ear and leaving him spitting up blood. They laid both bodies in the alley and Scatter then fished Chico's keys out of his pocket.

"You won't be needin' these, will you, bossman?" he quipped.

Guy pulled up in the stolen Buick Park Avenue. Hawk Bill jumped in the passenger seat while Scatter got in Chico's red Coup de Ville and pulled off behind Guy.

Bonk! Bonk!

Hawk Bill laid low in the front seat of Chico's Cadillac while Scatter was in the passenger seat. They were in the Bronx in front of Mo Jenkins' house on Tremont Ave. A young dude stuck his head out the door.

"'Ay, youngblood, tell Mo Chico said come here," Scatter

called out.

The young boy disappeared inside. Mo came out and saw Chico's car with a smiling Scatter looking at him.

"What up, Chico? Fuck you doin' way over here?" Mo asked as he rounded the trunk and came up to the driver's side window. But instead of seeing Chico he saw an unfamiliar face.

"Where's Chico?" Mo asked, instincts telling him to run.

Before he could, Hawk Bill gripped him by the shirt and put the .38 snub to his forehead. "Same place you gonna go!"

Boom! Boom!

Mo's lifeless body fell to the street, kicking and twitching as the Caddy skidded off.

Scatter was getting antsy. They had been sitting in Smitty's apartment for the last four hours. It was almost three in the morning. They had been there so long; Hawk Bill was in the kitchen frying bologna.

Smitty's wife sat on the couch, nervously wringing her hands.

"Sometimes he doesn't come home for days," she told them, hoping the men would get tired and go.

"Then we gonna wait for days," Guy assured her, his .32 resting on his knee.

"Please, let me go... what's between you and Smitty is between you and Smitty," she said, cursing herself for the hundredth time for opening the door for Guy.

She had known better. Smitty had beat it in her head, to never let another man in the house while he wasn't home. But she knew Guy's face. She had seen him around with Smitty and she had been at Nicky's party. She was one of the women that were eyeing Guy. That country charm and easy smile had enticed her to open the door; now her life was in danger because of a moment of indiscretion.

119

"Man, Guy, I ain't fo' all this sittin' 'round. Hawk fryin' 'loney like he home. Nigguh, smack that bitch up! She know where her old man at!" Scatter spat.

"I swear I don't!"

"She don't know, man," Guy confirmed. He knew Smitty kept his wife in the dark just like he kept Gloria in the dark.

"Man, god-damn," Scatter drawled. He had already rummaged the house, finding twelve hundred dollars and some jewelry he planned on giving his old lady.

It was another twenty minutes before they finally heard the key in the door. Guy put his hand over her mouth and Scatter got behind the door. When Smitty entered, he was looking down the barrel of Scatter's .357 Magnum.

"Yo, what the – "

Boom!

One shot echoed through the whole apartment, making Scatter regret using the gun instead of the blade. Without hesitation, Guy used Hawk Bill's blade to slit Smitty's wife's throat. The three of them then climbed out the window to the fire escape and descended to make their getaway.

"Guy? Man, do you know what time it is?" Eddie said half asleep when he opened the door.

It couldn't wait," Guy replied as he entered the apartment.

Hawk Bill had suggested being the one to hit Eddie, but Guy wasn't with it. He wanted to do it himself. He felt the most he owed Eddie was to do it himself. Besides, he was hoping Eddie would give him some reason, any reason, to justify what Guy came to do. Guy's mind may've been made up but his conscience was still at odds.

When Guy turned around, he saw the gun in Eddie's hand. His reflexes tensed as his guilt made him imagine Eddie raising the gun and shooting him.

Eddie saw Guy look at the gun. "Nigguh, I ain't know who it was bangin' on my door in the middle of the night," Eddie explained, putting the gun in his robe pocket. "Now what's so important it couldn't wait?"

Guy relaxed and sat on the couch. Eddie sat in the arm chair across from him. Guy just looked at him.

"Nigguh, I know I'm a pretty motherfucka, but goddamn, you just ain't my type," Eddie joked.

Guy laughed stiffly. Eddie was the only thing standing between him and a million dollar connect. But, he couldn't do it. So he said, "Man, it's Gloria."

"What about her?"

Guy rubbed his face.

"You want a drink or something'?" Eddie asked with concern. He remembered how Guy was acting earlier, so he knew he had something on his mind.

"Yeah," Guy sighed.

Eddie got up and went a few feet over to the bar. "Yeah, brah, I know Gloria gotta helluva mouth on her, but she a good girl and she love you," Eddie said, while fixing two drinks.

He had his back to Guy, so he didn't see Guy ease the gun out his coat. Guy only half listened to Eddie. He started to just sneak up behind him and shoot him in the back of the head, but Guy was too much of a man for that. So instead he said, "When was you gonna tell me about that Nicky shit?"

"Huh?" he replied.

Guy stood to his feet. "Nigguh, you heard me," Guy's voice got stronger.

He caught Eddie off guard when Eddie turned around and saw the gun.

"Guy? What the hell you — "

"Nigguh, don't play dumb wit' me! Nicky and half the Council got warrants. Shit about to hit the fan and you ain't tell me

nothin'??" Guy barked. He wanted Eddie to buck, he needed Eddie to buck so he could justify in his own mind killing his man.

Eddie was in shock. He didn't know where all this was coming from. He searched Guy's eyes to see if he was high, tripping off dust or something. But he could see that Guy was sober and intended on killing him. So he thought fast.

"Guy, listen, that ain't got nothin' to do wit' us. We okay, baby. We – "

"It's got everything to do wit' us! Or maybe you one of the nigguh's wit' the warrants! You plannin' on turnin' rat, Eddie??"

Eddie had long tuned out Guy's illogical rantings. His only concern was survival. He kept a close eye on Guy, waiting for his chance and when it came, he didn't hesitate. Eddie threw the drink in Guy's eyes, partially blinding Guy with the alcohol. Eddie went into his robe pocket for the .32 automatic. The barrel of the pistol got caught on the inside lining of the pocket just as Guy lunged at him, firing a shot wildly. Eddie shot through his pocket as he struggled to hold Guy's gun hand. The shot caught Guy in the side.

"Fuck!" Guy bellowed as he fell against Eddie. He had recovered his sight and was restraining Eddie's gun hand while Eddie was restraining his.

"Nigguh, what the fuck is wrong wit' you?!" Eddie barked. "What the fuck I'ma kill you for?!"

Guy didn't answer. He slung Eddie against the wall and began over powering Eddie with sheer strength, bringing his gun closer and closer to Eddie's head. Eddie realized that he was fighting a losing battle, so he opted to use both hands to restrain Guy's hand. With Guy's other hand free he hooked Eddie hard in the jaw, buckling Eddie. Guy stepped back and fired three times into Eddie's chest.

"What-what did I do?" Eddie questioned as he slid down the wall. It was a question he'd never get the answer to.

His dead body slumped to the ground. Guy stood over him and put two more in his head. Guy knew too many gunshots had gone off in the apartment, but Eddie didn't have a fire escape so he was forced to use the front door. He turned the door knob with his coat jacket then stumbled out into the hallway.

He felt weak from the loss of blood and momentarily leaned against the wall, holding his side. He stumbled off down the hallway. The lady across the hall was looking out of her peep hole when he came out. She had heard all the gunshots and called the police. She cautiously unlocked the door and peeped down the hallway trying to get a better look at the fleeing man.

⊙⊙⊙⊙⊙⊙

"You're where?! Oh my God, Guy, are you okay?! I'm on my way!" Gloria squealed over the phone.

Guy had Scatter and Hawk Bill take him to a hospital in Fort Lee, New Jersey, just across the border of New York.

"No, baby, I'm okay. The doc said it was a flesh wound... have you heard from Eddie?" he asked, trying to prepare her for what was to come.

"No, why? Is my brother alright?"

"I-I don't know, Glo. The nigguhs who got at me were looking for him," Guy lied.

"Oh, God please," Gloria moaned.

"Just sit tight, baby, okay? I'll be outta here in a minute. Just try and relax, okay? I love you!"

"I'll try, Guy. I love you, too."

But Gloria wouldn't get a chance to relax. A few hours later she found out Eddie had been killed. The stress of Guy getting shot then Eddie found dead was too much. She went into labor and had to be rushed to the hospital. The baby would be born prematurely but eight hours later, she gave birth to a six-pound three-ounce boy. He was named Kevin Edward Simmons.

The next morning Guy stood in front of the glass looking at his first born son. His chest swelled with pride. He could see nothing but good things in his future. He was ready to take on the world. Gloria's mother walked up.

"Hello, Mrs. Bell," Guy greeted her then hugged her. "I'm sorry for your loss."

Mrs. Bell didn't even hug him back. When he broke the embrace, she looked him in the eyes and said, "You may have everybody else fooled, but I can look through muddy water and see dry land. But it's all in the Lord's time, then all you do in the dark…will come to light."

With that she walked away, and it would be the last words she'd speak to Guy up to the day she died ten years later. She didn't even come to their wedding.

But Guy had succeeded in fooling the streets. Rumors abounded everywhere, from Chico had killed Mo, to Mo had Chico, to Nicky had all of them killed. No matter the rumor, Guy's name never came up. He spent the next two months keeping a low profile then when the Council started to get arrested left and right, he used that as an excuse to relocate to North Carolina. The Reign of the Council had officially ended in '81. But the Dynasty of the Simmons Family had just begun.

CHAPTER 12

Ty opened the door of his apartment for Kev. They greeted each other with a pound and a ghetto hug.

"What up, Kev, how you?" Ty asked as they settled down on Ty's couch.

"Chillin', Fam... what's that?" Kev asked gesturing to the 50-inch plasma mounted on the wall.

"You don't remember this shit? Benny Blanco from the Bronx," Ty remarked, imitating a Spanish accent.

"Naw," Kev shook his head.

"Carolito's Way! Remember when that shit came out and we was all hyped?" Ty smiled.

"Hell yeah and I remember my mother caught us skippin' school and beat our ass all the way out the theater!" Kev chuckled. "That's why I don't remember this part 'cause I ain't seen the rest since!" Both brothers laughed.

"And remember what Pop said?" Ty smirked.

"Serve y'all asses right for telegraphin' your next move," Kev said in a deep drawl, imitating Guy.

They laughed again. When the laughter subsided they both were silent a moment thinking how it all was so simple then. Ty paused the DVD.

"So, what's good?"

"I talked to ol' boy," Kev started, speaking of his Wolf Pack mole. Ty already knew who it was, and they never named names if it wasn't necessary, "you know Dino gettin' married Saturday?"

"Yeah."

"Well, I'm supposed to be the best man. Anyway, ol' boy said that's when the Wolf Pack is plannin' on gettin' at me," Kev explained.

"Oh word?" Ty growled. "Well joke's on them then 'cause that's when we'll be gettin' at them!"

"Exactly!" Kev seconded. "I convinced Dino to postpone the wedding. His fiancée' pitched a bitch, but I offered to pay for the whole family to have the wedding in Puerto Rico.

"Yeah well, better a late wedding than an early funeral," Ty commented.

"Word."

"Which is right on time for this New York shit," Ty told him.

"What New York shit?"

"Your peeps up top," Ty replied.

Kev sighed. "Ty, I told you that deal ain't —"

"Naw, naw it ain't about that deal right now. It's about Pops."

"What about him?"

Ty leaned forward, resting his elbows on his knees. "Look, I know you feel like Vee and them hit Pop but I know it *wasn't* them. But with all this shit goin' on, we ain't even consider the Bells."

"The Bells? Why would they come at us like that?" Kev wanted to know.

Ty shrugged. "I don't know, unless some how they found out our ol' boy mercked their ol' boy," Ty explained, speaking about Guy killing Eddie.

Kev nodded. "Yeah, but how?"

"I don't know… or maybe they felt like, wit' Pop out the way, I could convince you to move on the deal wit' me. They already know I'm for it."

Kev nodded again, thinking it over.

Ty continued. "I talked to fam up top and told him I needed his help. He's sendin' down a little crew. I 'posed to pick them up tomorrow from the train station."

"But how we 'posed to — "

Ty cut him off, anticipating his question. " 'Cause if he did it, I guarantee whoever he send to help had a hand in the hit, too. I can hear the nigguh now like, 'Yeah, son, the same nigguhs I sent to body the old man, I'm sendin' to help them dumb nigguhs cover they tracks,' feel me?"

Kev smirked. "I feel you, lil' brah. So now we run they names and see if they been down here befo' and when and if they have…" Kev's sentence trailed off.

"Then we take it to the Bells," Ty added. Guy had raised them the same so they thought alike.

"And if it ain't them, the only other thing I know is some old coon Pop was beefin' wit' back in the day. He just came home after doing twenty plus in prison. Cat named Brah Hardy," Ty explained.

"Hardy?"

"Yeah, 'cept I can't find this nigguh nowhere. I wanna look this nigguh in the eyes myself."

Kev shrugged. "That's nothin'. One of my youngens is a Hardy. He'll get us out Brah Hardy."

"Cool."

127

Kev took a deep breath. Silence filled the room. They both knew why, but no one spoke on the elephant in the room.

Kev stood up and shook Ty's hand. "Aw-iight... I'm out."

"I'll get at you tomorrow after I leave the train station."

"Bet." Kev walked slowly to the door. He opened it. Without turning to look at Ty he said, "Ty?"

"Yeah?"

Pause.

"Do you love her?" Kev asked.

Pause.

"Naw, Kev. I don't."

Kev looked over his shoulder and replied, "I do."

He left out closing the door behind him. Those two words along with the look on Kev's face were enough to convince Ty he had to end it with Karrin once and for all. No matter how much it hurt.

●●●●●●

Ty sat reclined in his Escalade, mellowing to the sounds of Jasmine Sullivan. He checked his watch then glanced around the train station in Wilson, NC. Looking around, he could pick out the undercover police mulling around. He shook his head with a smirk. Anybody with half a brain knew the Amtrak wasn't the move to smuggle drugs anymore, especially in Wilson. The spot had been blown too many times. He glanced down the tracks and saw the approaching train in the distance. He checked his watch once again. The train was fifteen minutes late.

He stepped out of the truck after the train pulled up and the people began to disembark. He scanned the passengers casually. He didn't know who he was looking for, but they knew he'd be pushing a navy blue Escalade.

"Hey, cutie," he heard a sweet feminine voice call out and he turned to see who was talking to whom.

A smile spread across his face when he saw his beautiful cousins, Asia and Brooklyn. They ran up to him and smothered him with a double hug, making every dude around wish they were him.

"What up, y'all? What you doin' down here? Tito sent the crew with you?" Ty asked.

Asia and Brooklyn looked at each other and bust out laughing.

"What?" Ty inquired, because apparently he had missed the joke.

Asia reached out and pinched his cheek, with a wink. "Baby... we are the crew."

"Ay yo, Tito, what the fuck is goin' on?" Ty huffed into the phone.

He was standing in his kitchen watching Asia and Brooklyn in his living room, dancing to music videos being girls.

"Fam, calm down. Believe me, the twins is official. They like pitbulls in a skirt," Tito assured him.

Ty shook his head in frustration. Watching them in the living room they looked like two dizzy broads.

"T, I'm tellin' you, this shit down here is serious. You may think this shit country, but ain't shit slow but our walk. That, set-a-nigguh-up-wit-a-chick is played! These nigguhs we gettin' at ain't goin' for it!" Ty barked.

"Don't let the smooth taste fool you, Fam. Put 'em to the test, you'll see."

Click.

Ty put his phone down wondering what kind of game Tito was playing. He already had their aliases being checked, so in the meantime, he damn sure intended on putting them to the test.

⬤⬤⬤⬤⬤⬤

Vee, Rome and Banks sat in a doublewide trailer outside of Durham that they used as a stash house. The TV was on, but no one was watching it. Vee eyed the two men evenly, his .40 caliber gripped in his palm. He knew, of the two men, one of them had betrayed him. He had known both men ever since he had came to Durham, since they had been broke. He had broke bread, did dirt and held them down, but the larceny in one of their hearts had caused them to go against the team. Greed had won out over loyalty, and now, one of them had to pay.

"Ay yo, dawg, I know shit is serious but is the gun really necessary?" Rome asked, shifting in his seat.

"Rome, you act like it make you nervous. It don't, do it?" Vee asked, scratching his ear.

"Naw, dawg, but goddamn, we 'posed to be family," Rome replied.

Vee chuckled. "I used to feel the same way... now... I'm not so sure."

"So what are we waitin' for? When we movin' on them nigguhs?" Banks wanted to know.

"I'm just waitin' on the call, then we out."

Five minutes of tense silence later, Vee's phone rang.

"Yo," Vee spoke into the phone.

"Ay yo, Vee, this hospital shit is cool. Same muhfuckas they got out here playin' the perimeter, no more no less. They ain't even move the old man," Mike G informed him.

Vee had put him down on the plan to trap either Rome or Banks.

"Cool," Vee responded then hung up. He looked at his two partners. "That's one," he told them cryptically.

They looked at each other in confusion. The phone rang again.

"Yo," Vee answered.

"Vee, you sure the wedding was today?" one of Vee's Lieutenants asked.

"Positive."

The lieutenant chuckled. "Well then, I guess the groom got cold feet or the bitch jumped the fence! Ain't shit happenin' at the church... not even a choir rehearsal!"

"Cool." Vee hung up then stood up slowly. "Y'all ready to do this?"

Both men visibly relaxed seeing that everything was on point... or so they thought. As Banks stood up, Vee slapped the shit out of him with the pistol. His forehead split and blood dripped down his face as he slumped on the couch.

"You'se a greedy piece of shit, Banks," Vee gritted.

Rome looked at Vee. "Naw, dawg, tell me this nigguh ain't set us up!"

"Tell 'em!" Vee shouted at Banks, kicking his leg. "Tell Rome you ain't do it!"

"I swear, Vee, it wasn't—"

Vee slapped him with the pistol three more times then put it to his head. "Tell him you did it, nigguh!"

"Vee, man," Banks sobbed, "Man I-I fucked up... this nigguh said he'd kill my family, dawg!"

"You expect me to believe that?! Huh?! You pussy muhfucka, you lyin'! You just a greedy nigguh, Banks!"

"No, Vee, I swear!"

"The nigguh promised to put you on, if you got rid of us, didn't he?!" Vee surmised correctly.

"No!" Banks lied.

"You had to have it all! Get us out the way and you'd be the man," Vee shook his head with a chuckle. "You was too greedy to see that once you got us, he was gonna kill yo' dumb ass," Vee laughed.

"No, Vee, man... man, I'm sorry, I'm sorry," Banks sobbed like a new born baby.

By now, Rome had his pistol out.

"Vee, let me be the one to kill this nigguh! Rico was my cousin!"

"Not now, Rome, 'cause first Banks gonna make shit right, ain't you, B?"

"Yeah, Vee, anything, Vee, anything," Banks assured him.

"You gonna call Kev... tell him you ready to do me yourself. Tell him Rome and Mike G is wit' you, but he gotta put them on, too. Tell him the price is fifty g's. When you meet him, you gonna kill him. You got that?" Vee explained.

Banks nodded.

"You sure? 'Cause if you don't, *we* gonna kill yo' family, B. One by one and make you watch," Vee told him. "You hear me, nigguh?!"

"Yeah, Vee. I got you man, I got you," Banks replied, wiping his tears. "But afterwards... what about me?"

Vee smiled. "You a dead man walking."

●●●●●●

Ty and Kev sat in the front of the late model Ford Bronco, while Asia and Brooklyn sat in the back. They were parked near the corner of the next block over from the church in

Greenville where Dino's wedding was to be held. The church block was quiet, except for a few cars parked on the block. Two of which held young Hardy and his crew and another crew of gunners that worked for Kev. Ty had a few cats posted up on each end of the block and one van full of shooters that circulated the block.

They had been sitting there for two hours and Ty was getting restless. Every few minutes, he'd chirp his team like, "Anything?"

Chirp! Chirp!

"Nothing."

The only sounds in the car were Asia and Brooklyn. It seemed like they talked non-stop, thought Ty. All the chatter about was designer clothes, hot music and what rapper probably had the biggest dick was getting on Ty's last nerve.

"Ay yo, Asia! Brooklyn! Goddamn, do you mind?!" Ty barked from the driver's seat.

Both girls got quiet instantly.

"My bad, Ty," Asia apologized.

"Yeah, Cuz, we just killin' time," Brooklyn added.

"Naw, y'all killin' my ears," he mumbled then he turned to Kev. "Yo, Brah, they ain't comin'."

Kev looked around before answering, "Just give 'em a few more minutes."

"A few more?? Kev, we been layin' on these nigguhs two hours already. I know Vee, if he ain't here by now, he ain't comin'."

"They already came through," Asia told them.

Ty looked at her through the rear view. "What?"

"They already came through. First, the cat came through in a grey Taurus. He came straight through the intersection," Asia explained. "Then the same Taurus came up the other intersection at the other end of the block," Brooklyn said.

"How you know it was them?" Kev inquired.

" 'Cause the same dude came through a half hour later in a burgundy Yukon," Brooklyn replied.

"Why you ain't say nothing?" Ty huffed.

Asia shrugged. "We thought you seen 'em, too."

Ty was hot. He didn't want to seem like he wasn't on point, especially by two cackling chicks. He had already had their aliases ran and they hadn't been in NC when Guy got shot. At least not under those aliases.

"And, yo, you see the woods behind the church parking lot? Look real close, see the path? You got muhfuckas on both corners, but that path—" Asia began but Ty cut her off.

Ty chirped his phone. "Yo, K. Step out."

A cat stepped out of the path that Asia pointed to. Ty looked at her through the rearview with a smug grin that said, *you ain't got all the sense*.

"Oh," Asia shrugged then turned back to Brooklyn like, "Anyway, you know what's real hot?" And they went back to their never ending conversation.

Ty just started the car, shaking his head. "Call off the dogs, Kev. We out."

Kev didn't protest, seeing that the spot had already been blown.

The four of them sat in Kev's stash apartment in Greenville. Kev and Ty were discussing the situation, while Asia and Brooklyn had a conversation of their own. Someone knocked on the door and Kev answered it. Hardy and his man Markie walked in.

"Aww look at the little cuties, Asia," Brooklyn chimed.

Hardy didn't pay them any attention but Markie smiled at the girls.

"What up, Kev, what you need me to do now?" Hardy

asked.

Kev smiled proudly. The young boy was a true soldier. "Just chill, Hardy. I'm waitin' to hear from my man now," Kev replied.

Hearing the name Hardy made Ty's ear perk up. "Oh... so you young Hardy, huh? Kev told me a lot about you, lil' homie," Ty greeted, shaking his hand.

Hardy smirked, proud to be acknowledged by the infamous Ty Simmons. "What up, Ty, how you?"

Markie was sitting between Asia and Brooklyn, smiling ear to ear. Hardy sat in the love seat across from Ty.

"Yo... you some kin to Brah Hardy?" Ty inquired.

"Yeah."

Kev's phone rang and he answered it.

"Check this out, dawg, I need to get in touch wit' yo' uncle. You know where he at?" Ty asked.

"Naw, Ty, I ain't really seen him since he came home. He around though... what up?" Hardy replied.

"Ain't nothin' really, I just need to holla at him. I got at a few of your other uncles, but they ain't seen him either. I'm like, damn, dude must be in the cut," Ty chuckled, attempting to mask his frustration.

Hardy could feel it though. He knew Guy Simmons had got hit in the 'boro and he knew how the Simmons' and Hardy's didn't fuck with each other, so he felt that Ty wanted to bring some type of beef to Uncle Brah. He may've been loyal to Kev, but blood was thicker.

"Naw, dawg, I wish I could help you. I see him on the fly sometime. I'll tell him to get at you," Hardy offered.

Ty looked at the young boy and could tell he was lying. Inside, Ty started to boil because he felt like Hardy was trying to play on his intelligence. Ty leaned forward in his chair. "My, nigguh... you know what happened to my pop?" Ty asked directly.

Asia and Brooklyn instantly ceased their chatter.

"Yeah, and like I told Kev, I was truly sorry to hear that. I fucks wit' Kev like that, so I'm wit' y'all nigguhs for whatever," Hardy vowed.

Kev ended his call. "Ty, what up, brah?" Kev wanted to know.

Ty didn't answer, instead he kept his eyes on Hardy. Hardy kept his eyes on Ty. It was becoming a test of wills to see which would break.

"Check this out," Ty began, standing up and pulling his pistol, "I'ma ask you one mo' motherfuckin' time, yo. Where… is… Brah?!"

Hardy could feel his pistol tucked in his waist. He wanted to reach but he new he'd never make it. He shrugged. "My, nigguh, I don't care how many pistols you pull… I can't tell you what I don't know."

"Yo, Hardy, we just wanna talk to Brah," Kev tried to assure him. He remembered Ty mentioning the name to him before, so he wanted to holla at Brah, too.

"Yo' guess is as good as mine," Hardy smirked, and it was the smirk that sent Ty over the edge.

Ty grabbed Hardy by his dreads and began pistol whipping the nigguh unmercifully. Markie started to go help Hardy and found a .38 snub under his chin courtesy of Asia.

"Be easy, playboy," Asia whispered, "stay outta grown folks affairs."

Ty beat Hardy until his arm got tired, then he relieved Hardy of his pistol. Blood covered his shirt. One of Hardy's eyes was swollen shut and blood ran down his face like sweat, but he was still conscious. He spit out his tooth.

"So it's like that, Kev? You just gonna flip on me like

that?" Hardy wanted to know.

Kev did feel a tinge of guilt, because he knew Hardy was a good nigguh. But Ty was his brother and blood was thicker.

"You brought it on yourself, yo. We just wanna talk to Brah, and you actin' like it's something to hide," Kev answered.

Hardy eyed Ty hard. "Nigguh, you might as well kill me —"

Boom!

Everyone looked in the direction of the sound of the gunshot to find Markie's brains all over the wall and Asia holding the smoking gun. "Ask him again."

Her actions surprised Ty because he truly didn't see it in her. But now he knew why Tito sent the twins.

"Bitch, you killed my man?!! My man?! Fuck all y'all! You, you, you, and you!" Hardy barked, looking at Ty. "Kill me 'cause I ain't tellin' you shit!"

Brooklyn stood up from the couch. "Oh I get it now, you a gangsta!" she chuckled. "Like, you for real? I wanna see. Kev, you know where the gangsta mama live?"

"Yeah."

"Take me there."

Just the mention of his mother made Hardy try to lunge out of the chair, but Ty caught him with a swift hook that crumbled him to the floor.

"Ty, you wait here wit' Scarface, boo. Let me handle this," Brooklyn assured him as she, Asia and Kev left out.

As they waited, Ty tried to talk to Hardy, softening his approach. "'Lil homie, word up, you a soldier... I know I gotta kill you and me being a soldier, you *know* I gotta kill you. But shit is real. I feel like Brah had somethin' to do wit' my pops. If he didn't, no foul. This shit end wit' you. But, yo, your moms ain't got shit to do with this."

"Nigguh, fuck you and your goddamn daddy! I hope he die chokin' on his own blood!" Hardy spat.

Ty spazzed out and beat the nigguh unconscious. He woke him up when Brooklyn called him from Hardy's mama house.

"Wake up, lil' homie, somebody wanna speak to you," Ty said, smacking him then putting the phone on speaker.

"Yo, Cuzzo, tell the gangsta this," Brooklyn said.

Hardy was groggy but he could clearly hear his two year old son crying and his mom asking, "who these women in my house?"

"Ask yo' son," Asia replied.

"Taveres! What's goin' on?!"

Hardy's baby mama was spazzin'.

Boom!

The shot seemed to rock the phone. The baby screamed and his mother prayed.

"What up blood, what up cuz, what up gang-sta!" Brooklyn sang the 50 Cent hook into the phone, giggling. "Don't worry, your baby moms wasn't all that cute anyway.

Hardy dropped his head.

"Talk to me, lil' homie," Ty urged.

Hardy remained silent.

"Yo, Fam, he still ain't talkin'," Ty told her.

"Say goodbye to your son, yo," Brooklyn hissed.

"Daddy!" the young child screamed.

Boom!

Hardy's whole body convulsed. He tried to get up, but his ribs were broke and every part of his body ached.

"Noooo!" Hardy bellowed, picturing his son's little lifeless body. His spirit was broke. He had called their bluff and lost. Now the only thing left was his mom or his pride.

"What's it gonna be?" Ty smirked at him. He was truly impressed by the young boy.

Hardy glared at him.

"Taveres, please! Tell them what they want to know!" his mother begged.

The pleas of his mother dissolved his pride instantly. He knew he was gonna die and he was okay knowing his son would be with him. But his mother was something different.

"Ay, Cuzzo—" Ty started to say, but Hardy cut him off.

"I'll tell you," he whispered through clenched teeth.

"Huh? What was that?" Ty taunted, leaning down close to his mouth.

"I said... I'll... tell you," Hardy gritted.

Ty smiled then said to Brooklyn, "Fall back, Cuzzo. I think me and lil' homie can work somethin' out."

"Handle yo' B.I. We'll just wait here until you say it's all good," Brooklyn replied.

Click!

Brah stayed out in the country, right outside of Goldsboro. It was a trailer that sat by itself, so Ty decided not to pull up to the spot. He parked in a little clearing down the road then guided a duct-taped Hardy back to the trailer.

"Remember, nigguh, yo' moms ain't safe 'til I say she safe, you understand? When we get to the door, I'ma knock, you talk. You alert this nigguh in any way, you'll be pullin' the trigger on your own mother," Ty explained menacingly.

Hardy walked in silence, like a man being escorted to the death chamber. He woke up every morning prepared to die, so there was no fear. His only thought was if he some how got away he would bring nothing but death to the whole Simmons family.

As they walked up to the door, the sounds of a woman being fucked royally moaned through the air. The small trailer was almost rocking from the dick Brah was laying down. Ty smiled because he had caught the nigguh with his pants down literally.

They stood on the short steps of the trailer and Ty knocked. The moans began to subside. He knocked again.

"Who is it?" a gruff voice called out.

Ty yanked Hardy's collar.

"Taveres."

"Who?!"

"Taveres," Hardy repeated louder through swollen lips.

Ty could hear the sounds of heavy footsteps nearing the door.

"Nigguh, fuck you doin' out here this time of night?" Brah mumbled as he unlocked the door. He would've sent anybody else away, but Taveres was his favorite nephew because Hardy took care of Brah, and he was the young live-type street nigguh Brah had been.

"Boy, I know you heard me fu—"

That's all Brah got out, because Ty shoved Hardy through the door and into Brah. The woman screamed on the bed.

"Nigguh, get down!" Ty barked, but the trailer was dark, so Ty's eyes had to adjust.

Brah was already adjusted. He had done twenty years sleeping with one eye open, so although the attack was sudden, Brah reacted on instinct. He shoved Taveres to the side and at the same time launched an overhand right square into Ty's nose.

Ty grunted and staggered; firing a shot wildly. As his arms flailed, he grabbed Brah's arm just as another punishing blow struck his temple. He raised the gun and fired.

Boom!

He felt Brah's body jerk out of his grip so he fired again.

Boom!

Ty heard a body slump to the floor. He felt along the wall until he felt the light switch and turned on the light. Young Hardy was gone! But that thought took a backseat to what he saw on the bed. His mother was sitting up on the bed, butt naked, with a gun pointed directly at him!

CHAPTER 13

Kev sat a block down from Hardy's house waiting for the twins. His phone rang. He looked at the number and smiled. It was Banks.

"Yo," Kev spoke into the phone.

"The nigguh had a change of heart, dawg. I think the nigguh feelin' like he over his head. He ain't tryin' to war wit' y'all nigguhs," Banks explained.

Kev smirked and nodded. He knew the young crew wasn't ready to war with the Simmons.

"But, yo," Banks continued, just like Vee had instructed him, "this shit done went too far. The nigguh know you ain't tryin' to talk after he tried to hit yo' pops."

Kev sat straight up in his seat.

"He what?! Muhfucka, why you ain't tell me that before??" Kev barked. He had known all along it was Vee and now he had his confirmation. All doubt was gone and now he tasted blood.

"I ain't know, Kev, I swear. The nigguh knew we wasn't wit' that shit. Now Mike and Rome, yo... they feelin' like Vee the cause of all this drama!"

"And?" Kev gritted.

"And... word, dawg, I'll get at the nigguh *myself*. Motherfuckin' Mike and Rome wit' me, but they want a spot too when it's all done."

Kev nodded. "No doubt, no doubt. They ride wit' you then they ride with you," Kev said, thinking, *a ride in a hearse*!

"Aw-iight cool. Gimme fifty stacks and the nigguh good as dead," Banks lied convincingly.

"Fifty?! That ain't shit, yo! You about to see *millions*," Kev gassed him up, "What the fuck is fifty cent?"

"I feel you my nigguh... but, yo, that's my price. I need fifty grand to make this move and you wanna get at Vee. Fair exchange ain't no robbery," Banks concluded.

Kev thought about it. He had to have Vee. A plan came to his mind that made him smile. "Okay, Banks, I'm cool wit' that."

"When can you get that?"

"Get it, nigguh, I got it!" Kev boasted. "Nigguh, that's wifey money." He laughed.

"Then it's whenever," Banks assured him.

"The sooner the better."

"I was thinking the same thing."

Kev looked at his watch. "Gimme an hour and I'm a hit you back."

"One."

Click.

Kev gripped the phone tightly. He was gonna get Vee one way or another.

"Tyquan?!" Debra gasped, dropping the gun and grabbing the sheet to cover her naked body.

Ty felt sick but his mind said find Hardy. While he and Brah were tussling, Hardy had crawled away. Ty took off through the trailer to find the back door wide open. He checked the back bedroom and bathroom to make sure the nigguh wasn't hiding. He went back to the back door and looked out into the pitch black woods.

"Fuck!" he yelled then went back up front. His mother had the sheet wrapped around her, kneeling over Brah. She looked up at Ty.

"He's dead."

"Ma, you fuckin' this nigguh?! What the fuck is goin' on???!" Ty barked, not believing what he was seeing.

"Tyquan, who was that that came in with you? Was it Kevin?" Debra asked nervously, jumping up and looking for her clothes.

Ty grabbed her arm and made her turn to him. "Ma, how you fuckin' this nigguh?! What the fuck is goin' on?!" Ty repeated exasperatedly.

"You-you wouldn't understand."

"Make me!" he demanded. His phone rang but he ignored it.

Debra slipped into her skirt, still wearing the sheet draped around her. "Ty, I'll explain later. But we have to get out of here, okay? We have to go!" she urged him.

"Ma, we ain't goin' nowhere until you tell me what you doin' in bed with the motherfucka that shot my father!" Ty barked. His phone rang again, this time he answered it. "Yeah."

"We good, Cuzzo?" Brooklyn asked.

"Yeah."

Click.

Debra got fully dressed then stepped into her shoes.

Ty stepped closer to her and hissed, "You gonna explain what you doin' here wit' this nigguh, or is it just once a ho always a ho?"

Debra's eyes were ablaze as she hauled off and slapped the shit outta Ty. "Nigguh, whatever I do, you gonna respect me! Do you hear me?!" Debra stated firmly.

Ty felt bad about calling his mother a ho, but he couldn't understand what she could possibly be doing there.

"You want to know what's going on?! Do you?! You think you ready to know about this family for real?!" Debra probed, looking her son in the eyes. "Yes, it was Brah who shot Guy... *because I set it up.*"

Kev, Brooklyn and Asia drove along after leaving Hardy's house. Once they got the word that Ty was straight, they murdered his mother then set the whole house ablaze. Their motto was, the murder mami's never leave witnesses.

Fire trucks shot by in the opposite direction. As Kev broke everything down about Banks, Asia sat in the passenger side and shook her head.

"I don't know, Cuzzo. The shit don't sound right. Send a lackey to meet 'em."

"Word," Brooklyn added from the backseat. "Don't nothin' beat the double cross but the triple cross."

"I feel you," Kev replied, "but he'll never meet with nobody but me. Besides, this ain't business... it's personal."

"We wit' you, Fam, but just make sure you on point."

"Always," Kev smiled.

"You what?!" Ty exclaimed. The words hit him like a sledgehammer and sat him down on the fold-out bed his mother had just got caught fucking on.

Debra kneeled in front of her son and caressed his face. "Baby, you don't understand what's goin' on. I-I did it for us, for *you*! It was the only way."

Ty snatched away and stood up. "How the fuck you sound, you did it for me?? You did it for him!!" Ty accused, pointing his finger at Brah. "You let that nigguh get in your head and mind-fuck you, just like he did when you was his—" Ty stopped talking and turned away. Debra stood up.

"Go 'head and say it. Say it, Tyquan. When I was his whore. Isn't that what you were going to say? No, baby, you definitely got it wrong."

"Then tell me why, Ma?? Fuck all this you did it for me! Tell me *why*?!" Ty wanted to know.

"Guy... Guy was talkin' about retirin'... about fallin' back. He said he was tired of the game and he was plannin' on turnin' everything over to Kevin," Debra explained.

Ty listened as she continued.

"You and I both know if that happened, Kev would push you back, push you out. Make you a peon in this family because Kevin is jealous of you. He's always been jealous, just like Gloria is of me," Debra told him taking a deep breath. "But with Guy gone, with everything up in the air then Kevin couldn't push you out, because they all know who should be the head of the family! You!"

"But, Ma, you ain't have to kill Pop. Why couldn't I just talk to him? He know what's goin' on between me and Kev," Ty offered.

Debra's eyes welled up and she dropped her head. "Guy... Guy would never choose you over Kevin."

"How can you be so sure?"

Debra looked at her son with a tear streaked face. "Because Guy isn't your father... Brah was."

●●●●●●

Vee, Mike G, Rome and Banks rode to Crabtree Valley Mall in Raleigh. The sounds of Tupac's "Hail Mary" blared through the speakers of the late model Lincoln Mike G was driving. Rome was in the passenger seat while Vee and Banks were in the backseat.

Vee eyed Banks with the .40 caliber in his lap. His finger itched to pull the trigger on Banks' rat ass. To Vee, the worst thing in the game was a rat ass nigguh, and what made it worse is that Vee had embraced the nigguh for so many years.

"Yo, Vee, please, man. We ain't gotta do it like this," Banks pleaded. "I-I know I fucked up but this me, dawg, Banks. I been there for you, dawg! When nigguhs tried to kill you in Charlotte, I laid 'em down! That gotta count for something'!"

Vee nodded. "You right, B. It do... I tell you what... bring Rico and Pappy back. If you can do that then I'll call it even," Vee said in deadpan tone.

"Man, you did it too," Banks mumbled.

"What you say?"

"I said you did it too, man!" Banks repeated firmly. He felt like he had nothing to lose, so he wanted to get off his chest what had been there for so long. "Yeah, Kev promised to put me on if I turned against you, but you did the same thing to Ty! Remember? He put you on and what did you do? You cut his throat and turned on him!"

Vee couldn't deny the truthfulness of Banks' words, but he wasn't hearing it. "Motherfucka, what I did was for *my* people, for *us*! What *you* did was turn on us for a motherfucka that don't even give a fuck about you. Ain't no comparin' the two!" Vee huffed.

"Wasn't Ty yo' peoples then, too?"

Vee smiled. "It took you to be dyin' like a lil' bitch to talk like a man, huh? I'm glad to see you got some heart left. Save it for Kev when you walk up and blow his brains out... then your own, next."

⬤⬤⬤⬤⬤⬤

Ty almost felt breathless. Like his whole world was turning upside down and topsy-turvy. "You lyin'!" he blurted. "You lyin'!"

"No, Ty, I'm not," Debra replied softly as she came over to Ty. "Brah Hardy was your father. Guy... Guy knew it because I was a few weeks pregnant when I finally left Brah. I can't lie; I respect Guy for taking you in and treatin' you like his own. He never denied you, but that was the only thing he would never give you... the right to run the family."

Ty couldn't believe all that he was hearing. Until Hawk Bill had mentioned it, he had never even heard the name Brah Hardy. His mother had never even hinted that Guy wasn't his father. Ty decided right then it didn't matter. Guy would always be his daddy even if he wasn't his seed. It renewed his respect for Guy, knowing he raised another man's child and the fact the other man was his enemy.

"What you saw... tonight... was just a part of the game, Ty. *My* game. I used Brah to kill your father. I had been writing him the last year, getting in his head. I told him about you, told him if Guy was gone, then *his* son would be head of the family! Brah couldn't resist having a Hardy run the Simmons organization and he went for it. Once Guy was dead, I intended on telling Kev who killed Guy, knowing he'd handle it and eliminate any connection to me," Debra explained meticulously.

Ty shook his head at how scandalous his mother was. "You'll use anybody... including your own son."

"We've all been used in this world, Tyquan. But a woman'll do what she has to in order to protect her own. Guy was going to rely on Kev's sense of family to keep you in the mix, but once Guy's back was turned... we'd be out in the cold... you know that," Debra replied.

"You got it all figured out, huh?" Ty said. "But what happens if Pop don't die?"

Debra had thought of that scenario before, and the consequences chilled her to the bone.

Kev and Asia drove toward the meeting place in silence. They were heading to Crabtree Valley Mall in Raleigh. Behind them was Brooklyn and Kev's lieutenant, Dino. He had tried to call Ty several times but it went straight to voice mail. So he headed for the usual meeting place. Banks always chose well populated places to talk. Kev waited patiently, but inside, his inner beast was rattling the cage, roaring to be released.

Banks walked through the parking lot feeling Vee's eyes on him the whole way. He hated the look Vee got in his eyes when he was mad, because they resembled a cobra's before it struck—hooded and slit tight. He also knew Vee fucked with roots, so he always felt leery of crossing him. But the deal Kev had thrown at him was too good to turn down. Finally, he'd be the man!

Yeah, he felt a way about crossing his childhood friends,

but at the end of the day, what they ate didn't make him shit... literally. He wanted a bigger piece of the pie, fuck that, he wanted his *own* pie so he could devour it unsliced. Just like any other man wants, except few are willing to do what it takes to get it. But Banks was, even if it was paid for in blood. Now the deal was in ruins and the ultimate price was his blood.

Vee had told Banks his mission. "Kill Kev then kill yourself." If he didn't, his mother, father, grandmother and little sister would be murdered. The Wolf Pack's shooters were at the house as he walked. He had heard them pleading on the phone so he knew it wasn't a game.

But Banks had other plans. There was no way he was going to pull the trigger on Kev, let alone himself. Kev was his lifeline to a jump-off somewhere else. Maybe he'd go to Milwaukee or Minnesota. Somewhere he could put his game down, but far enough from the Wolf Pack. He'd take the fifty grand Kev had for him and bounce. He had two hundred grand at the crib but he knew he couldn't go get it. He was out with just the clothes on his back. As for his family, that was in God's hands, he thought, but deep down inside he thought *better them than me.*

Banks sighed, ready to get the shit over with.

Debra's car was in the back of the trailer, which is why Ty didn't see it. He walked her to it then went back inside and torched the place. His eyes scanned the woods hoping to see a sign of young Hardy. He knew the young boy would be a problem, one they'd have to make a priority of handling. The little nigguh was a soldier and they had murdered his family. He wouldn't just go away.

At the same time, he thought about all his mother had said. He now knew who had shot his father, but instead of laying them to rest, he switched all the way around to protecting them. No matter how scandalous Debra was, she was his mother. He couldn't let anyone know the truth.

"What about the girl that was with Pops?" Ty had asked.

Debra sucked her teeth. "The bitch nutted up once Brah laid down the bodyguards, she was supposed to shoot Guy in the head. Dumb bitch dropped the gun."

"Who was she?"

Debra took a deep breath. "Some young bitch Brah recruited.

"And now Brah's dead," Ty reminded her.

"I didn't plan on you happenin', Ty," Debra replied sourly.

Ty had to find that chick. He felt like he was now his mother's accomplice, but if anyone found the girl then his mother would be exposed. As he drove, he turned his phone back on and called Kev.

"Kev."

"What up, lil' brah?" Kev asked, not knowing the new meaning the words "lil' brah" now held for Ty. "Dig, Banks spilled the beans! I *told* you it was fuckin' Vee!" he announced..

"Word?" Ty replied. He now knew the truth, but there was no way he'd tell Kev.

"We movin' on the nigguh now."

"Where?"

"Crabtree upper parking lot."

"I'm there," Ty assured him.

He knew Vee didn't do it, but shit had gone too far.

Besides, the Wolf Pack would make the perfect scapegoat. Ty pressed the gas and headed to the mall.

CHAPTER 14

A light drizzle had begun to fall on Banks as he walked. He could see Kev leaning against a car three rows ahead. Banks gripped the pistol tight as he neared Kev.

Kev saw Banks as well. "Here he come," he spoke into his Bluetooth.

Vee, Rome and Mike G were a few rows back from Banks and several cars apart, ready to blaze. They squat-walked from car to car, peeping up every few seconds.

Banks came up on Kev, looked around and whispered, "Vee came to kill you! I couldn't turn you, but you gotta hold me down!"

Kev handed him car keys. "See that blue Camry behind me?"

Banks nodded.

"The fifty is in the trunk. If Vee gets away, you handle your B.I., aw-iight?" Kev instructed him. He had anticipated Vee's presence, so he had a plan a, b *and* c.

"I got you, Kev," Banks assured him.

"This bitch-ass nigguh don't even care about his own grandma," Vee mumbled to himself, seeing Banks jog away from Kev. Banks knew his family was at stake, yet he chose to save his own ass.

Vee rose up and fired at Kev, barely missing him and shattering the back window of the car he was leaning on. From there, bullets rained. Shoppers caught in the midst screamed and scurried for cover. Asia and Dino came out of their hiding spots at the same time Mike G and Rome stood up to hold Vee down.

Kev was in a zone. All he tasted was revenge. With every shot he tried to get closer to Vee, while Vee honed in on him as well.

Dino was the first to fall, because he misjudged Rome's position. Rome was in the cut when Dino tried to cross the no man's land from one row to another. Rome aimed and caught Dino in the back of the knee, dropping him, then ran up putting three in his dome. By the time Kev squeezed off two in Rome's direction, he had dashed to safety.

"Don't shoot, please!" one of the women screamed, huddled by the dumpster. She was an elderly white woman.

Mike G had caught movement out of the corner of his eye and had swung his hammer in that direction. Seeing it was two women, he sucked his teeth like, "then stay the fuck outta my way." He turned to walk away, when he heard, *"Psst!"* He turned around to find the second woman huddled up was a young, black girl… with a gun.

Boom! Boom! Boom!

Asia's .45 lifted Mike G off his feet and he was dead before he hit the ground. Asia got up and ran off, leaving the old woman trembling in shock.

Ty pulled into the area just as Asia passed by the hood of his car. The sound of gunfire filled the air, and he wasted no time getting in the mix.

Banks wanted only one thing—to get away. He stayed low, moving when he could, trying to get to the blue Camry. He finally reached it and sighed with relief when he slid inside and started it up.

"Thought you got away??" was all he heard.

He looked up and into the barrel of Rome's Glock nine. He still had his pistol, but he knew he couldn't aim it quicker than Rome's bullet would enter his brain.

"Man, please—"

Boom!

Banks closed his eyes, waiting for death to claim him. But in the nano second it took him to realize he wasn't hit, he opened his eyes to see a blank look on Rome's face, then he just collapsed. Behind him was a female that looked just like a singer his mind was to frazzled to recall, except she wasn't holding a mic, she was aiming a gun. The gun that had killed Rome. She winked at Banks then ran off. Banks didn't know who she was, but he certainly wasn't sticking around to find out. He slid the car into drive and peeled out.

Kev quickly changed clips, pocketed the empty one then locked and loaded the .40 caliber. He had come prepared just in case Banks was trying to set him up and bring Vee. Now that he had him in his sights, he wasn't going to let him leave alive.

Vee gripped both pistols, squatting behind a car some seven cars away from Kev. He was just as determined to dead Kev. They had concentrated on no one but each other the full five minutes the shootout had been blazing. But Vee possessed an upper hand that made him smirk as he rose with a grunt and aimed at Kev's location.

Kev rose almost at the same time, but he was a hair quicker than Vee. His first slug threw Vee back against the car behind him, catching him square in the chest. Seeing he had shot Vee and the look of anguish on Vee's face, he squeezed off three more in his chest before Vee's body slumped out of sight. Kev waited no time rounding the car and running up on Vee.

Ty scoped the area, trying to get a lead on Vee's position. He saw Kev when he hit Vee up then ran around to finish him. Ty took off behind him to hold his brother down.

Kev aimed the pistol at Vee until he held it poised for a head shot. "For Guy, motherfucka!" he barked at the same time he pulled the trigger. The gun jammed.

He had been squeezing round after round fluidly, now the gun had jammed. He squeezed again and again, nothing. Vee could hear his own heartbeat as he lay on the concrete. His breathing was heavy and his chest felt like he'd been hit with a sledgehammer over and over. But the vest had done its job. Now with Kev standing over him, Ms. Sadie was doing her job. Her power had never failed him. He opened his eyes and squeezed the trigger.

"Kev!" Ty shouted, seeing his brother's body stumble back. He hurried to his side.

The first bullet entered Kev's open mouth and exited out the back of his neck. The second shot entered his right eye socket, killing him before his body hit the ground. As he fell back, his body tensed and his finger squeezed the trigger.

Boom! Boom!

The shot went towards the sky as he fell back.

Vee rolled over and stumbled to his feet in a crouching position. The sound of an army of sirens filled the distance. Mission complete, it was time to make his exit.

Ty ran up busting his gun recklessly, tears streaming. Car windows exploded and metal bumpers sparked from the gun shots in Vee's wake. Ty could make out the tail end of his movements and yelled, "Vee! Nigguh, ain't *nowhere* you can go! I swear on everything I love, you dead!"

He turned to Kev sobbing then dropped to his knees beside his brother. "Kev... damn, Kev. I'm sorry, man. I'm sorry!" he wept, thinking of his mother's conniving plan for mastery of the family. It was she who had set off the chain of events that ended his brother's life, and now that Ty knew, he too felt responsible.

"Ty, we gotta go!" Asia urged him, taking Kev's gun and cell phone. "Now!"

She grabbed Ty's arm and he allowed her to lead him away reluctantly. The shootout had lasted less than six minutes and in that short blink of an eye, the world had changed for Ty.

As Ty drove, Asia tried to call Banks to put Kev's Plan B into motion. He didn't answer. Asia smiled to herself because she knew Plan C wouldn't fail. She texted Brooklyn.

Kev's gone. Vee got away.

●●●●●●

Banks looked at his cell phone ringing with Kev's number, but he wasn't about to answer. His mind was filled with guilt and fear. The team Vee had sent to his crib called him. He reluctantly answered. All he heard was the sound of screams and tortured moans. They had stabbed them all repeatedly, his grandmother, mother, father and little sister. Then they punctuated the murderous statement with, "You next, rat ass nigguh!"

He was terrified. Banks didn't want any part of Vee, Kev or the whole beef. He planned on getting away as far as he could and then calling Kev from a new cell claiming to have lost the old one.

Matter of fact, he thought, lowering the window. He tossed the ringing cell out on to the street. He needed to dump the Camry then grab a cab and take it all the way to Charlotte. From there, he'd be home free.

He pulled the Camry over at McDonald's on I-40. He'd call a cab and eat while he waited. Banks brought his order out to the car and popped the trunk to grab the fifty grand.

Fzzztttzzz!

The metallic whoosh of a shot fired through a silencer caught him in the side and knocked him to the ground. Brooklyn quickly climbed out of the trunk and stood over a stunned Banks.

"Fifty thousand never looked this good, huh?" Brooklyn smirked.

"But you—" Banks gasped, remembering the angelic face that murdered Rome. His mind couldn't wrap around how the fuck she got in the trunk.

Brooklyn smiled, reading his mind. "I'm everywhere. Now," she replied, pulling him up by the collar, "show me where this nigguh rest at."

"You sure?" Brooklyn asked firmly, the silenced .45 to the back of Banks head.

He was too petrified to do anything but nod. Brooklyn looked at the plush apartment Cat lived at and scanned the area for signs of movement.

"G?" she asked.

"Yeah, ma, apartment G," he confirmed, feeling like he had fulfilled his part, but just to make sure, he added, "I was gonna dead the nigguh myself for Kev. I got Kev 100%... you want me to roll wit' you?"

"Naw," Brooklyn whispered.

Ppzzzfftzz!

The silenced messenger of death sparked, leaving Banks slumped against the steering wheel.

"You just wait here."

Brooklyn got out the car, tucking Banks' pistol in her waist. She slid along the edge of the parking lot, staying in the shadows and away from the street lights. She came up on Vee's apartment and cautiously checked the windows. When she got to the back door, she saw the ADT sticker on the window. She had toyed with the idea of breaking in and waiting inside, but the sticker deaded that idea. Even if it was a front, she didn't want to chance it.

Brooklyn walked through the breezeway to the front door thinking of her next move. Right across from Vee's door was apartment F. Brooklyn nodded to herself, concealed her gun behind her back, then knocked on the door. A few moments later a young white girl opened the door.

"Hi!" Brooklyn chimed, her face lit up with that little girl smile. "I'm Tammy and I'm staying with my brother across the hall, maybe you've seen him? Anyway, I was wondering and I really hate to bother you, but do you have any parmesan? I'm making this incredible lasagna. Do you like Italian? You look sorta Italian yourself. Anyway, can I come in?" Brooklyn talked so fast and smiled so sweetly, she talked herself right into the apartment.

Vee turned into his parking lot in the same late model Lincoln Mike G drove to the mall. Inside, he felt sick. Banks may have betrayed him, but they had come up together and put in work together. He regretted making the call that got his whole family slaughtered in cold blood, but he had to make an example and Banks' family became just that. It would also lead to an investigation that would ultimately come back to haunt him. He didn't know if Banks was dead, but Vee was determined he would be.

He also saw Mike G go down and there was nothing he could do. He didn't know if Rome had got away, but he had a nagging feeling that he hadn't. His whole team was gone and he still had Ty to contend with.

Vee opened the door slowly, rubbing his face, his mind heavy with thought.

Inside apartment F, the white girl and her boyfriend cowered face down on the floor with their hands behind their head.

"Please, take what—" the white boy begged, but Brooklyn cut him off.

"Sssshhh!" Brooklyn whispered harshly. She had waited patiently for Vee to pull up. When he did, she was ready. She couldn't see his face but her street instincts said it was him. She watched him get out the car, and she planned to catch him slipping as he unlocked the front door.

"That's it, boo, come to mami," Brooklyn sang, peeping out the window.

Vee closed the car door and took a step. His cell rang. He started to ignore it, but when he saw Cat's name, he quickly answered.

"What's up, baby?" he said, but heard nothing. "Baby?" he repeated then the call cut off. He stopped and looked at the phone.

"The fuck is he doin'?" Brooklyn thought out loud. She wondered if she rushed him right then would she be able to catch him before he got on point.

Vee dialed Cat's number. She answered.

"Cat?" he said with concern. All he heard was incoherent babble then she screamed and dropped the phone. "Cat???" he yelled into the phone.

All Vee could think was some how Ty had found out she was in B-More. His agile mind remembered the chick who was with Tre' when she recognized Cat from Morgan University. He didn't know what was going on, but he was gonna find out right then. He quickly back tracked and jumped in the car, peeling off.

"Shit!" Brooklyn cursed in agony. "Fuck! I don't know who that was but they just save yo' life, boo," she said as if Vee could here her. She texted Asia then turned to the white couple.

"Please! Anything you want!" the white boy offered.

"Anything?"

"Yes, yes!" he replied.

"In that case... I want no witnesses," Brooklyn smirked.

The two shots were quick, painless and above all, effective.

●●●●●●

Debra drove to the hospital after going home and taking a shower. She dressed casually in a cashmere track suit and sneakers, pulling her hair up into a ponytail. She thought about all that had transpired and she wondered how Ty was taking it. She knew he loved Guy and it hurt her knowing he was stuck in the middle. She didn't regret what she had done, but she did wish there had been another way. It wasn't that she didn't love Guy, because in her own way she did. She just loved herself more. Debra had always been a survivor and her first law was self-preservation.

She got to the hospital and headed to Guy's room. When she turned the corner, she saw a familiar site. Gloria. She started to say something, but seeing Gloria holding Guy's hand in tears, she paused and listened.

"Baby, please, I-I need you! Please God bring him back to me! Guy, fight, baby, please... fight! Oh God, I'll give up anything, just let him live!" Gloria cried out in an anguished tone of prayer.

Debra opened her mouth to say something, but her voice caught in her throat when Gloria screamed like she was in pain.

"Yes, Lord! God is great!" Gloria exclaimed loudly.

The pitch of her scream brought three nurses running into the room, brushing past a stunned Debra. Gloria had screamed not of pain, but out of joy when she felt Guy squeeze her hand back. The nurses joined in with Gloria, displaying degrees of excitement from professional to spiritual.

Debra had just witnessed the power of prayer right before her eyes; yet, it had brought about her worst nightmare as Guy opened his eyes and looked straight at Debra.

CHAPTER 15

Debra and Guy's eyes meet from across the room. Cliché to a degree, but a dream come true for Debra. It was 1985 and Guy was the man to see. From Charlotte to Wilmington and across South Carolina, he was the chief Heroin connect. Not many knew the extent of his operation, only the chosen few that he considered trustworthy.

Po' Charlie was schooling him well, teaching him to stay under the radar and make the kind of relationships that would be beneficial in the long run. Guy even associated himself with a church and became a mason. He was only thirty-three and well on his way to an illustrious career in the game. He had bought his parents a big ranch- style house in the Eastern Wayne District, a well- to-do area of Goldsboro.

"You know what somebody said to me the other day?" Willie had told him one day.

"What?"

"Some cat came in the pool room and said Simmons? Oh, you Guy Simmons' daddy!" Willie chuckled.

At first Guy was puzzled why it was funny. Then he remembered telling Willie that very thing would happen. He no

163

longer lived in his father's shadow.

Guy had Debra enchanted. She had heard so much about the infamous Guy Simmons. She had seen him from time to time, but never close enough to make her presence felt, and she knew she had a presence that needed to be felt. She was 5'9" and 160 pounds of southern comfort that curved around the scrumptious measurement of 34-26-42. Those were the types of numbers a poor man dreamed of hitting and the heavenly combination to a rich man's every fantasy. Her captivatingly deceptive hazel eyes, kewpie doll nose and long brown hair spoke of her Indian ancestry she inherited from her mother.

She could tell Guy liked what he saw from the way his eyes sparkled and he lifted his glass to drink to her. But then again, very few men didn't like what they saw in Debra, until they got to her heart. Her game was waterproof like fish pussy, so a nigguh had to play slick just to hold her attention. Guy not only held her attention, he owned it. He had that combination of southern charm and city slickness that was intriguing to a small town girl like Debra.

A small town girl with big dreams. Her parents were both hard workers and sought to instill morals and principles in Debra. Her mother, who was equally gorgeous, had told Debra at the time, "Your beauty can be a gift and a curse," but Debra used it like Voodoo. She had been fucking since she was twelve and selling pussy at fourteen. By seventeen, she had entered the young Brah Hardy's stable.

Brah wasn't a bona fide pimp, just the consummate hustler. Debra successfully manipulated Brah's bottom bitch out of the way then gamed her way to the prized position of being Brah's woman. This was how she came to be at Schroco's Lounge, sending subliminals across the room to Guy, while Brah sat inches from her.

To Debra, Brah was just a come-up. His name was definitely ringing bells, but Guy, he was in a whole other league. The big leagues, the level she had her sight set on. It was her 19th birthday and she decided right then Guy would be her birthday gift to herself.

"Punk motherfucka," Brah mumbled under his breath, violently stabbing out his cigarette in the ashtray.

"You okay, baby?" Debra chimed.

"Yeah." He had seen Guy come in as well. He couldn't stand how motherfuckas acted when he was in the room. It was like the second coming of Christ! Hustlers shook his hand and sent him bottles, while the women giggled and blushed at his slightest acknowledgement. Guy moved through the room with an undeniable swag, while Hawk Bill and Scatter stuck to him like Secret Service agents.

Guy stopped to show love to BooCore, another major player with a major organization except his product was cocaine. Brah despised both men, because he didn't see either one as real street nigguhs. They were ex-school boys that lived off of their family name in Guy's case and lucked up on a major connect in BooCore's case.

"Come on, baby, dance wit' me," Debra urged.

"For what?" Brah snapped.

"Don't act like that, Willie. It's my birthday," Debra pouted, grabbing his hand as she stood up. "And I wanna dance."

Brah took one look at the silk bodysuit that hugged her curves so lovely, he couldn't help but smile. He had the baddest chick in the club, so why not flaunt it?

But Debra had another agenda. They slid to the dance floor as the DJ played Teena Marie's "Casanova Brown." Debra purposely positioned herself so her ass was facing Guy and proceeded to let him see what he could have.

Brah grinded her close, dipping her smoothly the way a player slow dragged. He caught Guy looking at Debra's ass and smiled. He slid his hands to her ass and squeezed it lustfully.

Guy chuckled to himself, because he knew the bitch was in the bag. Besides, she was Brah's, which made taking her that much sweeter.

When Brah and Debra got back to the table, she noticed her daiquiri had been replaced with a fresh one. As she sat, she picked up the drink and saw a small heart had been drawn on the napkin. She smiled, dabbed her lips with the napkin then discreetly slid it into her bosom. She knew who had sent it and what was on it.

"Hello? May I speak to Guy?" Debra asked, calling Guy the next day.

"Yeah this is me, sweetness. I been waitin' for you to call me all day," Guy charmed, talking on the private line in Willie's pool room. It was where he handled most of his business and arranged his extra marital affairs out of respect for Gloria and their household.

"Mmm-mmm, I bet," Debra giggled, "you don't even know who this is?"

"You right, but I do know this is Debra and I thought that's why you were calling so I could get to know you."

Debra loved the way Guy's voice sounded. Smooth as warm brandy, intoxicating her senses. "Depends on what you wanna know?" Debra flirted, like a schoolgirl with a crush.

"Everything, sweetness, everything. But listen, I don't do too much talking on the phone, so I'm a see you in about twenty minutes. Cherelle and Alexander O'Neal doin' a show in Raleigh. That enough time for you to get ready and figure out what you gonna tell Brah?" Guy said, and she could hear his smirk over the phone.

Debra couldn't help but smile, because that was exactly what she was thinking. "I'm a grown woman, Mr. Simmons, and my daddy don't look nothin' like Brah Hardy. But you'll find all that out soon enough," Debra huffed with a feigned attitude.

"Beautiful, baby, 'cause what me and you do ain't nothin' but grown folk business. I'll see you in a minute."

Debra wasn't overly impressed with Guy taking her to a concert. Brah had taken her to plenty, but she was impressed when she found out not only were they going to see Cherelle and Alexander O'Neal, they were going to meet them as well!

Guy took her backstage and she got to meet and hangout with the duet that sang her favorite song, "Saturday Love." The song had just come out and it was all you heard in the clubs. Now to be in their presence was mind blowing. She held her composure well and never showed how star-struck she was. Besides, in her eyes the biggest star was Guy. Alexander and his manager treated Guy with deference while Cherelle played flirtatiously like she had fucked Guy before.

They hung out into the wee hours before Guy took her to the Hilton in Raleigh. They stood in the middle of the room hugged up like they were slow dancing to a rhythm only they could hear.

"So... did you enjoy yourself tonight?" Guy asked.

"Not as much as I am now," Debra replied, eyeing him seductively. "Them people acted like you were the superstar! Guy this, Guy that, Guy, Guy, Guy," she giggled, "I'm just happy to finally have you all to myself."

Guy chuckled, throwing his head back slightly. "Yeah, it gets crazy sometimes, but you've had my attention since the first time I laid eyes on you, sweetness," Guy crooned.

Debra closed her eyes and moaned. "Hmmmm, say that again."

"What? Sweetness?"

"That's it." She smiled, eyes still closed. She suddenly opened them with one eyebrow raised. "Who else you call sweetness?"

Guy smiled and kissed her gently. "Believe me, baby, I rarely call the same one twice. Now don't look at me like that 'cause we both know the life I live. But we also know, I'm not the chooser but I'm honored to be the chosen. So if tonight is all I have, I'm a use it to make the next man tomorrow pale in comparison."

Debra was glad Guy stopped talking, because another sentence would've made her cum on herself. "I wouldn't be here if it didn't include tomorrow, Guy," Debra replied, "and as for the next man... life goes on and people grow out of things that fit before. So if I am the chooser then I definitely choose you." She smiled then sucked his lip. "But I'm not the only one in a situation. What about your wife?"

She knew Gloria by face, every available woman around knew who Mrs. Guy Simmons was. From the furs to the jewels to the Benz, Guy treated her like a queen, so they all wanted to be her.

Guy caressed Debra's cheek gently as his smile gradually faded away. "My wife's position is rock solid with me, so you don't have to try and compete, because you can have your own position... if you willing to play it, ya dig? You think you can handle that?"

Debra knew if she played her cards right, she could have the world on a silver platter, so she didn't answer with words, she simply sealed it with a kiss. A kiss that started with his lips and traveled the length of Guy's torso as she removed his clothes along the way. If a man is truly in control, he has no problem in allowing a woman the luxury of assuming it. He relaxed as Debra covered him with kisses until she got to his silk boxers.

He heard the breath catch in her throat, but she didn't miss a beat, running her tongue along the entire length of his shaft and mouthing his nuts. Debra planned on fulfilling Guy's every fantasy so he would grant her every wish. And Guy definitely wasn't disappointed. It took her a second to get used to having so much dick in her, but once her womb adjusted she fucked Guy like she'd been doin' porno tricks for years.

Debra had never cum so many times in her life, nor passed out from the sheer intensity of an orgasm. But when she awoke, though her pussy would be too sore for sex for a few days, she had done what she had set out to do. Turn Guy Simmons out.

"Guy! Hell no, girl, I'm a see him now! Guy, you hear me??? Put your window down!" Shantelle yelled at her girlfriend in the passenger seat then at Guy out of the window of her candy red '85 Corvette.

She was in the middle of the intersection at Elm and Slocumb Street when she spotted Guy coming from the opposite direction. Guy stopped in the intersection and put the window down.

"Shantelle! We in the middle of the motherfuckin' street!" Guy barked, horns blaring at them from both sides of the street.

"So! You got yo' business in the street fuckin' with that bitch Debra!" Shantelle spat harshly.

"Just pull over," Guy sighed, then pulled up at the gas station called Darnell's.

Shantelle backed up and pulled in catty-corner to Guy. They got out about the same time. Guy could tell by her strut that she was on fire and her attitude made him chuckle. Shantelle Braswell was truly a piece of work. She was only eighteen and just graduated from high school. She was Hawk Bill's younger sister but Guy had had her for a year. Hawk Bill was cool with it because before she got with Guy she was already in the street hustling, and he'd rather see her with Guy, despite his age, than with some do-boy knucklehead in the streets.

Shantelle may've been young but she handled her business like a grown woman. She was 5'5" with the complexion of a Hershey chocolate bar, the waist of a wasp, the ass of a mule and the mouth of a sailor. She was the only woman besides Gloria that could spaz on Guy and get away with it.

When Shantelle reached him, he snatched her arm roughly.

169

"Bitch, you done lost yo' motherfuckin' mind, huh?!" Guy barked.

"No!"

"Then calm yo' ass down and get in the goddamn car," Guy seethed, opening the passenger door of his Eldorado, throwing her in then slamming the door behind her.

When he got in, she was sitting with her arms folded and her lip poked out.

"Now what the hell is you talkin' about?!" Guy asked, pulling off.

"You know what I'm talkin' about, nigguh! That bitch!" Shantelle huffed.

It had been a few weeks since he brought Debra into the fold. He had mainly taken her to spots out of town while she ended her thing with Brah, but in a small town, word travels fast, and Shantelle kept her ear to the street.

"I'm tellin' you, Guy, that bitch Debra ain't no earthly good! She a money grubbin' ho! Let that nigguh Brah have her 'cause you only want her 'cause she wit' him!" Shantelle read him correctly and it made Guy smile because she knew him so well.

"What's so funny?!"

"You. All in my goddamn business! Stay in yo' place 'cause I'm a grown motherfuckin' man!" he barked.

"Hmph, you need to act like one then," she mumbled.

Sssccrrrch!

Guy slammed on the brakes just after turning the corner. He grabbed Shantelle by her throat and pinned her against the window. "Aw-iight now, keep runnin' yo' mouth wit' that reckless shit and I'ma beat yo' ass, you hear me?!" he cursed.

"I hear you!" she replied, pushing his hand away. "I'm tellin' you, Guy, I put up wit' that wife shit, but you ain't gonna disrespect me with that bitch! I'ma end up killin' you or you gonna end up killin' me, but I ain't gonna keep goin' for this shit," Shantelle promised, tears of frustration forming in her eyes.

Guy sighed and softened up. "Dig, baby girl, you know you my heart. Besides my wife, you the only – "

Shantelle cut him off, "Nigguh, I'ma be yo' wife!" she blurted out with the same seriousness of a child, which made it that much more intense.

Guy smiled and caressed her cheek, but she slapped his hand away.

"Nigguh, don't try to hustle me wit' that sweet shit," she said, fighting back a smile.

"Hustle you?" Guy echoed, knowing that's exactly what he was about to do.

"Damn right! Just like you do on them Jew-ass prices you charge me. I'ma stop fuckin' wit' you and go see Cookie and them in Wilson," she chuckled.

"Yeah right. That shit been stepped on so many times you can still see the footprints." He laughed.

"Oh yeah, and ummm... I need five thousand dollars," she informed him sheepishly.

"Five grand? For what?" he questioned.

Shantelle explained how she had fronted this Army dude off the Air Force base a pound of weed. When it came time to pay he straight up laughed in her face. He thought because she was a girl and he was a soldier that he could take advantage of the situation. He didn't know she was a soldier, too. A street soldier. But when that hot lead hit his ass three times all the bitch came out of him, and he went to the police saying Shantelle tried to rob him. She bonded out, then sent word through a chick he was fucking asking how much would it cost to drop the charge and forget her name. He said five grand.

Guy listened, shaking his head. He already knew Shantelle was a wild child. She'd already been to training school twice, at twelve and fourteen.

"Why you don't use your own money?" he probed, making a right.

"Cuz." She pouted, hitting him with that baby doll look. "I don't wanna spend my own money." She pushed the arm rest and slid across the seat and eased into his lap. "Please, daddy, I'll be yo' friend."

Guy threw his head back with laughter as he made another right turn. "So now you gonna hustle me, huh? Just like you ain't wanna spend your own money on the car you drive and the apartment you live in and the – "

"I love you," she sang, kissing his mouth to stop him from talking.

Guy had mad love for this young girl. She was definitely a go-getta and went harder than some dudes he knew. He would give her the five thousand because he wanted her to stack her money and get out the game.

"Come by the pool room later," he relented.

She kissed him again as he completed the trip around the block and pulled up into Darnell's again. "Thank you, daddy, just keep the five and have me an ounce waitin'," Shantelle said.

He shook his head. Heroin was six grand an ounce. "You got all the sense, don't you?"

Shantelle winked. "I learned from the best."

Guy had definitely taught her well.

"And Shan, next time some shit like that happen tell me first," Guy scolded her.

"I know, I thought about it but I had to let that nigguh know, just 'cause I got a pussy don't play me for one," she replied. And Guy understood. "And I'm serious about Debra. Leave her alone. Everybody know you fuckin' Brah woman, now let it go. He talkin' 'bout what he gonna do to you, psychin' himself up. But don't worry, if I catch him, I'ma shoot him myself," Shantelle said, kissed him deeply then got out.

What she said to Guy was the last thing on his mind. It went in one ear and out the other, not knowing how much it would cost him in the long run.

CHAPTER 16

Vee wasted no time getting out of that hot ass Lincoln. He drove straight to the storage for his Bentley and the big guns. He grabbed two SK-47s and an AR-15 that he made fully automatic then he picked up his three most solid soldiers and jumped on highway 40 North, heading for Baltimore. The trip usually took five hours, but Vee made it in four. Guns or no guns, police or no police, his only thought was getting to Cat and Taheem.

"Yo, dawg, we in VA now. You know these crackers don't play," one of his soldiers said, watching the speedometer exceed 100 mph.

"Fuck them crackers," Vee gritted then didn't say another word all the way there.

When he arrived, he found the apartment complex filled with police. The front of the apartment door was yellow taped. Seeing that, his heart dropped. He pulled right up into the midst of the police and hopped out, leaving the door of the Bentley wide open and the car still running. His man discreetly slid over into the driver's seat and parked in a safer location, six apartments down.

"Yea, though I walk through the valley of death, I shall fear no evil," he whispered to himself, remembering that Ms. Sadie told him to recite Psalm 23 whenever he was in a tight situation.

Each step seemed to take an eternity as he approached the apartment door. He was trying to prepare his mind for the worst. All Vee could hear was the sound of his own heartbeat. All other sounds seemed distant. He attempted to duck under the tape but was restrained by an officer.

"Hey! You can't go in there! This is a crime scene," the officer informed him, looking at Vee suspiciously.

"This is my girl's apartment, yo," Vee replied calmly.

"And you are?" the police berated him like he was about to interrogate him.

"Baby, over here!"

Vee looked and saw the older woman that babysat Taheem. She was standing in front of her apartment talking to two plain clothed detectives. Vee approached her quickly and she threw her arms around his neck.

"Oh my, baby... I'm so sorry! I'm so sorry," she sobbed.

"What happened?" he said, just above a whisper.

"There's been an accident," one detective told him skeptically.

Vee's stomach dropped. The old woman took his face gently between her hands. "Baby... it... its Taheem. He's dead," the old woman sobbed, fighting to maintain her composure.

Dead?

Dead?

Dead?

The word bounced around in his head while his sense sought to make sense of it. "Dead?" he echoed. Hearing the word aloud made it real. He started shaking his head, praying that this was a dream, but Vee knew he was fully awake. He squatted then sat on the grass, holding his head in his hands. The tears welled up in his heart, but he knew he had to get to Cat.

"What happened?"

"The poor child was always tired. She... she left the patio door opened that let out to the pool." The old woman wiped her tears. "She didn't know, baby. She was a good mama, but...," her voice trailed off.

"Are you the deceased child's father?"

"Does your girlfriend have a history of depression?"

"Is she or has she ever been suicidal?"

"What's your name?"

The two detectives hit him with question after question, but he didn't hear any of it. His only statement was, "Where's Cat?"

"They took her to the hospital," the old woman replied.

"Please... take me to her."

The old woman drove him to Northwest Hospital. His team followed in his Bentley.

When they arrived, he went up to the front desk and asked, "I-I need to see Kionna Richards, please."

"And you are?" the woman behind the desk asked.

"I'm her husband," Vee told her.

The young lady behind the counter checked the computer then turned to Vee, "Yes, she's in the emergency room."

"Can I see her?"

"She's in... room 23."

Vee left the counter with the old woman behind him. He scanned each door until he got to 23. He knocked once then slowly opened the door. He saw Cat balled up in a fetal position, shivering like she was cold. Her eyes were open and she was just staring at the wall. She gave no indication that she heard them come in.

Seeing his woman like that made Vee feel so helpless and even more so alone. Not only was his heart aching from the loss of his only child, just looking at Cat, he could see that she would never be the same.

"Cat. Cat, baby, it's me… Vee," Vee said as he tentatively approached the bed, but Cat didn't respond. Vee looked at the old woman because he didn't know what to do.

"Kionna, we're here child," the old woman said in a comforting tone. "Are you cold, baby? Why don't you get under the cover?"

Cat still didn't speak. The old woman sat on the edge of the bed and stroked her hair. "Baby, I know no words in the world can take away your pain, but just… baby, the Lord's here. Lean on the Lord. This is one of them times when the only footprints in the sand are His. Give Him your burden, baby," she said to Cat.

Cat was still unresponsive. Vee walked around to the side of the room Cat was facing and looked into her eyes. They seemed empty and dim. The sparkle that made them light up the room was gone and had been replaced by a blank stare. It was then that the tears finally fell from Vee's eyes. He hadn't cried since he was a child. He knelt by the bed and hugged Cat's head. He felt her whole body become rigid as stone then she snatched away from his embrace.

"Don't touch me! Don't touch me you bastard, it was you!" she screamed like a woman possessed.

Both Vee and the old woman were taken by surprise by the outburst.

"Cat! What are you talkin' about?!" Vee asked, stunned.

"You know goddamn well what I'm talkin' about! It was you!" Cat screamed again, this time two nurses burst into the room.

"What's going on in here?!" the heavyset nurse wanted to know.

"Get him outta here! I don't ever want to see you again!" Cat cried. *"Get out!"*

Vee's heart felt like it had been ripped from his chest. To hear the woman you love deny you and push you away at the moment you needed each other most was too much for Vee to take.

"Sir, I'm going to have to ask you to leave," the nurse stated firmly, while the second nurse tried to get Cat to calm down.

"I needed you, Victor!" Cat cried in anguish. Those were the words that would haunt Vee for the rest of his life.

Outside, the old woman explained again what had happened. She told Vee she heard Cat screaming on the patio. Every unit had its own patio, but it let out to the collective pool area. When she got out there, Cat was cradling Taheem to her chest. He was soaking wet and his little face was so bloated. She said Cat kept calling for him and muttering how she had only went to sleep for a minute. Taheem had crawled out to the pool, fallen in and drowned.

As he listened, his mind went back to the dream he had told Ms. Sadie about. It all made sense to him then. How Cat was standing at the pool with her eyes closed; the beautiful fish that flew out of the pool. Fish usually mean pregnancy and water represents life, so fish leaving water can only mean death.

It's going to cost you everything you love, he again remembered Ms. Sadie's words.

The old woman suggested he let Cat rest. He knew he needed to call her parents and let them know what was going on. They were on the next thing smoking. There was nothing else for Vee to do but wait until the morning.

Vee spent the entire night in the parking lot. His team grumbled, but no one openly protested. They knew it was futile. At 6:30, Cat's mother and father pulled up to the hospital and called Vee. He met them in the lobby.

Cat's mother hugged him tight, and her father shook his hand firmly. They could tell by his disheveled appearance that he had no sleep and the pain in his eyes told the story of his heart.

"Victor, I know this is hard on you. I loved my grandson dearly, but we need you to be strong. Cat needs you," her father told Vee. He knew what Vee did for a living, but he respected how he cared for his daughter. Besides, he had been around too long not to know how to swim upstream himself.

They got a hold of the doctor who approached them timidly.

"Thank you for accommodating us so quickly, doctor. We'd like to know how our daughter is," Cat's father inquired.

"Yes, ahhh," he looked down at the memo in his hand, "Mr. and Mrs. Richards, there seems to have been a problem."

"What kind of problem?" Mrs. Richards gasped.

"Your daughter is gone. She left the hospital on her own some time this morning," the Doctor replied regretfully.

Vee dropped his head. Something deep inside told him he'd never see Cat again.

⚫⚫⚫⚫⚫⚫

The week since Guy's recovery had been bittersweet for the Simmons family. They rejoiced in the fact that Guy had recovered and cried bitterly about the death of Kev—Gloria especially. She had prayed in earnest for Guy to live, vowing to God that she'd give anything. She knew the saying, "be careful what you pray for," but never in her wildest dreams did she think she would lose her only child. So in a spiritual sense, Gloria felt responsible for her son's murder. They had to keep her heavily sedated because her mood varied from severe depression to fits of wild bereavement, and they feared she would harm herself.

Debra felt Gloria's pain sincerely. She had even embraced Gloria during one of her fits. After all, she had a son, too. So despite the fact that because of Kev's death Ty's ascendancy would be undisputed, she never wanted it at the expense of Kev's life.

Ty's mind was focused on revenge. He was relieved that Guy had recovered, but he felt somewhat distant from Guy. He too respected Guy for raising him as his own, but the bond would never be the same. So instead of dealing with the emotional confusion, he focused on the one emotion he knew best: anger.

The Wolf Pack and all their lackeys became the targets, the targets he used to take out his frustration on for not being able to find Vee. Once he found out from Brooklyn where Vee laid his head, he had his crib staked out 24/7.

Three teams alternated the task but Vee never showed his face. But Ty was determined. He kept the spot watched and intended on doing so until Vee lay dead in his own blood.

But the rest of the crew was no match for Ty's team. He all but shut down all of the Wolf Pack's spots and murdered anybody that repped the symbol. The carnage increased the police presence, but Ty didn't care. Until Vee was dead, he was ready to murder any and everybody even remotely connected to him.

Karrin was the only one that felt relieved across the board. She loved Guy like a father and she was glad to see he had pulled through. Kev on the other hand, was a different story. Theirs had been a marriage of convenience for her. She loved Kev, and human compassion made her regret his passing, but deep down she felt that the only obstacle between her and Ty getting back together had been removed. After their few fleeting moments of passion, Ty once again stopped taking her phone calls. His hot and cold streaks were driving her crazy and made her want him even more.

They rode in the funeral procession in separate limos. Ty and Debra in one; Guy, Gloria and Karrin in another. Debra understood why Guy rode with Gloria, so she didn't object. Plus, it would give her a chance to talk to Ty, because between the funeral arrangements and the war in the street, they hadn't had a chance to talk.

"You look tired," Debra commented, Dior shades protecting her eyes from the sun.

"I'm aw-iight," Ty replied dryly as he peered out at the streets, his reddened eyes hidden by the Versace's.

"I'm-I'm sorry for keeping it from you so long," Debra said, but Ty didn't respond, so she continued. "I feel so bad for Gloria. No matter the history she and I have, I wouldn't wish this on anyone. I keep thinking how easily this could've been you," her voice broke as she finished her sentence. She turned to the window and a tear fell from behind her Dior's.

She had thanked God many times that it hadn't been Ty. It would've killed her if the one person that she set off these terrible events for, was the one she lost because of it.

Ty hated to see his mother cry, so he reached over and took

her hand.

"I ain't goin' nowhere, Ma."

She squeezed his hand and kissed it. "I never wanted this for you, Tyquan. I wanted to see you do well in school... go to college... I don't know, maybe I should've been more persistent, maybe—"

"I made my own decision, Ma. You couldn't have stopped me anyway," Ty replied

Debra chuckled. "I know, Mr. Taurus the bull. So headstrong, just like your father," she said, but the look he gave her made her drop her head. "Guy."

●●●●●●

Gloria rode holding Guy's hand with both of hers, which rested on her lap.

"You know I love you, right?" Guy told her sincerely.

"I know you do, Guy," Gloria answered.

"And you know that, no matter what, we're going to find the bastards responsible for this."

"It-it won't bring him back."

"But he'll be able to rest in peace," Guy countered, and she could hear the rage concealed in his tone.

Gloria squeezed his hand. "There's nothing I'd like better than to know that my son's killer didn't go unpunished, but right now... I-I just want peace. I want this to be over," Gloria whispered, holding back the tears that came with being a wife of the game. She had practically been raised in the game, but all the money, the jewels, cars and fancy houses in no way amounted to the price she had paid for it. Her brother, her son and almost Guy several times.

"It will be," Guy assured her, "I promise you that!"

Karrin sat and listened without appearing to do so. She

smiled to herself at the way Guy always catered to Gloria. It made her wonder why they even got divorced. It was clear to anyone with eyes that they still loved one another. Sometimes love isn't enough, and the thought made her think of her and Ty.

"You okay? You haven't talked much the whole ride," Guy asked Karrin, leaning across the aisle to pat her knee.

"I'm-I'm okay," Karrin assured him.

"You sure?"

Karrin nodded her reply.

"You know, Karrin, you'll always be a part of this family. I love you like a daughter. Never forget that and never forget you're a Simmons," Guy smiled.

"Thank you, dad," Karrin replied, "You don't know how much that means to me."

She and Gloria's eyes met momentarily, and it made Karrin look away. Gloria didn't trust Karrin. She felt that she was a nice girl but she could sense another side of her, just beneath the surface.

The line of limos and Escalades looked more like a presidential envoy than a funeral procession. Tito Bell had come down with his mother and Gloria's sister, though they were still estranged. The twins were still in town, so they rode with Tito. Many of the old players, Mason and southern politicians came out to show their respect to the Simmons family.

Ty watched as they lowered his brother into the ground. Kev had a closed casket wake because of the nature of his death, but Ty had slipped into the back of the funeral home and slid a bullet into Kev's hand. It was his way of vowing to his brother that he would avenge his death.

Guy had to attend the funeral in a wheelchair because he was still a little weak. The doctors didn't think it was a good idea, but there was no way he wasn't going to attend the funeral of his son.

After the funeral, Tito approached Guy and Ty. He bent over to hug Guy in the wheelchair. "How are you doing, Uncle Guy?" Tito asked.

Guy shrugged. "As well as can be expected, nephew. It's good to see you," Guy replied. Tito was the spitting image of Eddie, except Tito had more of a physique and kept his hair short and wavy.

Tito shook Ty's hand and gave him a hug. "Peace, Fam. I hate that the first time I came to see you was under these types of circumstances, but like I told you, whatever you need, I'm here," Tito assured him.

"I appreciate that, T," Ty responded.

"The twins don't wanna leave 'cause they say it's hot and heavy down here, and they hate to start something and not finish it."

"I feel you, but I'm good. They more than showed me why you sent 'em," Ty smirked.

Tito nodded. "I told you, B. Pitbulls in a skirt," he said then turned to Guy. "I realize this is neither the time nor the place, but I would truly appreciate it if I could meet with you before I leave," Tito inquired.

"My door is always open for you, nephew, but it would do better to speak with Ty," Guy told him then looked at Ty, "He'll be makin' a lot of the decisions while I recuperate."

Ty felt a lump in his throat. Tito smiled at him with pride.

"That's what it is then, Unc. Ty, I'll be stayin' in Wilson. Whenever is good for you."

"I'll see you tonight," Ty told him.

They shook hands then Tito walked off.

"What do you think of this deal?" Guy questioned, watching Tito go over and hug Gloria.

"I think we stand to make a lot of money without assuming a lot of risk," Ty surmised.

Guy nodded. "A man only wants a partner for two reasons. One, he's weaker and he needs a protector or two, he's stronger and he thinks he can swallow you," Guy said then looked at Ty, "Do you know what destroyed Rome."

"No."

"It got too big to keep together. Everything else was just side issues. The man that put me on my feet told me that. With this deal, you'll be takin' us deeper in. Less risk? No, because Tito's issues become our issues, we take on his burden. I don't like it, but I'll support you whichever way you go, because the day will come when you'll guide the direction of this family," Guy explained.

Ty felt a mixture of guilt and pride, but he vowed inside not to let the family down.

"I got you, Pop," Ty replied.

Ty pushed Guy over to Gloria then went to find his mother. He had a lot on his mind and he needed solitude to weigh it all out.

"Ty. Can I speak with you?" Karrin asked as Ty made his way across the cemetery.

"Not now, Karrin," he replied dismissively.

She grabbed his arm and stopped him from walking away. "Then when? You won't return my phone calls or my texts and it's like you don't even live in your apartment because you're never home!" Karrin fought to keep from raising her voice.

"I been busy, okay?"

"Bullshit! You're avoiding me and I want to know why!" she demanded.

"Look, Karrin, let it go, okay?? It's over... I don't want to see you again," Ty spat, meaning it for the first time.

Tears welled in her eyes. "But why? What did I do to make you treat me this way?!"

"I-I gotta go," was Ty's unfeeling reply.

"Tyquan, don't walk—" she started to say with her teeth gritted, but Ty snatched himself away and a few people walked by with curious looks on their faces. Karrin gave a fake smile and moved the hair out of her face. Once they passed, she stared daggers in Ty's back as he walked away.

◉◉◉◉◉◉

The people at the cemetery weren't the only ones attending the funeral. Young Hardy and his man Dro sat across on a side street facing the cemetery. Young Hardy was behind the wheel of a grey hooptie and Dro was in the passenger seat. They both had AR-15s on their lap. Young Hardy gripped the steering wheel so tight, his knuckles turned red. All he could see was himself stumbling to the crib only to find it burnt to the ground, surrounded by police, a fire truck and a coroner's van. His whole family had been burnt up in the fire and young Hardy's heart along with it.

"Fuck that! I'm goin' in," Hardy hissed, tired of waiting.

"Yo, dawg, we'll never make it. You see them nigguhs got four guards at the cemetery entrance and ain't no tellin' how many shooters inside," Dro tried to reason.

"We about to find out," Hardy replied, starting the car. He went to put it in gear, but Dro grabbed it, "Ay yo, Dro, if you don't move your hand—"

"Hardy, listen to yourself! You ain't thinking! This ain't no goddamn Rambo movie, nigguh, shit is real! Ain't no way we gonna be able to make it inside *and* murder them nigguhs before we get hit or knocked or both!" Dro barked.

"Nigguh, I ain't got nothin' to lose," Hardy said from the heart. They had taken away his only source of peace forever.

"Yeah you do!"

"What I got to lose?!"

"A better opportunity," Dro replied simply. "I feel you, dawg. I know you don't give a fuck about death or jail, but if you want to get these nigguhs instead of *lettin'* 'em know you wanna get 'em then we need to do it right! You feel me? All we can do is go in there making a lotta noise. Fuck that. Let 'em have they day. The next funeral is on us!" Dro explained, and young Hardy saw the wisdom in his words.

"Your daughter... is very unstable. We felt it necessary to have her speak to a staff psychiatrist to determine whether or not she should be placed in our psychiatric ward for further evaluation. Unfortunately, it took some time to get the psychiatrist, and it was during that interval when your daughter escaped."

Vee thought about the doctor's words, as he drove through the woods leading to Ms. Sadie's house. They had spazzed on the doctor, threatening to sue the hospital for negligence, then they spent the rest of the day and into the night looking for Cat throughout the city. Her parents even went to the police so they could be informed if and when Cat was picked up.

They hoped Cat had gone back to North Carolina, but she wasn't at her parents place nor was she at the apartment.

"Did you know that your neighbors had been murdered, Victor?" Mrs. Richards (who's Mrs. Richards, the neighbor?) had informed him, because he didn't go to the apartment.

187

That confirmed for Vee that he could no longer rest his head there. He headed out to Ms. Sadie's to get his head together and see if she could help him find Cat.

When he pulled up, the sun was just setting, giving the woods around him an orangey hue.. The front door was closed. This was something that Ms. Sadie rarely did, unless it was bitter cold. He tried the knob, found it was open and went in.

"Mama, I'm—" those two words seemed to echo around the room because the place was empty.

Vee stared around in shock because every stitch of furniture, every artifact and picture had been removed. The old floorboards creaked with every step, showing their age. A spider had even spun a web over the front picture window.

"Mama!" he bellowed, going room to room, refusing to accept what his eyes told him was true.

Ms. Sadie was gone. Deep down Vee feared that she was dead. He knew that people who dealt with roots didn't want anyone to know where they were buried, so many would go off and prepare in advance to die.

"Mama!" he screamed again in anguish. It seemed like his world was coming apart at the seams. "Why didn't you tell me," he whispered as the tears slid down his cheeks. "Why didn't you tell me???" he yelled, referring to the dream about the pool.

He knew she must've known what it meant,and questioned why she didn't tell him. Then maybe he could've saved his child and his woman. His heart sank as he sank to the floor. Thinking of Cat's ranting at the hospital he answered, "Because I didn't know… I didn't know."

He sat on the floor with his head bowed, allowing his soul the cleansing it needed. He was all alone in the world.

No one to love and no one to love him. This was the punish-
ment for the choice he made. It was then that he thought
about the dreams about his mother. They hadn't stopped
since he told Ms. Sadie about it. They varied, but they
always involved his mother and the ring.

"The ring represents wealth and power. Once you get it,
the bloodshed will ensue, but death will assist you in
defeating your enemies," he remembered Ms. Sadie telling
him.

Vee stood to his feet. He had to find out what it really
meant, and the key to the woman that had abandoned him.
He had to find her. If wealth and power were all he'd ever
obtained, then he decided to live that to the fullest.

"Fuck love," he mumbled in an attempt to convince
himself as he headed out the door.

He already knew his mother's name, and in this day and
age it isn't difficult to find someone, no matter how far
removed. But when he Googled her name, nothing came up.
Her last name was prevalent in the Fremont area which was
a few miles from Goldsboro. He aimed for the oldest names,
hoping that one was the matriarch and could tell him where
his mother could be found. The first lady was unrelated, but
the second was an elderly blind woman. She lived alone but
had an attendant to help her get around. Vee sat down
across from the lady.

She said, "Would you like something to drink?"

"No, Ma'am," Vee smiled, "I won't take up too much of
your time. I just wanted to know if you knew a Shantelle
Braswell."

The old woman smiled. "Well I should, since she's my
youngest daughter."

Vee's heart jumped; excited to know he was on the right path. "Does… does she live here with you?"

The woman's smile disappeared. "I'm afraid not. Shantelle's been in prison since she was twenty years old. She's been gone 19 years this May," she informed him.

"Where is she locked up?"

"Troy, North Carolina."

He was familiar with the prison. It used to be a man's facility until the explosion of the female inmate population converted it over.

"I know where that's at."

"May I ask who you are? Shantelle doesn't get many people coming to check on her.

Vee smiled as he stood up.

"I'm… I'm an old friend," he replied to his grandmother, not wanting to reveal himself yet.

As he drove away, he felt relieved to know that his mother hadn't abandoned him out of her own free will, and he was anxious to meet her. He was so caught up in his destination; he didn't even realize he was being followed.

Hawk Bill drove behind him in an old raggedy pickup truck. In his lap was his trusty .38. He picked up the phone and called Ty. When he got an answer, he blurted out, "Youngblood! We got 'em!"

CHAPTER 17

"Nigguh, you got these bitches feelin' so comfortable they think they can call my goddamn house now!" Gloria based on Guy as he sat on the couch watching Monday night football and playing with a 2 year old Kev.

"Glo, what you talkin' about now?" Guy asked in a bored tone. He had been through this a thousand times, but he knew he had his chicks in check. They knew not to call the crib.

Gloria stormed over and turned off the TV. "You know what I'm talkin' about! Nigguh, you ain't shit! You do what you want in them streets but no bitch gonna be callin' my house!" she fumed.

Guy was getting too blatant with his shit. He used to try to be discreet, but even then Gloria knew. She knew how nigguhs in the game got down, and she had been raised to believe that's how men did. But now, Guy wouldn't even bother to come home for two or three days or, he'd come home reeking of another woman's perfume and body scent. When they went out, she could tell just by the way a woman looked at Guy if he was fucking her or not. She wanted her marriage with all her heart because she truly loved Guy. Now that they had a child, she wanted Kev to have a family, but Debra's call was too much.

Seeing his mother upset made Kev start crying. "Now look what you did," Guy huffed, "you happy now?"

"What _I_ did?? You betta check yo' hoes nigguh, or I'm a show you what I did!" she spat as she stormed out.

"Who was it?!" Guy call after her.

"Some bitch named Debra!"

Guy drove across town heated. It wasn't so much that Debra had called as it was the fact she had done something he told her not to. Guy was truly feeling Debra, but no woman in his life had the right to break his rules, so he went to her crib with the intent of breaking his foot off in her ass.

He got to the swanky little condo style apartment he had Debra in. They had just built them out by the mall, complete with tennis courts and swimming pools. He hadn't been fucking with Debra long, but she played her position well, up until then.

Guy rang the bell and banged on the door. "Bitch, open this mufuc – " he began, but when she opened it his heart dropped.

Debra's beautiful face was marred by a swollen right eye. It was turning purple. Her lip was busted as well.

"What the fuck happened?" Guy gasped, his anger towards her replaced with sympathy.

She fell into his arms, "It was Brah! He said he was goin' to kill me!" Debra sobbed.

Guy took her inside and shut the door. "Where the fuck is he???" was all Guy wanted to know. The nigguh was as good as dead!

"No, Guy, don't! Please don't! It's my problem, not yours!" she cried.

He grabbed her gently by both shoulders. "Of course it's my problem, baby. You're my woman," he crooned softly.

"You... you don't understand, Guy! Please, just go and I'ma be – "

"What you mean go? You want this nigguh or somethin'?" Guy asked angrily.

"I'm pregnant, Guy! I'm pregnant with his child!" she blurted out before the sobs made her slide down the wall to the floor.

Pregnant? Guys mind echoed. The thought of Brah fucking his chick made him sick. Pregnant?

"I'm sorry, I know I shouldn't have called but I didn't know... know what to do. He hurt me, Guy. He hurt me bad and he said he'd kill me and you if I didn't leave you alone," she informed him.

"How the fuck a dead nigguh gonna kill me?" he huffed. "I can't believe you was still fuckin' wit' this clown!"

"I know I fucked up, Guy, okay?! I wasn't thinkin'... I got... confused," she admitted. "I love you, Guy, I swear I do, but I ain't gonna be no fool! You gotta wife, a family. What do I have?! I don't just want to be a nigguh's whore for the rest of my life," she explained.

She did love Guy, but she wanted to keep her options open if and when Guy got bored with her. She wasn't going to get left out to dry. She had Brah wrapped around her finger, so she kept him on the side, just in case.

Guy understood her logic and his pride subsided.

"I know you don't want me no more, but I just wanted you to know what Brah said about you so you wouldn't be in the blind," she told him.

Guy sighed, kneeling down beside her. He gently took her hand away from her face. "You ain't my whore, sweetness. Believe me. You are my woman."

"Do you love me, Guy?"

"Huh?"

She looked into his eyes. "Do... you... love... me," she repeated.

"Yeah, Debra, I do," he admitted.

She threw her arms around his neck and hugged him tight. "I

love you, baby! I do! I just needed to hear you say it! I'm sorry, baby, I am. I'll-I'll get an abortion and — "

Guy jerked out her embrace quickly. "Hell no! That's out of the question! I ain't fuckin' wit' no woman that curse her womb like that."

"But, Guy, it's Brah's," she reminded him.

"I don't give a fuck whose it is! You ain't havin' no abortion. We'll get through this together, I promise," he vowed.

What he said touched Debra's heart like no man ever had and her respect for him grew a thousand percent. She had toyed with the idea of telling him it was his child, but she knew the truth was only a paternity test away, and she knew for a fact it was Brah's. But seeing that he was willing to raise another man's seed, made her heart leap.

"Now come on," he said, helping her to her feet, "we goin' to the hospital and get you checked out. Then after that, I got a run to make."

●●●●●●

"Nigguh, play! I said six-no uptown," Shantelle spat, throwing an ace of diamonds to the board. She was at Ms. Lillian's Liquor House playing bid whist for money.

"You make 'em, I'll rake 'em, partna," her girlfriend said, scooping up the books as Shantelle won.

"Y'all nigguhs know, Boston you pay double," Shantelle reminded them as she won book after book until she had won them all. "Double, nigguh! You know what time it is!" she laughed and slapped her partner high five.

The two dudes that were playing put five hundred on the table and got up.

"Somebody get me two mo' monkeys. These monkeys won't dance no mo," she bragged, sliding half the winnings to her partner.

"What up, Brah baby! What it is!"

She heard somebody say out in the front room. Her body tensed hearing Brah reply, "Nigguh, I is what it is! I thought you knew!"

Shantelle wanted to run out there and put a cap in his ass, but she looked around the room at all the potential witnesses.

"Girl, what's wrong with you?" her girlfriend asked, seeing the expression on her face.

"Nothin'," Shantelle grumbled.

"Ay yo, Brah!"

She knew that voice anywhere. It was Guy's.

"Nigguh, I know you ain't about to confront me about no bitch!" she heard Brah say then it was followed by the sounds of a bottle busting over someone's head.

The crowd in the back room ran to the door, so Shantelle had to push and throw elbows to get to the door. When she looked, she immediately went into action. Brah had Guy on the floor, choking the shit out of him. Guy's head was bleeding from the bottle Brah had smashed him with. He was clawing at Brah's hands and fighting to get his hands on his gun that had been knocked from his hand.

Shantelle ran up behind Brah and put the pistol to Brah's head, "Nigguh, get the fuck off my man!" she demanded though clenched teeth. The sound of her cocking the hammer made Brah instantly concede.

As soon as he was free, Guy punched Brah dead in the face then doubled over, fighting to catch his breath. When he did, he snatched the gun from Shantelle and put it to Brah's forehead. "You punk muhfucka, I'ma kill you!" Guy seethed, but Shantelle put her hand on his arm.

"Baby, no, not here. Look at all these motherfuckas. We'll have to kill every goddamn body to keep these muhfuckas from talkin'," she reasoned. "We'll get him."

"Nigguh, you pull a gun on me you better kill me," Brah

hissed, emboldened by the fact he felt Guy wouldn't shoot him in the crowded room.

Boom!

Guy squeezed the trigger but he aimed for Brah's dick. He narrowly missed it, hitting him in the upper thigh instead.

The crowd screamed and quickly vacated the room and someone had already called the police. Since Ms. Lillian's was a spot prone to violence, the police arrived in a New York minute.

"Freeze!" they hollered, looking at Guy's back.

Shantelle put her hand on the gun. Guy looked at her. Her eyes said, let it go. His said no, so she snatched it from his hand. The police ran up on Guy as he raised his empty hands. Shantelle dropped the gun and did the same. They cuffed her. Brah saw the whole thing, but he wasn't a rat. He dug Shantelle's realness even though he swore he'd kill her if he ever saw her again. Shantelle and Guy's eyes never left each other as the police led her from the room.

Guy bailed her out the next morning and got her the best lawyer he could buy. Her record was extensive and she now had two attempted murders since the D.A. decided to pursue the Army dude shooting even though the dude refused to say it was Shantelle. Everything was all good until Shantelle saw Debra and Guy driving in his car. Debra was all hugged up on him, laughing like she didn't have a care in the world.

She was sick. Here she was, facing serious time for this nigguh over a situation stemming from this trifling bitch, and he was sporting her like shit was sweet. Shantelle decided to go on the run. She vowed never to speak to Guy again or tell him about the fact she was pregnant.

She ended up at Ms. Sadie's because she too had used the Root Lady for many things. She had her son and planned on stacking her paper so she could bounce permanently, but she got popped in Kinston with six ounces of coke and another gun. The three charges combined got her twenty years and took her away from her only child and Guy's son.

CHAPTER 18

The twins, Ty and Tito sat around the small but plush suite at the Hampton Inn Hotel in Wilson. Ty sipped his drink as he listened to Tito talk. He thought about the words of wisdom Guy had dropped on him, and he could clearly see Tito was looking for a partner to strengthen his own points of weakness. He was reaching in too many directions. His plan was shrewd but the Bell family was definitely losing the powerful street presence they used to have in the 80's and 90's.

"So tell me, Fam... what you think? I know back in Aruba you felt my vision," Tito reminded him.

Ty sipped his cognac. "And I still do, Tito. A Simmons-Bell partnership could push a lot of nigguhs to the side."

"That's what it is then, so we got a deal?" Tito inquired.

"We can... we just need a few minor changes," Ty told him.

"Changes?" Tito echoed, one eyebrow raised, sensing there'd be nothing minor about it.

Ty sat his drink down and leaned forward. "Our percentage," he stated simply. "Instead of fifty-fifty, I'd be willing to do, say twenty percent but I want a twenty percent stake in Gotham Moon Records."

Tito downed his drink. Gotham Moon was half owned by the Bell family and had most of the hottest young artists on it. It served as the perfect front to launder money as well as generating millions on its own.

"Fam, you askin' me to give you clean money for dirty money."

"Which is why I'm only askin' twenty percent," Ty shot right back. "Look, Tito, the bottom line is you're looking to expand because the New York market has been steadily shrinking since the 90's. On top of that, you're askin' us to allow you access to our political and other connections across the south. Forgive me if I come off hypocritical, but the crack game got a whole lot more bad press than the heroin game. Now for us to go to bat for you when the time comes, I need something concrete for our risk," Ty explained.

"I can do fifteen," Tito offered.

"You can do what you want, Tito," Ty smiled, "but I'm only asking twenty."

Tito poured himself three fingers of cognac. "That's the best I can do," Tito shrugged.

"Come on, Fam, we're talkin' *millions*! The areas we can offer will make that twenty look like peanuts. Don't let five percent stop that," Ty reasoned.

Tito just sipped his drink without responding. Ty got up and hugged both Asia and Brooklyn. "I wanna thank y'all for holdin' me down."

"Anytime, Cuzzo."

"That's what family is for."

Ty extended his hand to Tito and he shook it. "Don't be a stranger, Cuz. Maybe one day we'll see eye to eye."

Ty tried to pull his hand away, but Tito held it then begrudgingly said, "Twenty percent."

Ty smiled and reaffirmed his grip. "Let's make it happen then."

Ty walked out content with the outcome, but Tito wasn't. He knew Ty sensed his weak position and had taken advantage of it, swooping in like a vulture and taking a chunk out of his cash cow. Tito was a competitor and he loved the art of the deal, so he hated to lose in a negotiation, especially to a country-ass nigguh. He felt that it wouldn't be long before his family would be back on top then he would see Ty again, this time on his terms.

⬤ ⬤ ⬤ ⬤ ⬤ ⬤

"This is Ty... leave it." Beep!

"Shit!" Hawk Bill cursed, hearing Ty's voicemail. He tried again but got the same results. He felt that Ty wouldn't answer because he didn't recognize the number. Hawk couldn't text him because he didn't know how. He threw the phone in the passenger seat and said, "Fuck it! I'll do this nigguh myself!"

He had been coming to see his mother when he saw Vee coming out with the attendant. He remembered Vee's face from when he was Ty's right hand man, and he knew he was the one that killed Kev. He was in the position to have caught Vee slipping getting in the car, but Hawk Bill had his own dilemma... what the hell was he doing at his mother's house?

Killing him on the spot wouldn't help, because if Vee knew where she rested, who else knew? The young nigguh would die, but not before he told Hawk what was going on. So Hawk followed him for miles. Hawk Bill was in no hurry because he was a patient man. He had once laid in a man's bushes eight hours before gunning the man down on his porch, so driving for miles was a piece of cake for Hawk Bill.

As Vee drove deeper into the country, he wondered where he was going? Maybe he was leading him to where he rested his head. Hawk Bill didn't know, but he intended on finding out. Hawk Bill saw the sign for Troy Correctional Institute and followed Vee as he made a right into the facility. Hawk Bill had been here several times to see his sister Shantelle.

Vee parked and headed inside. Hawk Bill definitely wasn't about to get at him in a prison parking lot so he picked up his crossword puzzle and waited.

●●●●●●

Guy Simmons is his father? The words weighed heavily on his mind. Vee walked out of the visitation in a daze. The whole visit had been an epiphany, a moment of clarity. From the moment his mother walked into the room and he saw himself in feminine form.

She embraced him tightly, and after a moment he allowed himself to embrace her back. She had been taken away from him, she hadn't abandoned him. She told him about her former life, before her incarceration, and he told her about the beef with Ty. He felt comfortable talking to her, not because she was his mother, but because he was just like her in his ways.

"Now all I gotta do is deal with is Ty because that nigguh Kev dead," he had explained.

"Dead?" she echoed. "Little Kev is dead?"

Vee chuckled. "Shantelle, he wasn't little Kev no more.

The muhfucka wanted it, so I gave it to him," Vee replied nonchalantly.

He was totally confused by his mother's sudden outburst of tears. Her vow never to speak to Guy again or tell him he had another son seemed so immature at that point, especially since Vee had just told her he had killed his own brother!

"What's the matter?" Vee asked.

That's when his mother filled in all the blanks she had left out in her earlier autobiography. How she was messing with Guy when she was sixteen and how he was her supplier as well. She also told him that one of the charges she was doing time for was really Guy's.

"I-I was young, Victor. I loved Guy Simmons with all my heart, but after seeing him wit' that… woman, after I done took a charge behind her shit, broke my heart in a thousand pieces. I wanted to hurt him back, take something he loved and I decided it would be my pregnancy. You." She looked up at Vee. She thought she'd gotten over the pain Guy had caused her, but nineteen years later it still felt fresh and vivid as if it had happened yesterday.

"Shantelle… what you tryin' to say?" Vee pressed her, even though the answer was already on the table.

"Guy Simmons… is your father, Victor," she told him as she continued to weep.

Vee sat back in the chair. His mind was blown. He had lost a child and gained a mother, lost a love and found a father. "My father?" was all he could say.

"Visitation is now over. Will all guests please prepare to exit," the C.O. announced loudly.

Shantelle and Vee stood up faced each other.

"Don't do anything, Victor, please. Don't mess with Ty. I'm going to write Guy as soon as I get back to the dorm... no, no! I'll call my brother Hawk Bill. Just don't do anything until we talk again, okay?" Shantelle begged.

"I won't."

"Promise me, Victor."

"I promise."

Shantelle caressed his face. He was no longer the child she had left. He was a man now. She pulled him to her and embraced him tightly. "I love you, Victor."

"I-umm-okay," Vee stammered, not knowing how to respond to a woman's love he hardly knew. But before he walked out he called to her. "Shantelle."

She looked up.

"I love you, too."

She smiled and blew him a kiss.

As Vee drove he tried to make sense of a life that had become totally topsy-turvy. He didn't know what to expect next, nor was he aware of what was behind him — Hawk Bill.

Vee pulled into a local McDonald's. He hadn't eaten in over twenty-four hours and he was famished. He parked and went inside. Hawk Bill pulled in behind him then entered the restaurant as well.

"Welcome to McDonald's. May I take your order?" the pretty doe-eyed brown skin girl chimed as Vee walked to the counter.

"Yeah, just... anything... a burger or somethin'," Vee mumbled, too preoccupied with his own thoughts.

"Excuse me, sir?" she inquired, eyeing Vee like he was candy.

"A burger, yo. Whopper or whatever."

She giggled. "This is McDonald's, sir. But don't worry." She winked. "I got you."

She could tell Vee was preoccupied. She hooked him up with two Big Macs, two fries, a order of McNuggets and her number.

"How much?" Vee asked.

"I'll tell you when you call me," she flirted.

Vee smiled and pocketed the number. He took his order to the back of the restaurant and sat down. Then it hit him. He had killed his own brother. He could see Kev's face as the first shot entered his mouth and the sick satisfaction he had gotten from seeing the back of his head explode.

Vee pushed his food away, his ravaging hunger having suddenly disappeared. He imagined what it would've been like to grow up with Kev and Ty, if he had grown up a Simmons. Everything handed to you on a silver platter. No grind, no struggle and now what would happen? Just because he was Guy's son, that didn't change the fact that he had killed Guy's other son, the one he had raised, knew, loved and buried. What if he was destined to kill his own family with his own hands? That would truly be a sick trick if God played that card, but what did God have to do with it? He had made a deal with Darkness, with black magic, so he was already cursed.

"Nigguh, you move and you're dead."

He heard the harsh whisper a second before the short stocky man sat across from him in the booth, concealing a revolver under a newspaper while resting it on the table. He had caught Vee totally slipping. He had taken off his vest and slid the gun under the seat before he went in the prison. Then after coming out, he had been so preoccupied that he hadn't geared back up. Staring at the gun, he felt naked and exposed.

Hawk Bill quickly assessed the young dude. He had seen many a man die, and most had showed some kind of initial reaction of fear or surprise. Even if they were able to regroup, Hawk Bill had already peeped it. With Vee, there was none of that. No fear, no surprise, just recognition.

"Killers don't talk," Vee said calmly, looking Hawk Bill in the eyes.

"Oh, you one of them tough lil' nigguhs, huh? Let's see how tough you is when I put this lead in you," Hawk Bill growled.

Vee leered across the table. "Do you?"

Hawk Bill saw there was no fear in the youngen, so intimidating him wasn't an option. He tried the direct approach.

"What the fuck was you doin' at my mama house, nigguh? Answer and I might let you live!"

"Who?" Vee asked. He didn't know which of his heinous crimes had finally caught up with him. But if he was to die he at least wanted to know why.

"Nigguh, you know who I'm talking about! Bertha Braswell, motherfucka!"

Hearing the name made Vee smile and made Hawk Bill think he was crazy.

"What the fuck is so funny?! Nigguh, if anybody so much as come near — "

"Nobody gonna do nothin' to my grandma, yo," Vee assured him calmly.

Now Hawk Bill was fucked up. "Your grandma? Nigguh, you think this a game?!" Hawk Bill sneered then raised the gun.

"Like I said, Ms. Bertha is my grandma, 'cause Shantelle Braswell is my mother."

"You lyin'! Shan ain't got no younguns!" Hawk Bill stated, but as he looked at Vee longer and deeper, the image of his sister's face began to take on the shape of Vee's. Hawk lowered the gun slowly, but he still wasn't convinced.

"That's where I'm coming from. I went to see Shantelle," Vee told him, not knowing he had been followed the whole way.

"That's who you went to see," Hawk mumbled to himself. Shantelle had a child? If his mother knew, she hadn't told him, but it was just like Shan to ensure that no one knew. Hawk Bill knew one thing, if she had a child it could only be one man's.

"What else did she tell you?" Hawk Bill probed, the gun no longer a factor in the conversation.

Vee smiled because he knew why he was asking. "You mean about who my father is?"

Hawk Bill nodded.

"Yeah... she told me. A dude named Guy Simmons," Vee smirked.

◉◉◉◉◉◉

Guy and Willie sat at the table in wheelchairs, along with Ty and another old coon. A few of Guy and Ty's soldiers stood around the pool hall holding them down. They were playing seven-card poker. The pile of money in the middle of the table was more than a working man's weekly wages, but to them it was pocket change for a family gathering.

"Gimme two," Guy said, asking for two cards. He turned to Ty. "I liked the way you handled that. Legitimate money beats street money any day."

Ty was happy his father was proud of him.

"Now that's out of the way, I need you to see if you can find that bitch I was wit' that night I got shot. She was a part of it. Hawk Bill can tell you who all was in there. Talk to *everybody*. The bitch is local 'cause I seen her before. Find her and we find them," Guy explained, not knowing the more he talked, the more Ty felt he was the 'them' Guy was talking about. He could never let Guy find that girl. Ty had his own reasons to find her — to kill her.

"And this fuckin' dude that killed Kev." Guy was choked up momentarily with emotion. "Whatever you got to do, you bring me his head *alive*! I want the pleasure of killing him myself."

"I got you, Pop," Ty replied, feeling like they were back on the same page.

Guy didn't have long to wait. They heard a knock on the door. One of Guy's men peeped out. "It's Hawk Bill and some dude."

"Yeah, let that nigguh in, goddamnit! He still owes me five big ones from the Redskins game!" Willie huffed in his husky voice.

Guy chuckled as Hawk Bill and Vee entered the room.

"Hawk, I hope you got five — " was all Guy could get out before Ty jumped up from the table and pulled his gun. He pointed it at Vee but Hawk Bill quickly stepped in front of him. It happened so fast, no one knew what was going on, but seeing Ty draw down, his team did the same. Guns were aimed at Vee from every direction.

"Ty, no!! Listen to me!" Hawk Bill yelled.

"Hawk, get the fuck outta the way or I swear to God, I'll drop you where you stand!" Ty demanded.

Hearing his son threaten his oldest and most trusted friend made Guy bark, "Ty, what the fuck is goin' on?!"

"That's the nigguh who killed Kev. That's Vee!"

Guy wasted no time and pulled his gun, causing his men to do the same.

"Guy, don't! You don't—"

"Hawk move!" Guy demanded. "What the fuck you doin' bringin' this nigguh in here?!"

"Guy, this Shantelle's son! *Your* son!" Hawk bellowed. There was no way he was going to move from in front of Vee.

The whole room got quiet.

"What did you say?" Guy asked. He had heard him clearly, but it didn't fully register.

Vee subtly moved a reluctant Hawk Bill to the side and looked into the face of the man that had sired him.

"I'm Shantelle's son... and she say you my father," Vee stated, standing in the shadow of death, but he truly feared no evil.

Guy saw instantly what Hawk Bill saw. It was like Shantelle had spit Vee out. Guy was speechless. Ty looked from Guy to Vee in total shock. His emotions were too wired, his adrenaline was too high. He gripped the pistol tightly...

And pulled the trigger.

Also by Dutch

Despite his humble beginnings, Maurice Sebastian, aka Money Mo, has always had lofty aspirations. An up-and-coming promoter, Maurice has his sights set on his biggest promotion yet becoming mayor of Newark. With politics in his blood and the streets as his playground, Maurice has devised a plan to combine the two and have the best of both worlds, a gangsta s paradise. With Maurice running the city and his ruthless squad handling the streets, can he rise to the top? Or will he fall victim to THUG POLITICS?

To purchase a copy, please submit $15.00 plus the shipping terms outlined on our order form for both regular mail orders and inmate orders.

Dutch

Hailing from Newark, New Jersey, Kwame Teague is the award winning, critically acclaimed, and Essence #1 bestselling author of the street classic Dutch trilogy. His other novels include The Adventures of Ghetto Sam, The Glory of My Demise, and Thug Politics under the pseudonym Dutch.

myspace.com/kwamefreedom
facebook.com/authordutch
facebook.com/freekwameteague
twitter.com/kwameakadutch

COMING SOON!!!

Chapter 1

I tried to stay as calm as I could with my father's front door being slammed in my face. I'd just walked from D.C. Jail, which was in the Southeast part of the city, all the way uptown, to Northwest, the equivalent of a New York City hike from Manhattan to the South Bronx.

My father died during my fourth year in jail, and my stepmother turned his home into a crackhouse. She had refused all of my telephone calls and straight dogged me out once my pops died. I just wanted to know why.

Now I knew!

So much for a welcome home party, I thought, and then banged on the door again until my hand began hurting.

"Bitch, if you don't open up this door, I'ma burn you up outta that ma'fucka!" I yelled.

"Carmelo! You better leave before I call the police on you!" she screamed.

"What!" I bellowed. "Look, ain't no need for all that. I'm gone." I lied. Now I was really pissed. This bitch had to die. Won't nobody miss her funky ass. She's just in a nigga's way for real, I thought, growing insane with anger because of her threats.

I stepped away from the door, which faced the short flight of stairs in the four-unit apartment building. She couldn't see me even if she looked out the peephole because the hallway was extremely dark. It even hid my bright-ass Albino complexion.

Once it grew quiet, I heard her leaning on the door. When I was certain that she was all the way up on the door, I spun toward the door and kicked it with all the strength I could muster. When the door flew open, this bitch had the audacity to run.

"Don't run now, bitch!" I growled, as I caught her by her bad hair weave.

I put her in a chokehold until she fainted. I peered at her, then left the front room to find my father's guns. After putting on a pair of gym socks, I began trashing the house, releasing a decade of pent-up anger, frustration and sadness. Raiding the closet, I found my pop's .45-caliber Colt automatic and his 15-shot Browning 9 mm. I was surprised her fien'in ass didn't sell them. I grabbed a few photographs of my pops and put them in my pocket. I cried silently as I left his bedroom for what would be the last time.

There was no future for me here.

I turned the volume on the stereo and the TV up to the max and nudged this black heifer's still frame. When I didn't get a response, I leaned in her ear.

"This is for my father, bitch," I whispered. "He told me if he died before I got outta jail, you had something to do with his death. So take this." I gently placed the .45 against her right temple and squeezed the trigger twice.

As her blood and brain matter soiled the dingy carpet, I left the apartment through the back door. Once I got outside, I saw all of my pop's neighbors standing around enjoying a cookout in somebody's backyard. I quickly reentered the scene of the crime and sprinted out the front door. My heart was pounding.

Within minutes, I created space between me and the crime scene. Whoever finds her body will assume it was a breaking and entering gone foul. But I knew the truth. And it will be a secret that I'll take to my grave, I thought, as I walked briskly down 11th Street.

2

Thirty minutes and thirty blocks later, I was in the projects around LeDroit Park. I was very cautious during my trek to Aaron's house. I was out of the loop for a while, but I didn't forget that there were a lot of ways to get killed in these parts of the city if you didn't know where your ass was at.

Standing 6 feet even and weighing a solid 215 pounds with a French vanilla complexion, I knew I stuck out like a Caucasian at a Nation of Islam pep rally. With my fresh-outta-jail glow and boyish good looks, all eyes were on me, and not too many guys appreciated it when their girlfriends nearly got whiplash trying to get a look.

I reached the middle of First and U streets and knocked on Aaron's front door. I knew he couldn't hear me because I heard music blaring loudly through his basement window.

"Ay Aaron," I yelled over and over as I tapped on the basement window repeatedly, only to get no response. I tried the door, and it was unlocked.

BigBoy is slipping like shit, I thought, before pulling out the .45 and slowly entering the house. As I walked through the doorway, I noticed the front room was trashed just like I'd done my Pop's crib. My heart began to race as all types of shit ran through my head.

"Aaron! I know you hear me! BigBoy?" I called out to my only true friend left in society and went farther into the basement apartment.

I hope ain't nobody crush my man. Slim is a good motherfucker and the only dude who looked out for me during my bid, I thought, as I reached his bedroom and opened the door.

"Who the fuck," Aaron yelled as he rolled off the king-size bed and went for a big-ass gun.

"Hold up, Aaron," I yelled. "Whoa, Aaron! It's me, Carmelo," I explained, watching Shantice jump up and quickly wrap the sheets around her naked frame. The stench of weed mixed with sex invaded my nostrils while I watched Aaron and Shantice hurry to get dressed.

3

Aaron Whitmore has been my friend since Gage Elementary School. When Aaron got arrested for hustling back in the day, his folks worked out a deal with the courts, and sent him off to Job Corps somewhere in Drums, Pennsylvania, for two years. When Aaron completed the program, he returned to the city and began doing big things on the legal tip. At age thirty, Aaron already owns a four-story home, which he obtained legally and now rents out to boarders. And no one can take that away from him.

Shantice Carmody has been a friend of ours since our days at Shaw Junior High School. She got pregnant by Aaron and had an abortion, but they've managed to stay together since they were teens.

I don't know how because Aaron and Shantice have always argued and fought like cats and dogs. They had the hood convinced that they hated each other's guts. I guess opposites do attract, I told myself, and decided to tease my partner and his girl.

"Hurry up and bring ya'll freak asses on up outta there," I laughed, noticing that Shantice didn't think it was funny at all.

In the hood, Shantice was more sought after than some potent drugs. The 5'6", 135-pound dark-skin beauty with a fully developed 32-24-40 body always kept her hair and nails immaculate. And since junior high, Shantice always had the latest gear and shoes, which had a lot of guys in D.C. trying to snatch her up on some wifey time.

"Slim, how in the fuck did you get out," Aaron asked, interrupting my thoughts. "And how the fuck did you get up in here? You almost caught that hot shit."

"Ease up, BigBoy," I smirked. "My appeals came through, and you left that ma'fuckin' door open. I thought a ma'fucka peeled your shit back after I saw the front room all fucked up," I said as Shantice slow got dressed.

Shantice rolled her oval eyes at me, then slid on a yellow thong and matching bra. After checking out her assets, my equipment stiffened. I'd never noticed how sexy Shantice was until now. Maybe it was the decade without any pussy in my life.

4

"Shantice, I think you should go out for a few so I can holler at Carmelo. I'll see you tonight," Aaron told her. She nodded without disagreeing, which surprised me.

Shantice had always been the drama queen and confrontational type. I watched Aaron's 6' 2" foot 2 hulking frame exit the bedroom. He had flawless caramel brown skin covered in tattoos, which made him look like a larger version of the rapper Styles P from the L.O.X. with 2-Pac-like tattoos.

Seconds after we entered the raggedy shackled living room, Shantice came out and kissed Aaron on the lips.

"See you later, Boo. Remember who loves you, okay," she said softly and left the basement. Before she closed the door, I could've sworn she gave me a seductive glance and nod.

I was jive flattered but quickly shook that shit off. I was free for one purpose: to rid the city of all snitches and fake motherfuckers who ruined the game. I wanted to fuck something badly, but that shit would have to wait for now. Now it was time for me to holler at Aaron in hope of getting some help.

"Fuck is up, slim? What's up with this messy-ass crib?"

"Shantice was tripping again. You know how she gets when she feels like I played her out of pocket. Even though I know she's a lunchbox, I can't cut her sexy black ass off," Aaron confessed, shaking his head.

"You gotta stop being soft on them broads and start checking them bitches," I admonished him.

Although the thoughts of having a female going crazy over my dick jive turned me on, you can never lose focus when dealing with a bitch. They're evil by nature and not to be trusted.

"I did check her ass, and it lead up to a fight and some bomb-ass make-up sex—until you popped up," Aaron joked, picking up a pre-rolled blunt.

"Looka' here, BigBoy, I'ma come all the way clean with you. I'm broke, homeless and fucked up. I really need you to throw me a bone until I get on my feet."

Aaron looked away and lit the blunt as he answered, "Slim, I'm not in the game no more. It's too many hot ma'fuckas out here," he said, as he looked out the basement window. "Melo, this house is my only major source of income, and I do temporary plumbing work sometimes. I'm fucked up too, slim, but I'll do whatever I can to look out. I got an open room up on the third floor. It's yours for however long you need it.

"Thanks, slim." I hugged him tightly.

"Cut all that freak-ass shit out, Melo," Aaron joked and pushed me away playfully. "I mean, we cool but not that damn cool. Naw, but on some real shit, we boys, slim, and if I can help you out, then I'ma do it without blinking."

There were no words that could express the gratitude that I felt at that moment, so instead of speaking, I just remained silent as we smoked. I listened to Aaron fill me in on everything he knew that had happened during my ten-year absence from the streets.

I listened to stories about niggaz going to prison because of a snitch, so-called gangstaz hanging out with these chumps who got a rack of good men caught up in the justice system and so-called hustlers making DVD movies glorifying a hot nigga who really fucked the game up in D.C. and made it seem like it was okay to start snitching.

Coming soon!!!

Part 1
February 1989

"Yo, B, I'm sayin' (sniff) we eatin' (sniff-sniff) but we ain't eatin' eatin'... you know what I'm sayin', B?" YaYa said between sniffs of heroin. He held the wax paper carefully between his heavily jeweled fingers, using his pinkie nail to powder his nose. "Now Fell and them? They out West Virginia gettin' they weight up."

"I hear you, B," Shameeq replied, smoking a blunt and pushing his cocaine white kitted Benz 190 down Market Street.

"And not only Fell," YaYa added, "Beeb and them down South, Fu Ak up in Connecticut, Mel Kwon out in Ohio... I'm tellin' you, B, we need to migrate! Get the fuck up outta Newark and fuckin' feast," YaYa emphasized, thumbing his nose as he sat back in the plush piped interior and lit a cigarette.

Shameeq looked over at his man, shearling coated up and truck jewelry'd down, looking like a dark skin version of Rakim. If it wasn't for the system banging out the truck, every time YaYa moved it would've sounded like slave chains clanking together. He had on that much jewelry. They were barely twenty and already heavy hitters.

Shameeq handed him the blunt, chuckling. "We ain't eatin'. How you sound, B? Avon doin' five of them things a week, 17th Ave doin' eight on a bad week, not to mention—"

"I ain't say we wasn't eatin'. I said we wasn't EATIN' EATIN'," YaYa replied, eyelids getting droopy.

Shameeq sucked his teeth like 'stop playin'. Word is bond, Ya, if you was stackin' yo' shit instead of putting it around your neck and up your nose, you'd be EATIN' EATIN', B," Shameeq argued, even though he was damn near as jeweled up as YaYa.

"Fuck that, B, I'm a muhfuckin' Don," YaYa replied, going into a dope lean

"Whatever, B."

Shameeq pulled over and double parked in front of Ali's jewelry store to pick up the nugget bracelet Ali was fixing for him. He threw on the hazard lights and hopped out into the frigid early morning air.

Downtown Newark on a Saturday seemed to stay crowded, even in the coldest weather. Shameeq was on his way in the store when a brand new burgundy Acura Legend Coupe at the light caught his eye. The system was pumping "Like This" so loud, it even drowned out Shameeq's system sitting only a few feet away. His eyes followed the car as it made a left on Halsey Street. He got a glance at the driver and his eyes got big as plates.

"Oh shit!" he cursed, jogging back to the car. He snatched the door open and got in so quick his entrance made YaYa snap out of his dope nod and snatch the pistol from his waist.

"Meeq, the fuck wrong wit' you?" YaYa growled, mad he disturbed his nod.

Shameeq threw the car in drive and pulled out, making a right on Halsey in pursuit of the coupe.

"I just seen KG bitch ass," Shameeq gritted.

"From Elizabeth?"

"I know this muhfucka ain't buy no new whip wit' my paper," Shameeq growled. He had to run the next light to keep up with the Acura. By the time they reached the end of Halsey, Shameeq flashed his lights until the Acura pulled over. Both cars double parked then Shameeq hopped out and stepped up to the driver's side window as KG lowered it.

"Sha—"

"Yo, B, this you?" Shameeq asked angrily. He had already peeped the temporary license in the back window. "Please tell me you ain't buy no new whip!"

KG thought seriously about just pulling off, but the look in Shameeq's eyes seemed to dare him to do just that, while Shameeq's hand rested under his Giants hoodie.

"Yo, yo, Sha, word to mother, I was comin' to see you. I just been—" KG tried to explain, talking so fast the words tumbled out over each other.

Shameeq opened the door. "Get out," he told KG calmly. KG hesitated, so Shameeq repeated it more firmly. "Yo! Get the fuck out!"

KG got out slowly, watching Shameeq's hands. "Yo, Sha, this word to mother, B, I was coming to see you —"

"When? After you spent my shit up?! I ain't seen you in two months, now all of a sudden you was comin' to see me?!" Shameeq blazed him, getting madder with every word.

KG could see it building in him so he quickened his plea. "I got like two on me now —"

"Two?!" Shameeq echoed, spit flying out of his mouth and lightly sprinkling KG's face.

"Two?!" You owe me seventeen, niggah, not two!!"

"I… I know."

"You tryin' to play me, B?!"

"No, 'Meeq, never that—"

"Huh?!"

"Sha, word to mother!"

"Fuck your mother, gimme the keys," Shameeq demanded, looking around, scanning for the police.

"Sha, man, I swear I'ma—"

Smack!

Shameeq cut off KG's weak pleas by smacking the shit out of him.

"Yo, B, chill!" KG hollered, holding his face.

"You think I'm fuckin' playin?!" Shameeq hissed, hooking KG with a vicious left that crumpled him against the trunk of the car. He stood KG up and went in his pockets. "Punk muhfucka, you gonna disrespect me like that, huh?! You think shit is sweet?! Shut up, don't say shit, you disgust me," Shameeq barked while he beat KG ass, pocketing KG's money.

"Yo, Sha, you dead wrong for that, Ock," YaYa yelled from the car laughing.

"Come on, Shameeq man, don't do it like that. I swear I'ma get yo' money, yo," KG mumbled as his lip swelled.

Shameeq smirked like, "Then get it. But until then… the 'Ack me, B." He shoved KG off the car and got in under the wheel. It was then that he realized there was a chick in the car. He looked at her as he closed the door.

"Yo, your man owed me money. You part of the payment or something?"

She sucked her teeth like, "Picture that."

"Then get the fuck out!"

"Hmph! And freeze? Please… somebody takin' me home," she sassed then crossed her arms over her breasts.

Shameeq looked shortie over. She was a fly chinky eyed cinnamon bun with mad attitude. Her hair was cut like Anita Baker and she wore two sets of bamboo earrings. One pair had her name across it.

"Okay, Nikki," Shameeq shrugged, reading her earrings. He pulled off watching KG standing in the street behind him.

"Whatever... Drama," she replied, smirking.

He looked at her. "Yo, who is Drama?" he asked, playing stupid.

Everybody in the streets called him Drama except his crew. He would answer to it, but he never called himself by it.

"Who don't know Drama?" she replied, adding in her mind, *wit' your fine ass.* She was holding her composure, but on the inside, her stomach was doing back flips and semis. With his Egyptian bronze skin tone, hazel eyes, wavy hair and dimples, every ghetto chick wanted his type of Drama in their lives. He was 6'1", bow-legged and his swagger gave chicks chills.

"So you fuck wit' clowns like that?" he asked, looking through KG tape collection.

"No," she answered quickly.

"I can't tell. All them bags back there. Sh... you must be one of them bitches that juice nigguhs, huh?" he said, popping in 3XDope's "Funky Dividends."

"Like I need a man to take care of me," she replied dismissively, "all that's for his son which he too sorry to provide for. Shit, the only reason he in town is 'cause I threatened to take his ass to court," she explained.

"In town? Where. he was at?" Shameeq's ears perked up.

"Virginia."

"Doing what?"

"What you think?"

Shameeq's mind went back to what YaYa was talking about earlier.

"That's why you nor I seen him. He owed me too," Nikki chuckled.

Shameeq looked at Nikki. She was a dime, no question, but she ran her mouth and had no loyalty to a man she had a child

5

with. Still he could tell she was open on him, so he planned on making fucking KG's baby mama part of KG's payment. But first he had to fuck with her head.

"Where you live?" he asked.

"Brick Towers."

At the next block he pulled over in front of the bus stop. She looked at him confusedly.

"What? You thought I was takin' you home? Picture that. I got shit to do," he said, holding in a smirk.

"Like you can't take me a few more blocks, Drama. Brick Towers ain't that far," she snapped.

"Yeah well, I ain't goin' that way," he answered, looking at his Movado, then glanced in the rearview. "Here comes the bus now. You betta hurry up."

She eyed him to see if he was serious then sucked her teeth. She reached in the back for the bags but Shameeq stopped her.

"What you doin', yo? Didn't I tell you he owed me doe?"

"What my baby's clothes got to do wit' that?" Nikki probed.

"Like I ain't got a son," Shameeq lied, but she kept reaching. He jerked her arm like, "Fuck you deaf? That shit mine. Now beat it, your bus is coming," he said, bopping his head to the music.

Nikki was close to tears. "That's foul, Drama, word is bond, that's foul," she said, but Shameeq turned up the radio rapping along with E.S.T.

Nikki got out. She pulled her earmuffs out of her pocket and put them on her ears. Shameeq pulled off then headed straight for the bus stop on the corner of Elizabeth and High Street, where he knew she'd get off. He knew with her good looks, she was used to dudes fawning over her every whim. So he decided to put down the demonstration so she knew it was all about him, not her.

A few minutes later, the bus pulled up and Nikki got off. Shameeq blew the horn then pulled up beside her.

6

Nikki rolled her eyes and kept walking. Shameeq lowered the passenger window, smiling. "Ay, yo, Nikki, my fault, yo. I ain't mean to flip on you like that. I was just mad at your man."

She ignored him and kept walking, so he rolled at a creep beside her.

"Come on, get in. I know it's cold out there," he said, holding back his laughter.

"I'm fine," she replied, but he could damn near hear her teeth chattering.

"At least come get yo' baby's clothes," he offered.

"Keep it."

He slammed on the brakes and barked, "Ay yo, Nikki, bring yo' ass here! I ain't tryin' to have all that attitude, word up! I said I apologize 'cause I like you, but if it's like that, fuck it then!"

Nikki's ears perked up when he told her he liked her, so when Shameeq began to pull off, Nikki called out, "Drama! Hold up!" She pranced over to the car and got in.

"So this mean you accept my apology?" He grinned.

She gave him the eyes like, "Maybe... and like I told you, he ain't my man!!"

Fifteen minutes later, Shameeq was nine inches deep in Nikki's guts. She straddled him as he reclined on the couch, riding him like a thoroughbred. Her firm C cup sized breasts bounced with every stroke, the gushy sounds of sloppy sex filled the room punctuated by her screams of passion.

"Yeeessss, Drama, ohhh right there! Fuck this pussy." She moaned, grinding her hips into him and biting her bottom lip.

Shameeq grabbed her around the back then laid her on the floor. He cocked her legs over his shoulders then started long dicking her like he was trying to knock the bottom out.

"Drama, unnnoooo," she gasped, clawing at the floor trying to squirm away from the dick, but she was pinned beneath him helplessly.

"Ahhhh, baby, I-I feel it in m-m-my stomach," she squealed, eyes rolled up in the back of her head.

"Take this dick, bitch," he growled, "tell me you want Drama in your life!" Shameeq slid in as deep as he could go, grinding her spot until her body shook with her fourth orgasm.

"Oh I doooo, I do, I do, I want Drama in my life! I wanna have your baby," she moaned.

Picture that, he thought, being careful not to bust the condom. Shortie definitely had the type of pussy that would make a man rush home, but she played herself by giving it up too quick.

Shameeq fucked her three more times then fell asleep. Shortie woke him up, washed him, fed him and fucked him once more. She wanted him to know the pussy was his when he wanted it. He already knew that because his dick game was crazy.

By the time he left, it was after nine that night. He drove around to his spot on Avon, laughing with his workers about the whole incident with KG and his baby moms. But little did he know the joke would soon be on him.

A black Monte Carlo SS had been sitting in the cut waiting for him to come through. They knew his crew was too deep to try anything right then, so they waited. They had been paid to do the job right. They followed him to YaYa's block on 17th Avenue, but couldn't make their move. Once he left YaYa and hit Irving Turner Boulevard, they finally got their chance.

He pulled up to the light pumping "Ain't No Half-Steppin'" by Big Daddy Kane. The SS pulled up beside him on the passenger side and an Uzi Sub machine gun was stuck out the window. The only thing that saved Shameeq's life was the light turning green and he pulled off a split second before the Uzi began to spit. That split second made all the difference. The shot that burst through the window aimed for his head exploded the headrest, making Shameeq duck and mash the gas.

"What the fuck?!" he barked, but the only answer was a shower of bullets.

The staccato sound of the automatic burst filled his ears as he desperately tried to weave in and out of traffic and still stay low. The Acura was fast, but it was no match for the SS. They tried to pull up beside Shameeq, but he veered hard to the right, trying to ram the nose of the SS into a parked car. The screeching sound of metal on metal and shooting sparks danced across the SS head as the driver fought to maintain control. He had the better car but Shameeq had the better driving skills.

Shameeq aimed his Beretta through the back window and opened fire on the SS then he made a hard left, momentarily losing them. The SS came up behind him and bumped the rear. They accelerated trying to push the Acura into the next busy, intersection.

Shameeq turned completely around in the seat and took aim straight at the driver. He shot out the windshield of the SS, causing the driver and shooter to take cover. He used the opportunity to speed up, throw up the emergency break, fish tailing the Acura. That made the SS slam into the rear flank of the Acura and the air bags to explode in the driver and shooter's faces, coming to a screeching halt.

In a second, Shameeq was out of the car and pumping shot after shot at the driver. The air bags exploded on impact and the driver's head jerked back, blood flying everywhere. The passenger, still discombobulated by the accident stumbled out of the passenger door and took off in a drunken sprint. Shameeq let off one more round before his clip was empty.

"Shit!!" he cursed then sprinted off in the opposite direction with the sounds of approaching sirens in the distance.

Not knowing when or what was waiting for him at his crib, Shameeq took a cab up to Vailsburg, where his twin sister Egypt lived. She greeted him at the door with a hug. He peered over her shoulder at the dude sitting on the couch, broke the embrace and said, "Yo, B, you gotta bounce."

"Excuse you?" Egypt quipped, one eyebrow raised.

Shameeq ignored her, grabbed the dude's coat and put it in his lap. "She'll call you later."

"Shameeq!" Egypt bassed.

Dude looked at Shameeq then at Egypt confused.

"Yo, B, I'm the one talkin' to you, not her. Family crisis and I ain't tryin' to repeat myself," Shameeq said calmly, but eyed dude firmly.

When Egypt heard him say family crisis, she sighed and said, "Jerome, let me call you later, okay? Let me speak wit' my brother."

There was no denying Shameeq was her brother, because Shameeq and Egypt were the spitting image of one another. Even down to the long eyelashes and thick eyebrows, although Egypt's were slightly arched. She was slim and flat-chested but her hips and ass more than made up the difference. At six feet even and bowlegged just like her brother, the only thing distinctly different was the fact that Egypt wore long skinny salon locs. No extensions, it was all her own hair.

The dude grabbed his coat, like "Yeah aiight." He was eyeing Shameeq hard, but Shameeq had his back to him, talking on Egypt's cordless.

"I'll call you," Egypt whispered, giving dude a kiss on the lips. She closed the door just as Shameeq hung up the phone and sat down.

"Ohhh! This better be good! Bustin' up my groove and I was about to get me some," Egypt fumed with a smirk. She tied two of her dreads around the rest to make a ponytail.

"Watch yo' mouth," Shameeq warned, "Don't make me chase duke down and smash his ass, yo. I'm already heated, don't make it worse."

"Whatever, Shameeq."

"I know whatever. Wait until you get married," he huffed.

"Too late." She giggled, going in the kitchen. "Now what's this crisis or you just here cock blockin'?"

"Muhfuckas tried to kill me."

The sound of silverware hitting the floor was all you heard as Egypt rushed back in the room. "What?! Who?! When?! Are you —" she rattled off, coming over to check his face, but he swatted her hand away.

"I'm ai-ight. Damn mother hen, I said tried."

Egypt stood back with her hands on her hips. "So what we gonna do?"

"We? We ain't doin' shit," he replied.

"Oh so you gonna play me lame now? Hell no, Shameeq! You all I got, yo, you think I'm just gonna stand by and let these punk muhfuckas take that?!" She was so vexed, she was close to tears, but she had murder in her heart.

"See, that's why we ain't doin' shit. Look at you 'bout to cry and shit. What you gonna do, huh?" He pointed his fingers like a gun, shaking like he was scared. "You shot at my brother, boohoo, I'ma kill you." He chuckled.

"Fuck you, Shameeq," Egypt hissed, and stormed in the kitchen.

"Yeah that's right, you in the best place for a woman," he yelled, although he knew his sister wasn't the average female.

They had grown up parentless since they were eleven, after their mother killed their father then killed herself. She had found him in the bed with another woman. They refused to be split up by the system, so they took to the streets and either hustled or starved.

When crack hit Newark around '85, they used the opportunity to come up. They never looked back. It was him and her against the world, taking the trips to New York, posted up on the corners and handling any beefs that came their way.

When YaYa came home from Caldwell, he and Shameeq took their hammer game to the next level, earning the name Drama Squad, and Shameeq, the name Drama. They stayed in some shit because none of them had a cool head, all three live wires. They were young, black and reckless getting paper and making a name for themselves in the street.

As shit got heated, Shameeq made Egypt fall back, get her G.E.D. then go to Community College, which was where she was then, her second year for business management.

Despite his jokes, Shameeq knew Egypt was serious because she loved her brother to death and she was no stranger to putting in work.

YaYa got there in no time with Trello and Casper. Both were fifteen and hungry to be made in the Drama Squad. Trello was a short brown skin dude that weighed a buck fifty soaking wet, but his Uzi weighed a ton and his hammer game made him a beast. Casper was called that because he was an albino. Red eyes and a deadly temper, he had hands so nice that he was a two time Golden Gloves Champion. He had a promising career awaiting him in the ring but the streets had a hold of him and wouldn't let go.

Shameeq explained the scenario to YaYa and they both came to the same conclusion.

"KG," YaYa surmised.

"I feel like that, too," Shameeq concurred.

"Yo, I told you you was dead wrong, B. You can't play a dude like that in front of his bitch," YaYa said.

"Shameeq, I know this ain't over no pussy," Egypt remarked, knowing her brother. "That shit gonna be the death of you."

"Don't mark me like that, girl. And I told you duke owed me money!"

"But you fucked her though, didn't you?" Egypt inquired, knowing she was right because Shameeq didn't answer.

"Trick."

"Watch yo' mouth."

"But yo, B… yo, it might not be KG," Trello added, "it might be them dudes on Renner still in they feelings 'cause we housed they block."

"Or that kid off 20th Street," Casper added.

"Drama." Egypt smirked, shaking her head at her brother. The streets had named him well.

"So what up? Word to mother B, somebody gotta bleed, rightly or wrongly," YaYa growled, ready to set it.

"Indeed, indeed. So, yo, first thing in the morning we gonna snatch that bitch up!" Shameeq exclaimed.

"What bitch?" Casper asked.

"KG baby moms. If duke did do it, I know exactly how to find out," Shameeq smirked.

The next morning, the Drama Squad waited on the corner of West Kinney and High Street in a brown conversion van, watching for Nikki. She had told Shameeq she worked at the Marriot on 1 & 9. So he knew she'd be coming out any minute. She came out of the building, bundled up in a pink goose parka and matching earmuffs. The wind whipped furiously around her as she trekked to the bus stop.

"There she go," Shameeq said from the passenger seat. YaYa pulled off, making a U-turn so he could come up beside her. Nikki didn't notice the van until it was too late. Casper threw the sliding door open then he and Trello jumped out. He cuffed her mouth and snatched her inside the van so fast she didn't have time to scream until she was laying on the back of the van.

"Shut the fuck up!" Shameeq growled, backhanding Nikki. He didn't try to hurt her he just wanted her to know shit was serious.

13

"Dra-Dra, what did I do?" Nikki sobbed, holding her reddened face.

"You know what you did, bitch! You set me up for your man so he could kill me!" he bassed in her face.

"Noooo! I didn't," Nikki protested, but Shameeq grabbed her by the throat.

"Bitch... don't... lie," he seethed, hazel eyes a crimson red.

"No... I mean... argh," she gagged, "I ... I don't know, no!"

"What you mean you don't know, huh?! You must know somethin' if you know it's somethin' not to know!!" Shameeq grilled her, relaxing the grip on her throat.

"No, Drama, No! I meant I don't know what you're talkin' about! I swear!" she cried, but Shameeq just eyed her without answering. She continued. "K-KG, he called me flippin'... askin' me why I didn't get out wit' him and where you take me."

"And what you tell him?!"

"I told him you dropped me at the bus stop, that's it," she stressed.

Shameeq snorted like, "You expect me to believe that shit?!" he hissed.

"I swear on my mother, Drama!"

"So you sayin' you ain't know he did it?" Shameeq's tone lowered, but he was still skeptical.

"No," she sobbed, "I would never do something like that to you, Drama," she vowed, leaning up and hugging his neck hard. He winked his eye at Casper and Trello then untangled her arms from around his neck. "Naw, yo, I can't trust that shit, yo, I can't trust you!"

"You can, baby, you can trust me," Nikki replied quickly, looking him in the eyes and willing him her heart.

"I can trust you? You sure?"

She nodded then hugged him again.

"Then I need you to do something for me," he began.

Nikki wiped her eyes with the back of her hand and answered like she was down for whatever. "What?"

"I need you to call KG. Don't ask him about shit, just go at him and clown him about me takin' his whip. Ai-ight?" Shameeq instructed her.

"That's it?"

"Yeah."

"What if... what if he did it?" Nikki asked timidly.

"What you think?" he replied, and she could already see KG's blood in his eyes.

"Word is bond Drama, KG ain't much but he all I got. I-I don't care either, but if... who's gonna do for me and my son?" Nikki inquired, hoping this show of loyalty would bond her to him.

He smiled and caressed her face. "You won't have to worry no more, Nikki, I got you," he promised.

She nodded and kissed the palm of his hand. Shameeq and Nikki waited in her apartment. It took awhile for KG to finally call back, after paging him repeatedly. When he did call, Shameeq picked up on the kitchen phone while Nikki had the cordless.

" 'Bout time," Nikki huffed, the sassiness back in her voice, "what? You was fuckin' some bitch?"

"I ain't got time for that shit, Nikki, fuck you want?" KG spat back.

"You ain't got time? I could be callin' 'cause yo' son is sick! What you mean you ain't got time?!" Nikki winked at Shameeq, knowing she was doing her job. He smiled back, but he was thinking, scandalous bitch.

"What... do... you... want?" KG repeated, gritting his teeth.

"I need some money."

"I just took yo'ass shoppin' yester—" KG tried to say.

"And I told you that dude that took your car wouldn't let me get my shit!" she replied.

15

"Ain't nobody take shit from me! I gave that bitch muhfucka that shit," he exclaimed.

"I can't tell. But anyway, what you gonna do because yo' son still need clothes. It ain't his fault you got stripped." She giggled.

"Bitch, you think that shit cute?! His faggot ass had a gun, that's the only reason I ain't beat his ass! But trust me, after what I sent at his ass last night I bet you he respect KG now!" he boasted, not knowing he had just signed his own death warrant trying to save face with a chick that didn't give a fuck about him.

Shameeq was fuming. He pressed mute on the receiver and whispered, "Get him over here!"

Nikki nodded. "Whatever. Just when you comin'?"

KG sucked his teeth. "I'm 'bout to bounce. I'll wire it to you."

"Oh hell no, Kevin! That's that bullshit! The last time you said that, I ain't get shit. But fuck it I see how you wanna play. Monday morning I will be up in Essex County—"

"You a triflin' bitch, you know that?!" KG spat, "I'll be through there."

"When?"

"Later." He hung up.

"Beep him again," Shameeq ordered. He wanted KG right then.

Nikki did as she was told. She beeped him three times back to back, until KG called back, vexed.

"Bitch, didn't I say later?!" He wanted to strangle Nikki's ass, but he was ready to get back to VA, and he damn sure didn't need a child support warrant hanging over his head.

"And I gotta go to work now! Just come gimme the money so you can go back to your lil' hoes!" she replied.

"Have yo' ass downstairs when I get there. I ain't climbin' all them damn steps!" KG roared then hung up.

"So... what-what you gonna do, Drama?" she asked nervously. "What if he don't come up?"

"He will," he assured her.

"And then?" she probed.

"Nikki."

"Yes?"

"You talk too much. I told you I got you," Shameeq answered, peeping around the curtain like Malcolm X, glock in hand. He could see the front side of Brick Towers, nine stories below. Down the block, YaYa had the van parked.

As they waited, Nikki debated several times whether or not to break the silence. She finally got up the nerve and said, "Drama."

He looked at his watch then at her.

"I... I love you," she blurted out before she lost the nerve.

"You what?" he snickered.

She came over to him. "You probably think I'm foul 'cause I'm doin' this to KG and he my baby father... but I really do have feelings for you. You ain't like all these nigguhs out here... you different. Just give me the chance to show you I'm different, too," she vowed, never losing eye contact. Nikki felt that by being willing to commit an act of murder with him, it was the ultimate show of loyalty. Drama would see she was a down ass chick and take her under his wing.

Shameeq pulled her close then kissed her forehead, nose and lips. "So you want Drama in your life like that, Boo?"

Nikki smiled seductively and bit her bottom lip. "And other places, too," she replied, grabbing his dick.

Shameeq eyed her body thinking about a quickie, but one glance out the window killed that thought.

"He here."

Nikki looked. KG was driving his old Black '88 Seville with the beige rag. She looked up at Shameeq questioningly.

"Just chill," he told her, eyes trained on the car.

They could vaguely hear him blowing the horn repeatedly and the faint thump of his system.

"He's not comin up," she surmised.

17

Shameeq stayed vigilant.

KG blew the horn several more times then began to pull off. Nikki was about to breathe easy thinking he was leaving, but KG made a U-turn and parked across the street. He hopped out and crossed the street. He kept his head on swivel, looking both ways back and forth, because he was looking for more than cars. He kept his hand tucked under his Avirex coat as he disappeared inside the building.

Nikki's knees got weak knowing what was about to go down. Shameeq peeped her expression so he cupped her chin in his hand and said, "Everything is cool, ok? I got you."

Nikki nodded.

"You wit' me now. Walk like a champion." He winked.

Nikki's eyes lit up with her smile. "I'm good, baby," she assured him, although her stomach was in knots.

"When you let him in... turn your back and walk over to the couch, ai-ight? I'll take care of the rest."

Shameeq went and got in the closet by the door. Nikki stood in the middle of the room hoping it would all be over soon. The knock on the door made her jump!

"Nikki! Open the fuckin' door!" KG demanded.

She took a deep breath, drawing her last ounce of sass then barked, "Boy, wait! Knockin' on the door like you the police!" She unlocked all the locks and opened the door. She turned and walked to the couch like Shameeq had instructed her. "Just let me get my coat!"

"Didn't I tell you be downstairs?!" KG fumed. He felt safer now that he was in her apartment.

KG came deeper into the apartment, allowing Shameeq to ease out of the closet and put the gun to the back of KG's head.

"What up, B? Remember me?" Shameeq hissed like a cobra ready to strike.

18

KG froze up and damn near shit a brick. "Sha?" he gulped, in a voice so high pitched he sounded like a mouse.

He held his hands where Shameeq could see them.

Shameeq reached around and took the pistol off his waist then he spun KG around to face him.

"Surprise, nigguh." Shameeq smirked.

"Man, my word, I got yo' money!" KG confessed.

"Keep that shit duke, this about that shit last night!"

"What sh—" KG began, but Shameeq smacked the shit out of him with his own gun. KG fell flat on his back while Shameeq continued to pistol whip him.

"Muhfucka you tried to body me?! Huh?! Bitch ass nigguh you missed!" Shameeq huffed then put the gun to his forehead.

"Sha, I swear I don't know what you talkin' about," KG lied, his whole mouth swollen and several teeth lost on the floor.

"I'ma ask you one time and one time only, B... do you want to live?"

KG nodded vigorously.

"Where the other muhfucka? I bodied one of them faggots but I want 'em both or word is bond, I'll body you here and now," Shameeq gritted, cocking back the hammer.

KG quickly weighed his options. Any hope of survival was enough for a coward, because a spineless nigguh can fit in the smallest places.

"You tell me K and I'll give you a pass, because a dead nigguh can't pay me my paper. But if you lie...,"

"Shameeq, he a cat from Grafton Avenue. Cat named Hameef. He 'posed to beep me so I can give him his money," KG blurted out.

"What code he usin?"

"1-1-1."

Order Form

DC Bookdiva Publications
#245 4401-A Connecticut Avenue, NW
Washington, DC 20008
dcbookdiva.com

Name: _____

Inmate ID _____

Address: _____

City/State: _____ **Zip:** _____

QUANTITY	TITLES	PRICE EACH	TOTAL
_____	Up the Way, Ben	$15.00	_____
_____	Dynasty, Dutch	$15.00	_____

Coming Soon

QUANTITY	TITLES	PRICE EACH	TOTAL
_____	Dynasty 2, Dutch	$15.00	_____
_____	A Killer'z Ambition	$15.00	_____
_____	A Beautiful Satan	$15.00	_____
_____	The Hustle	$15.00	_____
_____	Trina	$15.00	_____

Sub Total $_____

Shipping/Handling (Via U.S. Media Mail) $3.95 1-2

Shipping $ _____

Total Enclosed $ _____

FORMS OF ACCEPTED PAYMENTS:
Certified or government issued checks and money orders, all mail in orders take 5-7 Business days to be delivered. Books can also be purchased on our website at dcbookdiva.com and by credit card at 1866-928-9990. Incarcerated readers receive 25% discount. Please pay $11.25 per book and apply the same shipping terms as stated above.